"Mark my words, Angelena. You'll be in my bed by the end of the week."

She was mesmerized by him, by the shimmering intensity he exuded, his breath warm against her face, eyes flaring with desire.

It wasn't fair! Somehow, for all his arrogant behavior and raw language, he drew her like a magnet. He'd more than insulted her, yet his touch was a temptation.

Though she yearned for the strength to turn away, to disallow him access to her heart, her honest soul would not allow the deception. Wes Tanner held her fate in his hands. Though she might be separated from her past by a dark curtain in her mind, her future loomed before her, and it was linked to this man. She was immutably drawn to him, knew a yearning to rest in his embrace.

And that fact was more frightening than the fury in his gaze...!

Dear Reader,

Spring is in full bloom and marriage is on the minds of many. That's why we're celebrating marriage in each of our four outstanding Historicals romances this month!

The ever-popular Carolyn Davidson returns with a darling marriage-of-convenience tale, *Tanner Stakes His Claim*, book two of her EDGEWOOD, TEXAS miniseries, which began in February with *The Bachelor Tax*. Known for her to-die-for heroes and her sensuous portrayal of marital love, Carolyn once again delivers, with a squeaky-clean Texas sheriff and the new gal in town, an amnesiac—and pregnant—saloon singer he *can't* stop thinking about!

We also have two outstanding medieval tales this month that capture the essence of our celebration. *The Bride of Spring*, by Catherine Archer features an intrepid heroine who must marry to protect her young brother, and decides to orchestrate her own "forced" marriage. In *My Lady's Choice* by Lyn Stone, an English lady heals King Edward's best knight. Her reward? She'll take marriage to the semiconscious and oh-so-handsome warrior!

Award-winning author Cheryl Reavis brings us a powerful story about a second chance at love and marriage in *The Captive Heart*. Here, a British officer's wife is imprisoned by her own husband, but rescued by a daring Native American. Don't miss this tale of forbidden love!

Enjoy! And come back again next month for four more choices of the best in historical romance.

Sincerely,

Tracy Farrell,
Senior Editor

Carolyn Davidson

Tanner Stakes His Claim

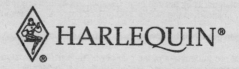

HARLEQUIN®

TORONTO • NEW YORK • LONDON
AMSTERDAM • PARIS • SYDNEY • HAMBURG
STOCKHOLM • ATHENS • TOKYO • MILAN • MADRID
PRAGUE • WARSAW • BUDAPEST • AUCKLAND

ISBN 0-373-29113-2

TANNER STAKES HIS CLAIM

Copyright © 2000 by Carolyn Davidson

All writers need a cheering section—those who offer words of encouragement, and who are oblivious to the faults and failings of our rough drafts. I have been fortunate to find several who qualify for that position. One is my sister Nancy, who thinks I'm wonderful and sings my praises to anyone who will listen. Another is my sister Norma, who touts me as the wunderkind of the family, and ships copies of my books hither and yon.

And finally, Joyce Austin, a fellow member of the Lowcountry Romance Writers of America; she offers undiluted praise for each chapter I send her, and even though I know better, she tries to convince me that my work is without blemish. To all of them I offer my love and appreciation for their support during the writing of this book.

And to the man who has been my hero for more years than I can count, I give full credit for all that I accomplish. I love you, Mr. Ed.

Chapter One

No wonder they called her Angel. From the top of her gleaming golden hair to the tips of her silver slippers, she was the epitome of a heavenly being.

So what the hell was she doing in the middle of the stage at the Golden Slipper Saloon? Wes Tanner leaned his elbows back against the long walnut bar, intrigued by the sudden hush as the piano player performed a simple introduction.

A full house met his gaze, every table filled, with several cowhands leaning against the wall near the swinging doors. Hats were removed, as if this woman were a creature to be honored. One man nudged another into silence when his whisper sounded loud within the room. Another fuzzy-cheeked cowhand cleared his throat and grinned at his companions.

Wes lifted one eyebrow, idly noting his own sense of anticipation. He'd heard, from more than one man over the past weeks about the new singer on Jason Stillwell's stage.

Before tonight he'd not allowed himself to enter the saloon to attend her performance, maybe because he doubted the tales that circulated. Perhaps because his own well-ingrained bent to cynicism would not allow the image of an angel on the stage of a saloon. He'd walked that path once and learned his lesson well.

Then too, he felt, as sheriff of Edgewood, Texas, he must refrain from the temptation of frequenting the saloon. Even if he hadn't been the sheriff, he'd likely have steered clear of the place. Having Nate Pender for a father had created in Wes a fear of traveling the same path his drunken parent had walked.

The pianist was silent, the air hushed, as the young woman tilted her head, allowing her eyes to sweep the width and depth of the room, her mouth forming the faint semblance of a smile. She inhaled, the visible lifting of her breasts beneath the blue dress she wore bringing a soft sigh from the lips of more than one watching man. Wes tore his gaze from her modestly covered bosom and shifted his stance.

Then, within a heartbeat, she opened her mouth, and a tone so sweet, so pure it threatened to bring tears to his eyes, penetrated Wes's hearing. Cascading into a melody, undergirded by the simple chords from the piano, her song flowed over the crowd and held her listeners immobile.

"What do you think?" The whisper behind him broke the spell and Wes shrugged. "They don't call her Angel for nothing," Jason Stillwell murmured.

Wes turned his head, aiming his reply toward the man behind the bar. "Costs you a pretty penny, I'll warrant."

A rancher beside him darted an angry glare at Wes. The silent complaint was valid, Wes thought, and he nodded his understanding. He'd listen, he decided, and hold his comments until later. One thing for sure, the lady could sing.

Angelena closed her eyes, sensing a depth of emotion within herself that filtered through into her song, knowing she had never performed better. The song was of heartbreak, of a woman's love for a wayward husband, and though she had no recollection of such a happening, she felt the pain of the forgotten creature mourning the loss of her love.

A tear slid down each cheek and she lifted one hand to wipe away the evidence of her emotion, even as her voice soared to the final note of the ballad. A hush surrounded her and she bowed her head, knowing the applause would follow. It burst into sound, wrapping her in the audible appreciation of the men who gathered to listen to her music.

For more than six weeks she had performed here. Edgewood, Texas, the sign on the station platform had read. The Golden Slipper was the name of the saloon in which she sang. Upstairs was a room that held all she owned in the world. There she was safe, promised by Jason Stillwell that she would not be molested or disturbed.

She lifted her head, opening her eyes, viewing with blurred vision the room full of men. They clapped, cheered and whistled, calling loudly for an encore. She nodded her head at the piano player and waited for the short introduction of another song.

The words came to her as through a mist, a line at a time, and after six weeks she had learned to accept the phenomenon of her memory. It was empty, blank of all knowledge, except that her name was Angelena and that music was her life.

She scanned the room as she sang, this time an aria that

was simply written and easily performed. Her gaze passed over the man leaning on the bar and then returned, captured by the dark, cynical expression on his face. He lifted his glass to her as she watched, his mouth twisting in an uneven smile. Then he tilted his drink, his gaze piercing her for a moment before he turned aside.

She shivered, her voice faltering for a second, and a concerted gasp escaping from her audience caught the attention of the man who scorned her. He looked at her once more, his smile widening, and whispered to the man next to him. In the glow from a lantern over a nearby table, a shard of light caught and reflected from the star pinned to his shirt.

A lawman. The legendary sheriff of Edgewood, no doubt. Angelena looked away, focusing instead on the men directly before her. They smiled their admiration and she played to her audience, swaying as the rhythm of the music increased. Her voice lifted to swell upon the notes that brought to mind a happiness she did not know.

She would not dwell on that thought. A barely perceptible shake of golden curls disallowed the sadness with which she lived. The aria rose to a finale and she held the last note for an interminable time, then released it and bent her head. The applause again swelled around her and she acknowledged it with a wave.

"One more, if you like," she said quietly, nodding at her accompanist. He obligingly slid into another ballad, one of love offered and accepted, of man and woman finding happiness together. She sang with a will, her heart lifting, her very being exulting in the words and music that poured from her mouth.

Across the room, the tall man at the bar shifted, caught in her peripheral vision, and made his way to the door. The men stepped from his path, their interest taken by the music and the woman who performed. Unwillingly, Angelena watched the straight back, the broad shoulders and the hand that lifted to settle a wide-brimmed hat upon dark hair.

Angelena was given an escort after every show, protected from the crowd as she made her way to the stairway and climbed slowly to the upper floor. Lily, wise of eye and voluptuous of form, followed Angelena tonight, leading the way into the room assigned to the new singer, then crossing to where an oil lamp sat upon the small dresser. A match struck and the wick caught fire quickly as long slender fingers settled the glass chimney in place. Lily turned.

"You sure do sing nice, honey. You know you've got pretty near every man in town wantin' to buy you a drink, and every cowhand from miles around tryin' to buy their way into this room." She lifted a hand to still the protest Angelena uttered.

"I know you're not for sale, Angel." She laughed, and the sound was not without a trace of envy. "Jason likes it better that way—makes you more mysterious. And the men are eatin' it up."

"He told me I didn't have to worry," Angelena whispered. She felt the apprehension escalate as her fingers gripped the small reticule she carried. It held little: a few coins, a lacy kerchief and a locket with a broken clasp. And it was never out of her sight.

"Come on, sit down and take a load off," the other woman encouraged her, sinking into a slipper chair next to the window. "You sure wear yourself out singing, don't you? If you're gonna go on down again tonight, you need to put your feet up for a while."

Angelena closed the door behind herself and shot the bolt, a feature of the room newly installed since her arrival in town. "I just need to rest a little," she said quietly, stepping to the bed and sitting carefully, lest she muss her gown. "I want to thank you for being so kind to me, Lily. I don't know what I'd have done without you and the other girls, too, for that matter."

Lily smiled, adjusting her snug costume as her gaze slid over the contents of the small room. A rack held three dresses, all tastefully designed to complement the woman who had become a nightly attraction at the Golden Slipper. With sweetheart necklines and puffed sleeves, they lent an air of purity to their wearer that was seldom seen in the atmosphere of the saloon.

Beyond the performance wardrobe was a trunk that held Angelena's belongings: a few dresses, underclothes and an assortment of books. Nothing within that piece of luggage held a clue to the woman who wore the clothing it contained.

"You really don't know who you are, do you?" Lily asked, not for the first time. Her lush bosom and exaggerated hairstyle, along with her kohl-lined eyes, had appalled Angelena at first. Now, after days and nights in this place, she had come to look beyond the flash of sequins and rouge to the woman beneath the satin dresses. A woman whose interest in her seemed sincere.

Yet there was no answer to Lily's query and again Angelena shook her head. "I really don't, not one little bit." And that fact was enough to keep her on edge, wondering if the next man through the doorway might hold a key to her forgotten past.

Lily crossed her legs, exposing a long length of silk stocking, topped by a ruffled garter. "You know, at first, I didn't believe you, honey. I figured you were runnin' from somebody, maybe a husband who'd been mean to you. Maybe folks who'd treated you bad."

Wrapped in the darkness of not knowing, Angelena shook her head. "I only know I awoke on the train with a throbbing headache. When it pulled into Edgewood and I saw the sign on the platform, I knew I had to get off." Her shrug was telling, as was the sigh that escaped her lips. "I'd thought by now I'd remember something. Anything."

Lily shrugged, rising from the small chair and sauntering toward the door. "Well, sweetie, at least you've got a place to stay and job givin' you pocket money. That's more than some folks can say. Now, you better put your feet up and take a load off. I've never seen anybody get so ragged after singin' a few songs. Sure takes the starch outta you, don't it?"

Her smile bore a trace of sympathy as she paused by the door. "Come lock this behind me, honey. Don't want any of those cowhands thinkin' they can come for a visit, do we?"

Angelena shivered at the words and stood quickly, her steps swift as she followed Lily to the door. Her mouth was dry as she considered the threat implicit in Lily's remark, and her fingers trembled as she closed the wooden barrier and shot the bolt home.

The fear that was her constant companion swept through her and she closed her eyes. If only…

If only he'd stayed out of the damned place. Wes Tanner allowed the thought to drift through his mind, not for the first time tonight. He rolled over in his bed and looked out the window. The sky was clear, stars shining brilliantly, only a barking dog to mar the peacefulness of the night.

He'd left the saloon in the midst of her song, unwilling to listen any longer, unable to admit the impact her music had made upon him. She was a woman who knew how to cast a net and gather in the suckers, that was for sure. She'd had those men in the palm of her hand. At least now he knew there'd been a damned good reason to stay away from Jason's place lately. Something told him the new gal there was named trouble.

Angel? Not likely.

And he, fool that he was, had almost fallen prey to her, just like the ranchers and cowhands who'd been enthralled by her performance. He rolled over again, the sheet tangling around his naked body. She had him randy as hell, he thought glumly.

Him and about fifty other men. At least that many, if Jason Stillwell was to be believed.

They'd flocked nightly to the Golden Slipper for more than six weeks now, ever since the morning Angel had appeared, just after the train from Shreveport had made a quick stop. He'd heard about her walking down the boardwalk, past the bank and the general store, directly to the saloon, where Herbie had stopped his sweeping long enough to call Jason from his bed.

She'd sung for the first time that night, accompanied by Dex Sawyer on the piano, who'd been put into service at a tidy sum, Wes had heard. Dex's days of playing in the saloon were long past, but the word was he'd been captivated by the young woman's talents and agreed to accompany her.

Wes thought of Dex, the man who'd befriended him in his boyhood, those long ago days when Wes had been called Scat Pender, before salvation came his way. Salvation in the form of Rosemary Tanner.

Now, there was an angel, he decided, thinking of the woman who had reared him ever since his new beginning. Between her and Gabe… He shook his head, rising from the bed. Sleep was far off tonight.

He strode to the window, standing back so as not to be seen from the street below. Across the street, the final light flickered and faded inside the saloon, and on the second floor only one lamp remained to glow through gauzy curtains. He watched as a slight figure paused before the window, cast a slender shadow, then moved on.

He'd warrant it was Angel herself. Not another woman in Jason's place was that slim, that finely built.

Maybe she entertained Jason there tonight, he thought, his mouth twisting distastefully. And then he shook his head, dispelling that thought. Probably not. Lily would snatch her bald-headed. That female was a possessive woman where Jason was concerned, not fearful of speaking up for herself after the years she'd spent in his place. The slender form passed the window again and Wes bent forward to catch a better look.

He sighed. Damn woman was keeping him on the edge, that was for sure. Twenty minutes leaning on the bar, drinking a glass of fizz water, and he was acting like a schoolboy.

He'd have to pay her a visit one of these days, as a lawman of course, to find out what she was doing in Edgewood. In fact, that visit was weeks overdue. He returned to his bed, resigned to a sleepless night, yet strangely satisfied as his decision was made. He'd give a bundle to be invited up to that room, to hear her speak his name with desire.

Tomorrow. Tomorrow, he'd stop by and pay her a call.

The women who slept in the rooms over the Golden Slipper Saloon were seldom seen in daylight, most of them preferring to spend their waking hours in private pursuits. Their nightly endeavors were of no concern to Wes since, being a discreet man, his preferences did not lie in that direction. Thus, the sight of Angelena walking past his office at nine o'clock the next morning came as a surprise.

She was an early riser apparently, and that thought was at variance with her late hours the night before. He watched her, noted the slight sway of her skirt, cocked his head to one side as he envisioned his hands circling her narrow waist.

How many men, he wondered, had seen the inside of her room, had shared her bed? He shook his head, memories from his wandering years surging into his mind, scorching him anew with the pain of rejection he'd survived.

Rejection dealt out by just such a creature as *Angel.*

His jaw hardened as he considered his past and Kitty, the golden-haired beauty who'd sung in a saloon in Abilene when he was still wet behind the ears and too eager to keep his pants buttoned. He banished the thoughts with the ease of long practice. Then he buckled on his gun belt and strolled through the doorway onto the wide boardwalk that fronted the jailhouse.

His pace was slow, his gaze fastened on the woman he followed. She stepped briskly, nodding occasionally at the men who stood in the dusty road and watched her pass.

As she turned to go into the general store, Wes increased his gait, following her inside. She faced the counter, speaking with Phillipa Sawyer, the flame-haired proprietor, whose husband, Dex, had performed so ably at the piano in the saloon last evening.

"I'm afraid we're out of tea in the kitchen, and coffee is not my drink of choice," Angelena said quietly.

"I expect I can rectify that problem," Pip answered cheerfully, reaching behind her for a metal box on the shelf. "We've several varieties. What's your preference today?"

Angelena nodded. "Green if you have it. Otherwise black will do very well."

Phillipa glanced his way as Wes neared, and her eyes lit with welcome. "Sheriff! What can I do for you?"

Angelena stiffened, her shoulders squaring as if she prepared for battle, and Wes stepped forward to stand by her side. "Just looking around town, Pip," he answered lazily. "Thought I'd see if your shipment of new boots came in yet."

The storekeeper shook her head. "Nope. Just placed the order last Monday. It usually takes a couple of weeks."

Her eyes were sharp, glancing from one to the other of her two customers, and she stifled a chuckle, clearing her throat instead. "Have you been introduced to the new musician yet, Sheriff Tanner? This is Angelena, possessor of the finest voice this side of the Mississippi, according to my husband."

Wes lifted a brow and cast a look at Angelena's profile. Her face was flushed, her eyes focused on the countertop before her. "Can't say that I've met the *lady*," he drawled. "Not personally. Stopped by the saloon last night and heard her sing for the first time though." Not to mention watching for her through his window for half an hour when he should have been sleeping, he thought ruefully.

Angelena glanced up, her smile aimed in the general direction of his chest. "I hope you enjoyed the performance, Sheriff." She lowered her head again, and Wes inhaled, recognizing the scent of lilacs. Her hair was a mass of brilliant waves, pulled back into an untidy bun at the nape of her neck, a small blue hat perched atop her crown.

His fingers twitched to eager attention as he considered the pins that held her abundant locks in place, and he smiled as he considered how easily he might undo her efforts. He'd thought her appeal might fade upon closer appraisal, but banished that hope as he scanned her face.

Her skin was unblemished, her eyes a brilliant blue, and her features finely drawn. Bar none, she was the loveliest creature he'd seen in his life. Not even the unforgettable Kitty could measure up. It seemed a shame that all that beauty was wasted in a place like the Golden Slipper.

At his continued silence, she glanced higher, her eyes meeting his, her expression quizzical.

His manners came to the forefront and he nodded cordially. "The music was beyond my expectations, ma'am. It was hard to believe that talent such as yours would be on exhibit in Jason Stillwell's place."

"On exhibit?" Her query was faint, her voice soft as she repeated his words. "I don't care to think of my performance in that way, sir."

He tipped his hat and stepped back, taking in the full length of her. She was neatly dressed, like most any other lady in town, yet there was an air of elegance about her unlike that of any woman he knew. "I suppose any time a performer steps on stage, he's on exhibit."

She nodded slowly, her gaze braver now, searching his face as if she could see beyond the set of his jaw and the narrowing of his eyes. "But did you enjoy the music?" she persisted.

"The view from where I stood was superb," he said formally, aware of Pip's lifted brow at his comment. "The music was extraordinary and the woman beautiful. I've never seen men so dazzled."

"Dazzled," she repeated, her frown apparent. "I don't suppose I've ever endeavored to dazzle an audience. I prefer to think that I provide them with a few minutes of pleasure with my music."

Pleasure. Wes felt the word against his tongue and relished the flavor. "Pleasure?" he echoed. A smile curled his mouth and he allowed it full bloom. "I'd say you were a pleasurable sight to behold, ma'am, even if you'd never opened your mouth."

She stiffened, her chin lifting in defiance. "I think it is safe to assume you are not a connoisseur of music, sir."

"Maybe not," he returned, his voice a low rumbling baritone. "But I sure enough know a good lookin' woman when I see one."

"Wesley Tanner!" Pip's voice was sharp, the rebuke implicit. "Miss Angelena is owed an apology, sir."

"Think so?" he asked. He swept his hat from his head and bowed in the young woman's direction, leaning forward until his nose almost brushed the crown of her hat. He inhaled her scent again. Lilac, sure enough.

"I surely meant no offense. I'm sure Miss Angelena has been called good-lookin' before today, and probably by finer gentlemen than I."

Angelena stepped back, the counter pressing against her hips. "Your apology is accepted, sir. You're right, I've received my share of compliments during the past weeks. The men who frequent Mr. Stillwell's establishment are very kind."

"And before the past weeks, Miss Angelena?" he asked, drawing out the syllables of her name. Surely the lady was used to extravagant praise from the men who sought her charms.

Her mouth twisted, her eyes darkening with an emotion he could not decipher. "I fear my life is not up for discussion, sir."

Wes rocked on his heels. "Secrets? Don't tell me a lady like you is hiding a past? Is there anything the sheriff should know?"

Pip's mouth dropped open and she sputtered, her words

confused, as if she could not place them in order. "Of all the nerve! My word! I can't imagine, I surely can't imagine what you're thinking of, Sheriff."

Wes glanced at her. "I only want to assure the lady that the law in this town is interested in newcomers. We like to keep an eye on things."

"I appreciate your concern, sir." Angelena's words were low and well modulated, but her eyes sparkled with an anger she fought to subdue, if he were any judge of it. "But be assured. You need not be concerned about my actions in your town. I am not a lawbreaker."

Wes bit his tongue, vainly wishing back his remarks. She was more than beautiful, he decided, with a passion bursting to be set free. The memory of that golden hair falling over her shoulders as she sang was foremost in his mind. In less than five seconds, he could pull those miserable pins from place and release the beauty she hid within the confines of that wretched bun.

Stepping back, he turned aside as he sensed the burgeoning of his manhood. The woman made him feel like a callow youth, anxious to find a willing girl. He held his hat before him and gritted his teeth.

It had been more years than he wanted to think of since a female had affected him so strongly, back in those days in Abilene. Maybe it was time to loosen his self-inflicted bonds and take a chance. Just once more.

He gritted his teeth. He'd probably managed to alienate her beyond redemption, if he wasn't mistaken. The urge to prod and push at her, to get beyond that façade of elegance had been too much to resist. And a façade was what it was. Bottom line—she was a saloon singer, and he needed his head examined.

He bowed his head in deference. "I overstepped, ma'am. I beg your pardon. Perhaps we can speak again."

Her eyes hidden behind lowered lashes, she nodded shortly, and probably unwillingly, he thought.

Her reply was soft, sweet, succinct and, unless he missed his guess, far from sincere. "Perhaps, Sheriff. Perhaps."

Chapter Two

"I can't believe one of my sons would be so rude!" Rosemary Tanner shook her wooden spoon in Wes's direction, and he winced, whether at her scornful words or the gesture with which she emphasized her scolding, he did not know.

It was sufficient that Rosemary glared in his direction, let alone shot him with verbal darts. That such a slender, soft-spoken woman held such power had always puzzled Wes. He felt properly admonished and searched for words that would excuse his misdeed.

"Honestly, Mother—" He hesitated, aware that he'd been rightly subjected to Rosemary's words of discipline. His shrug signified defeat. "You're right. I was rude, way out of line."

"Well, I should hope to tell you," Rosemary huffed. "When Pip told me about it the other day, I swear I could hardly fathom you treating a lady so badly."

Wes's brow lifted as he drew a breath. "Now, hold on for just a minute. Who ever said the woman is a lady?"

Rosemary turned to stir a kettle on the stove, the contents of which Wes had about given up hope of ever tasting, now that he had his mother on a rampage. He'd probably have to eat crow first. Then maybe he could wangle an invitation to dinner.

"You know," he began cautiously, "I did offer her an apology. I begged her pardon."

"Were you truly apologetic, or just making the gesture?" Rosemary's retort hit the nail on the head.

Wes considered for a moment and grinned. "You may be right. Even then, I probably didn't sound properly sincere."

"According to Pip, Miss Angelena is every bit a lady, no matter where she sings. And Phillipa Sawyer is a fine judge of character." As if that settled the matter, Rosemary turned her back on the sheriff of Edgewood.

Wes eased his way around the big kitchen table. One hand rose to rest on Rosemary's shoulder, and he bent to deliver a quick kiss to her cheek. "If I promise to apologize nicely to Miss Angelena, and act like I really mean it, can I stay for beef stew?"

Rosemary released a deep sigh and shot a glance at her son. "Today? This very afternoon?"

"The stew or the apology?" he countered with a grin.

"You can't have one without the other," she said, her mouth softening as she allowed it to tilt at the corners.

"You know I'd do most anything for a meal at your table, sweetheart. I'll eat the stew this afternoon and do the apology thing tomorrow morning."

Rosemary eyed him judiciously, a familiar dimple appearing in her left cheek. He'd grown more than attached to that dimple over the past fifteen years, not to mention the woman who possessed the beguiling mark of good humor.

Her hair was still dark, her eyes as blue as they'd been the first time he saw them, the day he fell in love with Rosemary Tanner. If there was one woman on God's green earth who deserved sainthood, it was this creature who held a firm grip on his heart.

"Go ring the bell," she said, elbowing him out of her way as she bent to check the oven. "Then watch out for yourself. Those boys are probably starving. Your father put Adam and Seth to work in the hay field with the men, and the little ones have been pulling weeds in the garden."

Wes headed for the porch, looking over the buildings of the farm that had been his home for the best years of his life. That he lived over the jailhouse now did not count. The ranch belonging to Gabe Tanner would always be home.

The bell rang with gusto as Wes pulled the rope, and from the garden patch, the barn and the corral beyond, a stream of figures headed to the pump.

Damn, it was worth looking like a fool in front of the new saloon singer, just to sit at Rosemary's table and be one of the family.

He'd promised to do the deed, and true to his word, Wes approached the Golden Slipper before noon the next day. A familiar melody sounded from inside, and Wes hesitated as he stood before the swinging doors. The early-morning crowd was usually sparse—a shop owner stopping for gossip, or a rancher wetting his whistle before he headed home.

If he was going to do this, he'd as well make his apology when the audience would be smallest, he decided, pushing the louvered doors aside.

He hesitated, allowing his eyes to become accustomed to the dim light, glancing the length of the bar where Jason Stillwell held court. Two men shot him a look, one lifting a hand in greeting, the other looking away quickly.

"Sheriff." Jason held up an empty glass, his grin welcoming. "It's on the house."

Wes shook his head. It was a ritual they went through, one that never changed. A movement in the far corner caught his eye and he recognized the figure of Dex Sawyer at the piano. *Damn.* Pip would get it from the horse's mouth once Dex went back to the general store or home for supper, or wherever he next saw his wife.

It couldn't be helped. Maybe the sight of Miss Angelena would be balm enough to make it worthwhile. Dex's gaze lifted to the balcony, the melody he played coming to life as the woman standing there gave it voice.

Wes looked around, noting the absence of conversation as the three men at the bar gazed upward. His eyelids closed and he inhaled sharply, unwilling to acknowledge the sharp edge of his attraction, even to himself.

Surely she wasn't as perfect as he remembered. Of a certainty her golden hair would fade into an ordinary hue, here in this shadowed place. She was, after all, a saloon singer. Nothing more, no matter that Pip Sawyer gave her the status of lady.

And how Rosemary could condone such an occupation was beyond his imaginings. He should have thought of that argument. It might have saved him from her ire.

The music ceased abruptly, and Dex muttered a phrase beneath his breath. "Sorry, Miss Angelena," he said quickly. "I'm in the wrong key."

Her laughter was quiet, melodic and forgiving. "I thought it was a little high."

"Sounded fine to me," Jason said from the bar.

"You're a true gentleman, sir," Angelena said softly, her voice carrying in the empty room.

How he was supposed to get from here to where she stood was his major problem, Wes decided. His apology would be easier to make if it didn't have to be spoken in front of four men, one of whom was a blabbermouth when it came to sharing things with his wife. Everyone in town knew that Dex Sawyer was crazy in love with the red-headed woman he'd married.

Wes moved with a firm stride across the floor, heading for the curving stairway. One hand gripped the gleaming banister as he swept off his hat with the other. "Dex," he said quietly, catching the pianist's attention easily. "Hold it for a minute, will you?"

Dex nodded, his eyes agleam with curiosity. He glanced at the woman who waited on the balcony, as if asking her permission, and at her nod glanced back at Wes. "If it's all right with Miss Angelena, have at it, Sheriff."

"Problem, Sheriff?" Jason asked.

"Nope. Just want to have a word with the lady," Wes replied, his gaze pinned on the woman above. She'd backed from the railing to lean against the wall, and he noted the movement with satisfaction. She was wary of him. It put him at an advantage.

His foot touched the upstairs carpet and he hesitated. Maybe her room might be the place to do this. And as quickly as that thought entered his mind, he dismissed it. That would be temptation beyond bearing. The scent of lilac drifting from her hair, back in Pip's store, came to mind. He'd be willing to bet her whole room held that aroma.

"Sheriff?" Her greeting was barely above a whisper, and her gaze flickered from his.

He'd been wrong. Her hair was just as golden, as if each strand held rays of sunshine, and the form beneath a simple cotton gown was enticing, slender, yet rounded. At her waist, long, elegant fingers were clasped, gripping a lacy handkerchief for dear life.

The lady was nervous.

* * *

He was here, hat in hand, a crooked smile fixed on those wide lips. She'd thought never to see him again, to be rid of him after the fiasco in the general store. He'd tendered an apology there that was almost as rude as the words preceding it. Oh, it had contained the proper terms to be considered an admission of wrongdoing, but the man who delivered it had done so under duress, and his gaze had burned its way past her defenses, charring her with derision.

"Ma'am?" His eyes were dark, almost black in the shadows of the balcony. They searched hers as if seeking entry to her thoughts.

"Sheriff." Thankfully, her voice was firm as she spoke the single word.

His long fingers gripped the hat brim firmly, holding it before him. "Could we speak for a moment?" His gaze shifted across the balcony to where a door stood ajar.

She turned her head to follow his line of sight. "I think this is as good a place as any, sir," she said quietly.

He nodded tersely. "Whatever you say, ma'am." Still, his eyes moved, darting to her left where the hallway loomed, lit only by the sunshine that poured in a window at the far end. His nod in that direction needed no explanation. He asked for the privacy that long corridor would offer.

She hesitated, conscious of the females behind almost every door, four in all, most of them awake and aware of the footsteps outside their rooms. It would be as he asked, she decided, turning away. He followed her several paces down the narrow hall.

"Is this private enough?" As if listening ears were not already pressed against wooden doors.

"Yeah." His voice rasped the word, and he cleared his throat as though the words he considered were lodged there and must be stirred into being. "I came to offer you an apology, ma'am."

"You did that already, Sheriff, in the general store."

"I fear it was not spoken in earnest, Miss Angelena. I mistook you for another sort of woman, and my words were not kind."

She glanced at him, then away. "I understand. You were concerned for the morals of your town."

He shifted from one foot to the other, and she heard a distinct giggle from Sarah Jane's room.

"Ma'am? I was wrong," he said quietly, glancing toward the nearest door. "I am aware that you are no danger to this community. I made an error in judgment. You did not deserve the words I spoke to you. My apology is most sincere. I beg your pardon, ma'am."

She glanced up in surprise, and her gaze was caught by the crisp, masculine planes of his face. If his eyes weren't so sharp, she could have been a true believer. If his mouth didn't curve so subtly at one corner as he spoke, she might have taken him at his word. As it was, she knew a modicum of doubt colored her expression and her reply.

"I'll accept your apology, Sheriff," she said slowly. "I'm not sure why you felt it necessary to come here, but I appreciate the gesture."

Dark color rose to ridge his cheekbones. "My mother said I'd wronged you, and she's a pretty smart lady. If Rosemary says I owe you my regrets, then I reckon I do."

His degree of discomfort gave her courage. She could not hold back a small smile. "Your mother?" This was unbelievable. "Your mother sent you to apologize?"

His mouth tightened. "You laughin' at me, ma'am?"

She shook her head. "No, certainly not. I just find it odd that the sheriff is so compliant to his mother's wishes."

His mouth turned down at the corners. "She heard from Pip, old Dex's wife, that I hadn't been nice to you. I suspect she got chapter and verse, if I know Pip Sawyer. You don't know my mother, Miss Angelena. She's got the whole bunch of us on a pretty tight string. It doesn't pay to get on the wrong side of Rosemary Tanner."

She touched her teeth to one side of her lower lip, considering his words. "This wasn't your idea, then."

"Damn!" The oath was softly spoken, but no less emphatic than if he had roared it from the rooftop. "I went about this all wrong, didn't I?"

A thump from the room just beyond where they stood caught her attention, even as his gaze shot to mesh with hers. "Are we being spied on?" he asked, his eyes narrowing, a touch of anger glittering from beneath his lashes.

Angelena nodded toward the balcony. "I'll talk to you in the kitchen, if you like, Sheriff. Unless you've said all you had to say."

"Not nearly," he said shortly, following her as she descended the wide staircase to the lower floor. She cast a look at Jason, aware that his full attention was concentrated on her, even though his damp cloth wiped the surface of the bar with methodical strokes. Surely if he considered the sheriff dangerous to her in any way, he would call a halt before they reached the back room. Talking to the man in the middle of the saloon was not an option, as far as she was concerned.

The kitchen door fell into place behind them, and the aroma of coffee greeted her nostrils. "Smells like good coffee," the sheriff said, taking a seat at the long table. He looked around the cheerful kitchen, his gaze hesitating on the potted plants she'd placed by the window, the checked curtains she'd hung only this week.

"Didn't look like this the last time I was here," he said finally.

"What did you want to talk to me about?" Angelena asked bluntly. He'd apparently given up on insulting her. But what his next foray would include was yet to be heard.

"I just thought we might get acquainted, ma'am." He waved his hand at the stove, and an unexpected grin was aimed in her direction. "Can you spare a cup of that coffee?"

Angelena nodded, pulling a thick mug from the cupboard. "Cream, Sheriff?"

"No, straight up." He tilted his chair back and watched her. "You're not havin' any?"

She shook her head. "I drink tea. I'll make some in a minute."

"I remember you sayin' that."

A grin curved his lips again and she felt an answering curl deep within. *Glory!* Somewhere inside her chest a hundred hummingbirds were fluttering. Angelena's gaze dropped to the coffee she'd poured, and she considered it witlessly. Her fingers gripped the handle and she lifted it, noting the contents sloshing as she took it to the table.

"Let me get that, Miss Angelena," he said, rising quickly, taking it from her, casting her a questioning look. "You all right?"

"Yes, of course. I'll just get the tea." She turned back to the cupboard, searching for her tea ball, sorting through the assortment of utensils. It gleamed dully at the bottom of a crock and she fished it out, filling it quickly from the metal tin that held her prized green tea.

"What's that thing?" he asked, peering over her shoulder. His breath was warm against her skin, penetrating the fabric of her dress, and she closed her eyes. Allowing him access to the kitchen had been a mistake.

"A tea ball," she murmured. "I know a man who makes them, and he gave it to me." And how she knew that was a puzzle, she realized, aware that she'd just peered into a part of her past. "It holds the leaves and it brews without leaving a residue in the bottom of your cup."

"You'll miss out on having your fortune told that way," he announced, returning to the table with his coffee.

As though a stone settled in her stomach, she was struck by his words. What she wouldn't give for someone capable of seeing her future. Her eyes misted, and she blamed it on the steam from the hot water she poured into her china cup.

Better yet, she'd give all she owned to know the secrets lurking in her past.

"You planning on staying on here?" the sheriff asked, settling in his chair. Angelena pulled out a chair for herself, and slid onto its seat.

"I'm not sure what my plans are yet."

He eyed her over the rim of his mug. "Jason's damn lucky to have you here, but I have to wonder why you chose a place like this to work in. I'd think your voice belongs in a music hall, with an orchestra in the pit. Or maybe in one of those theaters where they bring in a different troupe of singers every once in a while."

She nodded, swishing the tea ball back and forth in her cup. "I don't think I've ever sung in a place like the Golden Slipper before. But I didn't see a theater here in Edgewood, when I arrived." She shook her head and lifted her gaze to his.

"Why Edgewood?" His hands embraced the mug and he leaned forward. "Where'd you come from, ma'am?"

She drew in an unsteady breath. "Is that an official question?"

"No, just my curiosity talkin' out loud, I guess."

The kitchen door opened and Jason stood on the threshold. "Things all right out here? Miss Angel?" His eyes slanted a look at the sheriff, and Angelena felt the comfort of her employer's protection.

"Dex went on home," Jason told her. "Said you had the songs down pat anyway. He'll see you later on."

Angelena nodded, sipping at her tea.

Wes stood, drinking the last swallow from his cup. "Everything's just fine, Jason. I'm about to leave. Miss Angelena was kind enough to offer me coffee."

"Anytime, Wes. Pot's always on the back of the stove," Jason told him.

Angelena watched as the two men left, her gaze measuring the shoulders of the man Jason had called Wes. And then he was back, broad shoulders nudging the door open as he allowed it to rest against his back.

"Thanks for the coffee, ma'am. I forgot to introduce myself, I'm afraid. Name's Wesley Tanner." He placed his hat squarely atop his head, nodded a farewell and was gone, leaving her shaken, only too aware of his dark eyes, the curve of his mouth.

She searched her mind, hoping for a glimmer of remembrance. Somewhere in the shadows of her past, there must have been another such man who had stirred her senses. Else she would not have recognized the sheriff as a danger. And for certain, he was that very thing. His warmth, his scent—the very sound of his voice—spoke to her womanhood, and some inner voice gave warning of peril.

Yet, for all his masculine bearing, he allowed one part of himself to answer to the woman he called mother. It was that soft center she was drawn to, that kernel of concern that lent him an air of vulnerability.

Angelena shook her head, as if by that small action she could rid her thoughts of the man. Her hands sought the comfort of daily tasks, performed for the past weeks as an early-morning ritual. The freshening of the coffeepot, the baking of cinnamon rolls in the big oven, a skill she seemed to have brought with her from another life.

Her movements were automatic as she uncovered the plump, raisin-filled specimens atop the warming oven. With barely an admiring glance for her creations, she slid the pan into the yawning oven and closed the door. By the time they were done, she would have a dozen eggs ready to scramble and a panful of thickly sliced bacon on a platter.

Somewhere in her shadowed past, she had learned to cook, and that alone would have earned her a haven here, according to Jason Stillwell. He'd watched her closely, that second day she'd spent in this place, his sharp eyes aware of every move she made as she cooked and served a late breakfast to his girls.

And then he'd offered her a place to stay, a stage to sing upon and the security of a locked door at night. A proposition she'd grabbed. The women had been another matter, their reticence understandable once she'd recognized the vulnerability of their livelihood.

Now she heard them clattering down the back stairway, approaching the kitchen, their voices blending in a chorus of teasing remarks. She recognized a kinship with each of them. Not because of their positions here, for she tried to ignore the activities in those upstairs rooms. Instead, she sensed the precarious situations they lived with, and hers was perhaps the most likely to collapse around her.

At least they knew why their paths had led them to the

Golden Slipper. Only a blank wall faced Angelena when
she turned to search out the memories she'd once known.
And that fact made her the most vulnerable of all.

The bevy of women, in various stages of undress,
pushed through the door and clustered around the table
behind Angelena.

"How'd you get the sheriff upstairs?" Sarah Jane asked,
an edge of spite coating her words. "I been tryin' for two
years to coax him into my room, honey. Less than two
months, and you've got him at your heels."

"Cut it out," Mary Ellen admonished her. "Don't mess
with the cook, my mama always said. Besides, Angel
didn't have to coax Wes Tanner up those stairs." Her voice
lowered to a seductive undertone. "I saw him watchin' her
sing the other night." The boa she wore lost a feather, and
Angelena caught it midair before it settled into the pan of
scrambled eggs.

"Don't mess with my breakfast," Jolene warned, sashaying to stand guard beside Angelena. "Angel makes the
best food we've eaten since Henry Tolliver left, bless his
heart." She bent to peer into the pan. "Sure looks good,
honey."

Angelena held her breath as the residue of perspiration
and stale perfume met her nostrils. Later on, when they'd
all had their share of hot water and soap, the women would
regain some semblance of cleanliness. Now, in the confines
of the kitchen, their bodies bore the odor of men and
booze, mixed with the scents of cologne each woman pre-
ferred.

She'd kept herself apart for the first few days here, and
then, to her amazement, found that beneath the feathers
and froufrou of their attire dwelt four women who clung
together because they had no one else with whom to share
their lives.

Lily took her place at the foot of the table, a spot she claimed as senior member of the group. "How about pourin' some of that coffee, Sarah Jane," she murmured, her smile lazy as she watched Angelena turn to face her. "You girls need to lend a hand. Angel's been workin' hard over that stove."

Their meal was long and drawn out, each woman set on outdoing the next as they discussed the men who frequented the saloon. It was a topic they never seemed to tire of, but as the comments grew more ribald, Angelena rose, excusing herself, and left the kitchen.

She'd left Dex hanging earlier, and as she climbed the back staircase, she resolved to visit the general store and extend her apologies. He made it a point to run over her music each day, usually in the morning. Before long he'd be off to share dinner with his wife, a meal he'd cook and carry through town in a covered basket.

His devotion to the woman who ran the emporium with an eye to business and a genuine smile of welcome to each customer was well known.

Although Jason paid Dex well to play, Angelena was only too aware that his nightly appearance at the Golden Slipper was because of her own presence there. They shared a bond, tacitly understood by each of them, that in no way infringed upon that which involved his wife.

Music was the focus of Angelena's narrow existence in Edgewood, and Dex respected the talent that drove her to perform.

She changed her dress, smoothed her hair into place and left the saloon by the back door, not wanting to appear in public view from the doors that opened onto the sidewalk. The whole town might be aware that she sang nightly in the Golden Slipper. But she didn't need to advertise the fact.

Pip greeted her with a grin as she entered the store. "I hear you had company."

"Your husband talks too much," Angelena answered, looking around the store for the man in question. "Is he here?"

Pip nodded toward the curtained doorway that opened into the back room. "He's working on the books and watching the baby while I get some remnants marked."

"Would you offer my apologies to him? I fear I walked out on our rehearsal and then, what with cooking for the ladies, I truly forgot to speak to him."

Pip nodded, folding a length of yard goods into a neat square and pinning a price tag on the selvage edge. "He said you really didn't need the practice anyway. One of these days I'm going to come with him and listen to you sing." She looked up from the neat pile of fabric she'd measured and priced for sale.

"I heard you the other day when you rocked the baby in the back room, and I swear, my heart was in my throat when you were singin' to him."

Angelena's eyes misted at the honest words of praise. "I must have sung lullabies at some time in my life. Somehow, the words come to me whenever I touch that blessed child."

"Well, that 'blessed' child is about to wake up from his morning nap, unless I miss my guess." Pip cocked her head, listening to the soft sounds coming from the room beyond the curtain. It held a crib next to the desk, both wedged between tall shelves of merchandise.

"Maybe I'll stay for a bit then," Angelena decided. "He smells so sweet and sleepy when he first wakes up."

"Depends on which end you're sniffin'," his mother stated. "I'll just run in and make him sweet for you, if you want to play with him awhile. Besides, you haven't told me yet what Wes Tanner had to say to you."

Angelena felt a flush climb her cheeks, and she turned away to run her hand over a bolt of dimity laying on the counter. "This would make a lovely dress, don't you think?"

Pip laughed aloud. "You won't get out of it that easily. I intend to hear all about your visitor. It's about time the sheriff took an interest in a woman. I'd about given up hope for him."

Angelena's hand hesitated, then halted. "I don't think you're on the right track, Pip. He's not a man to be interested in a saloon singer. Not in the way you mean. And contrary to what some of the women in this town think, I don't entertain gentlemen in my room."

"Well, I'm glad to hear that." From the far corner of the store, a sharply spoken retort brought Angelena's head up as new color surged to her face.

A matronly figure made her way toward the counter, a pair of shoes in hand. "I was settin' over there tryin' on shoes, Phillipa. I think these will do."

"Mrs. Comstock." Pip's eyebrows rose as she greeted the woman. "I forgot you were in the store. May I introduce you to Miss Angelena?"

"I reckon so," Bernice Comstock said. Her gaze was piercing as she scanned Angelena's slender form. "My husband tells me you have a fine voice, young woman. I have to wonder why you're wastin' it on a bunch of drunken cowhands."

Angelena was torn between amusement and embarrassment. Amusement won the tussle and she smiled at the shrewd-eyed matron. "I needed work, and Jason Stillwell offered me a job. I needed a place to stay, and he gave me a room."

"Makes sense, I suppose. You don't make much singing in church on Sunday morning. And there aren't many positions open for young ladies in this town. It just seems a shame that you spend your days in the company of fallen women."

Angelena felt led to disagree but found no words to dispute the woman's statement. Fallen women needed friends as much as anyone else in this world, she wanted to say. Yet it was true that she had little in common with the four ladies she cooked for, only that they faced a bleak future, as did she.

"Where you from?" Bernice asked bluntly.

"Back east." Since the train she'd been travelling on had come from that direction, Angelena thought it a logical conclusion.

"Humph. No family?"

That was a stumper, and only the baby's squall from the back room saved her from a reply. She turned grateful eyes in that direction as the curtain was pulled aside and Dex thrust his son through the doorway.

"I'll freshen him up for you," she said eagerly.

"You won't be in such a hurry when you get a little closer," Dex drawled, offering the child into her care.

Angelena took the teary-eyed babe in her arms and nodded a brief farewell to Bernice Comstock. Her steps carried her quickly past the curtain and into the back room.

No family? She shivered as the two words resounded in her head, comprising a question she had no way of answering.

Chapter Three

He would not. He definitely would not take one step in the direction of the Golden Slipper. His jaw clenched, his hat firmly in place, Wes fingered the gun belt he had just put aside. If he stepped outside the door of the jailhouse, the belt would be buckled into place. On the other hand, if he climbed the steps to his rooms upstairs, he could put his gun next to his bed and forget for a while that he was responsible for law and order in Edgewood, Texas.

His door was open; the evening breeze played with the papers on his desk, and in the distance he heard the unmistakable sound of Dex Sawyer's piano. A roar sounded from the direction of the Golden Slipper and Wes closed his eyes as he imagined the sight that multitude of men was cheering with such gusto.

He snorted his derision. All this fuss over a saloon singer, a woman who probably wasn't any better than any run-of-the-mill— He shook his head. She was different, maybe not better, but she sure enough was different. Even his jaded soul had to admit that. Left the men panting every time.

Sashaying her little butt up those stairs with not a look

over her shoulder, knowing that every eye in the house was on her.

"Damn!" His curse was softly spoken. "You're no better than those ranch hands, all wet behind the ears and half in love with a woman who plays them like the strings of a harp." It was an admission of attraction he'd been fighting for longer than a week, watching for her, wondering about her.

It was time he did something about it.

His hands buckled the gun belt as he crossed the doorsill. He reached back to shut the door and then watched as the doors of the Golden Slipper swung open, allowing a wide beam of light to form a path across the dusty road. He headed for that beam the way a ship would gravitate toward a beacon from shore, then stood watching as the doors swung shut once more, leaving only the glow from the top and bottom of those louvered doors to lure him there....

From within the saloon a cheer arose, followed by a hush announcing the arrival of tonight's entertainment. He could see her in his mind's eye, center stage, her golden hair curling over her shoulders and halfway down her back. The doors were before him and he pushed against one, angling his big body to edge inside the smoky room.

She was there, hands clasped loosely before her, eyes on Dex Sawyer as an unspoken message passed between them. Dex nodded and his fingers touched the keys of the upright piano. As if the notes spoke to her, Angel tilted her head, her eyes closing, a small smile flirting at the corners of her mouth.

Dex's fingers paused and Angel tilted her head back, her mouth opening as a sound emerged that sent chills down Wes's spine. The note ascended, becoming a series of words, then dove to the bottom of the scale and whispered of heartbreak. A sigh rose from the men assembled, and Wes inhaled sharply, not willing to join in this mass worship.

Looking deliberately away from the woman on stage, he made his way to the bar, meeting Jason's grin with a cynical glare of his own. Turning his back on the stage, he leaned both elbows on the bar, glancing against his will toward the mirror that cast an image of the room behind him.

Damn, she even looked good through the smudges Jason had allowed to mar the surface of his new mirror. The sea of men surged to its collective feet as her song ended on a low, subdued note. Their cheers resounded from the walls, and Jason's laugh was taunting as he slid a glass half the length of the bar to where Wes stood.

"Drink up, Sheriff. Your lip's hangin' low tonight. Never saw you frown so much in all the years I've known you."

The glass held an amber liquid, and for a moment Wes was tempted. That second of seduction, when the scent of Jason's best whiskey reached his nostrils, brought back almost forgotten memories. He shoved the glass to one side and turned away, its odor no longer an appeal.

Now there was an appealing sight and sound, and if he were only close enough, he'd guarantee the aroma surrounding the woman on the stage would far outclass the finest bottle of hooch Jason could come up with. Angel bent forward, just a little, listening to a ranch hand at a front table, as he sang out his request.

Standing erect, she nodded to Dex Sawyer and folded her hands at her waist as Dex's fingers swept the length of the keyboard, chording an introduction to the song she'd agreed to perform.

"I want to see her afterward," Wes said in an undertone,

aware of Jason's presence behind him. Unbidden, the words had left his lips as if they'd hovered there, waiting only for a breath to spin them into being.

"She doesn't entertain," Jason said softly. "I told you that already."

"I want to talk to her." As though underladen with steel, his words were a barrier to persuasion.

Jason shrugged. "Can't deny the sheriff his rights as a lawman, I guess. Here." Loosening a key from a ring at his waist, he handed it across the bar. "Your word, Sheriff?"

With a nod, Wes agreed, palming the key and sliding it into his front pocket. The door to the back room beckoned and he made his way there, moving behind the men who barely noticed his passage.

The murmur of voices and the sound of tumblers rearranging themselves inside the door's lock brought him out of the chair he'd claimed. His footsteps were slow as he rounded the bed and then paused, watching as the door swung open and Angel stepped over the sill.

"Want me to come in, honey?" Lily asked from the hallway.

"No, I'll just rest awhile." Angel's voice was weary, her head bowed. She closed the door, and in the dim light from the window, he watched as she leaned against the wooden panel, her white dress outlining her slender form.

His conscience twinged, knowing she thought herself alone; yet he waited, unable to draw his gaze from her shadowed face. Her chin lifted and one hand rose to brush the hair from her face.

"Miss Angelena?" Reluctantly, he broke the silence, stepping forward as his words brought a gasp from her lips.

"It's Wes Tanner, ma'am." He spoke hastily, lest a scream should call Jason from behind the bar.

"Sheriff?" Her head turned, and she flattened her arms and hands against the wall behind her.

"You want to turn on a light?" he asked quietly.

"How did you get in here?" She moved then, edging past the bed to where a kerosene lamp sat on the dresser. Her fingers were unsteady, allowing the glass chimney to clink against the metal that held it in place. A match flared, then the wick caught its flame and she settled the chimney once more.

The light was behind her as she turned to face him, her eyes wide and wary. "Jason gave you a key, didn't he?"

Wes nodded. "I told him I wanted to talk to you. I came up the back way."

"You're the man in charge, it seems. What do you want?"

He stepped closer, his hands trembling as he shoved them into his pockets. "I've never done anything quite like this before, ma'am. Can't say for sure why I'm doin' it now."

Her eyes pierced him with a knowing look. "I don't have men in my room, Sheriff."

"I don't want to visit you in your room, Angelena. Not the way you're talkin' about, anyway." He allowed his gaze to move from her face, although heaven knew there was enough there to appeal to him for a good long time. Her breasts were full and youthful beneath the bodice of her gown, and he clenched his fists, cramping them inside the confines of his pockets. She was almost too perfect, too appealing, too much woman for his needy body to ignore.

"Where, then, would you like to visit me?" she asked evasively.

"That easy, ma'am? You're willing to see me, away from here?"

She shook her head. "No. I can't be 'easy,' even for you, Sheriff." She lifted her chin and met his gaze, her eyes dark with weariness. "I'm not even sure I've ever been with a man. And it isn't what I want now." She turned her head away. "That is what we're talking about, isn't it?"

His hand waved aside her query as a given. "What do you mean?" His voice was an incredulous whisper. "How can you not know whether..." One hand, then the other, slid from his pockets and he stepped closer to her.

"I have no memory," she said bluntly. "I only know my name, and that I can sing. I remember words and music, and once in a while a picture flits through my mind."

He reached for her, his fingers tightening around her waist, and she stiffened, a shiver running the length of her body as her hands rose to press against his chest.

"You don't like to be touched?" His hands curved to mold her, long fingers almost meeting in the center of her back, yet he made no move to draw her closer.

She closed her eyes, and from beneath each lid a tear slid, hovering a moment before falling to her cheeks. Dark lashes lifted and blue eyes were awash. "What do you want with me?"

Harshness edged his words. "You know damn well what I want, Angelena. My hands have been itchin' to touch you from the first time I laid eyes on you."

He lifted his shoulders, hesitating, weighing his words with persuasion. "I can take good care of you, make sure no one else bothers you."

She shivered. "Jason is already doing that. I don't have men in my room, Sheriff."

He shook his head, his jaw taut. "There'd only be me,

Angel. Nobody else but me. I'll make it worth your while, and I'll be good to you.''

Her eyes widened, glossy with tears and her teeth bit harshly at her bottom lip. The whispered denial of his offer came as no surprise. ''No, I can't do that. I can't be a whore for any man.''

It took every bit of self-control in his possession to allow her the distance she had set between them, and Wes felt a fine line of perspiration break out across his forehead and above his upper lip as he thought of what he might find in her arms. ''Look, I can help you, if you want.''

''No, I won't do what the other girls here do. I'm not like that. I know I'm not,'' she whispered after a moment.

''Yeah?'' The single word was doubt-filled, and he cocked his head, one eyebrow lifting. ''I've seen your sort before, Angel. But that doesn't make you any less appealing, knowing you've probably...''

She glared at him, frustration livid in her eyes. ''How do you know anything about me? I don't even know myself what I've done or haven't done in my life.'' Her voice broke and her whisper was barely audible. ''There's a dark hole behind me, and I'm afraid to fall into it. I feel safe here. No one bothers me.''

His grunt of derision brought a flush to her cheeks. ''Here? You feel safe in a two-bit saloon in a town in Texas? Honey, you're only as safe as that door over there. One good punch with a cowhand's heel and you'd be fair game. Jason can't guarantee you protection any farther than that.''

''I have a key,'' she said staunchly. ''The men don't bother me.''

''Give 'em time. One of these nights some drunk is gonna plow his way into this room and you'll find yourself in a pile of—'' He hesitated, unwilling to sully her ears

with crudity. Unwilling to think about another man pos-
sessing those curves.

And yet, he reminded himself, he let her know he was
more than willing to claim her body himself. Hell, he was
beyond willing. Eager was a better word, maybe even
champing at the bit.

She tilted her head, and golden strands of hair glittered
in the lamplight. "This is blackmail, isn't it?"

Damn if she wasn't about halfway to giving in, he
thought exultantly. His lips twitched and he forbade the
smile to appear. "Lawmen don't do blackmail, ma'am."

She leaned forward, her lips opened, and she bravely
whispered words that put paid to his good humor. "What
will your mother say?" Her lips curved in a trembling half
smile as she awaited his reply.

"My mother? You think I'm gonna tell my mother?
She's got nothing to do with this, honey. I doubt she's
gonna be visiting you anytime soon." And yet the vision
of Rosemary Tanner chastising him held not a whit of humor as he glumly surveyed the woman facing him.

"I'm not sure you're as tough as you'd like me to think,
Sheriff," she said softly, her voice stronger. "You gave
yourself away the other day." Her smile widened, and he
half expected her to laugh aloud. At him.

Damned if the female wasn't taunting him.

She stood there in front of him and mocked him, her
head tilted just so, hair gleaming in the pale glow of lamplight. It was more than he could bear, this woman turning
down the first offer he'd made to a female in a coon's age.

He growled a curse, leaned forward to muffle it against
her mouth and took possession of tender lips. He'd meant
to take what he wanted, show her his anger, but it was not
to be. This was not what he'd expected, this fresh, sweet

revelation of innocence, soft breath exhaling in a surprised gasp. It was beyond his experience.

He held her with a tenderness that was rare to him, inhaling her scent, tasting heaven for the first time in his life. One hand slid, finding its way to the rounding of her hips, the other the slender span of her shoulders, and he lifted her against his body, there, where his arousal was quickly becoming a fact.

His lips shifted, softened and settled again. Beneath their pressure her mouth trembled, tensing as he brushed its surface. A soft, pleading sound whispered against his mouth and he ignored it, unwilling to heed her distress.

"Hush. I won't hurt you," he whispered, barely allowing room for the words to exit his mouth, intent on savoring the sweetness of soft flesh. His teeth clasped her bottom lip, a primitive gesture, pleading for entrance. She inhaled sharply, her lips parting.

It was the opening he sought. His tongue explored the inside of her lower lip, then touched the ridges of her teeth before venturing further. He was avid, tracing the roof of her mouth, hearing, yet almost ignoring, the broken sounds of her breathing.

She sobbed, her body shuddering, and it was that note of distress that brought a halt to his foray. "Angelena...." He lowered her till her feet touched the floor, one hand lifting to cradle her head, bringing it to his chest. "I said I wouldn't hurt you, honey. Did I lie?"

And if he had, if he'd done her harm, he'd walk out the door and not look back, he decided ruefully. To hell with taking her as his mistress. Much as he wanted this woman, he'd not be accused of using force.

She was silent, her trembling ceasing as she leaned against him, her breathing quiet as he held her with careful touches. His hand slid from her hip to span her waist, and he offered support without coercion, as if he would release her if she so desired.

"No, you didn't hurt me," she managed to whisper. Her head lifted from its place and his flesh was chilled where her warmth had been. She tilted her head back, seeking his gaze, and he met it uneasily.

He'd exposed himself, allowing his need for her to run rampant, a need he'd managed to keep under control for more years than he wanted to count.

He knew she could make him look a fool if she wanted to. One shriek, one call for help, and he would lose his reputation as a man of honor among the people of this town. They might grin behind his back and class him with the rowdy cowhands, looking for a quick roll. Or they might relish the thought of Wesley Tanner stooping to force a woman to his will.

He straightened. His reputation reflected the upbringing he'd received at the hands of Gabe Tanner, a man he would gladly die for. He bent his head, nodding slowly.

"I won't deny I want you. I'd be a fool and a liar if I did. But I'd be a bigger fool if I tried to talk you into something you couldn't live with." He molded his palm to the nape of her neck, his fingers tangling in curls and waves that clung to his skin. His other hand left her waist, and with hesitant fingers he traced the damp line of her cheek, where so recently a tear had traveled. Her skin was like soft velvet, her features fine and delicate, and he was stricken with the urge to lift her in his arms and take her from this place.

"Miss Angelena." From outside the door, a voice called her name, and she turned from him, his arms falling to his sides as she crossed the room.

"Who is it?" she asked quietly.

"It's Sarah Jane. Jason wants to know if you're all right."

Angelena leaned her forehead against the door. "Yes, I'm fine. I'm going to rest for a while before the second show."

The reply was dubious. "I'll tell him what you said. You're sure you're all right?"

Angelena's shoulders rose and fell. "I'm fine." She faced the door, her head tilted as she listened to the footsteps fade from hearing. Then turning, she leaned against the heavy oak panel. "Have I sealed my fate?" she asked quietly. "Jason will think..." As though she could not speak the words, she hesitated.

"He won't think anything has gone on here," Wes said quietly. "He knows me better than that. I gave him my word."

"Really?" A dubious smile flickered into being and she straightened, walking toward the bed.

"You were never in any danger from me, not here. When I have you in bed, it won't be in a room over a saloon."

"*When* you have me in bed?" she repeated as if she had not heard him aright. *"When?"*

"When. When you're ready, when the time is right."

Her look was more confident, as if she recognized the absence of danger. "You don't want to be tangled up with a woman who doesn't even know who she is. Who doesn't know anything about her past."

"Your past doesn't enter into it," he said bluntly. "It's your future I'm interested in."

"Wes Tanner hiked out to the kitchen tonight while Angel was singing," Dex said in the midst of a yawn. He settled himself contentedly next to Pip and reached one long arm to haul her to him.

Aiding his cause, she scooted closer after one last look at the crib against the far wall of the bedroom. Within his nest, her child slept the dreamless sleep of the young and innocent. She sighed contentedly, and then, as if she pondered Dex's statement, she frowned at him. "Where did he go?"

His grin was wide. "Well, when he came back into the saloon, he walked down the stairway, like he'd been visiting one of the rooms upstairs."

"Wesley Tanner? I don't believe it." Her words were vehement, her mouth pursed. "He wouldn't be looking at those women for…well, for anything, unless he's fooled me for a lot of years."

Dex leaned closer and whispered in her ear. "The only one of the girls upstairs was Angelena. Sarah Jane went up for a minute. I think old Jason sent her up to check on Angel, and then she trotted right back down."

Pip looked at her husband disbelievingly. "Are you saying that Angelena entertained the sheriff in her room? I don't believe it," she repeated.

He shook his head. "I'm not telling you anything. I'm just saying it looked to half the men around these parts like Wesley Tanner had been visiting our new singer. He walked down those stairs and out the door, looking neither right nor left. Had a grim sorta look about him, like nobody'd better ask him any questions."

"Humph." It was an indescribable response, Dex decided. His usually agreeable wife was stymied, and that fact probably did not bode well for his chances tonight. He'd set her to thinking, and with a sigh, he wished silently that he'd kept his mouth shut until the candle had been snuffed and good-nights said.

"Dex? You don't really think—no, of course, you don't," Pip said decisively, answering her own query. She turned to face him. "Angelena's a good girl. I don't care where she lives or works, she's an innocent young woman. I can tell."

"She's lonely," Dex offered. "Might do her good to be friends with the sheriff."

"I doubt being friends is what he'd have in mind, now that I think about it," Pip muttered. "You'll keep an eye on her, won't you?"

"You're not afraid I might…you know?" His drawl was meant to tease, and his lifted brow accented the gibe.

Pip lifted herself on one elbow and leaned over her husband. "For whatever reason, Mr. Sawyer, you married the town's old maid. You didn't have to, you know. She'd have given her eyeteeth to belong to you in any way, shape or form." She leaned over him to plant a lusty kiss next to his mouth.

"You haven't looked at another woman in twelve years. You've given me three redheaded boys who about run us both ragged, and a beautiful yellow-haired baby to boot. You come home to me every night of the week. Now, tell me why I should start watchin' over your shoulder at this late date?"

He lifted a hand to cup her cheek, his eyes filled with the simple beauty of the woman he loved. "There's something about her, Pip. I can't explain it, but she tugs at me, like there's this tie between us."

"It's the music," Pip said quietly. "You're filled with it, Dex, and so is she. It's a gift, God-given and pure, and you share it. Don't be thinking I'll ever fear such a thing."

"I love you, Phillipa Sawyer," he said solemnly, pulling her closer for his kiss.

"Yeah?" she said with a grin. "Wanta cuddle?"

* * *

The sheriff's office was dark, but a light glowed from the rooms above. Angelena sat just inside her window, the curtain hiding her from onlookers below, watching the shadowed form of Wes Tanner pace the floor. He hesitated just in front of one window, drawing the lace curtain to one side, and she felt his gaze as if it were a living presence against her flesh.

He couldn't see her, she was certain of that, hidden as she was in the darkness. And yet an almost palpable sensation brushed her skin as he watched from across the street.

"Wes Tanner." She whispered the name, tasting the syllables. And then she touched the roof of her mouth and the inside of her lips with her tongue, remembering the taste of his mouth, the flavor of mint he'd left behind.

She'd have been willing to swear that she'd never been kissed in such a way. She'd searched her mind for the past fifteen minutes, attempting to envision such a happening somewhere in her past. It was not to be. The dark walls of the room where she stood were no more impenetrable than the blank areas of her mind shielding her past.

Tears rolled down her cheeks and she brushed at them impatiently. Crying never helped. She'd spent hours at it for the first few days here; then she'd dried her tears and spent her energy on better things.

If she lit the lamp, he could see her. He'd watched one other night. She'd known his eyes followed her movements and had ignored his presence across the street. She leaned closer to the window, holding the curtain aside just a bit, unwilling to allow its filmy beauty to cast an additional blur on his image.

He was before the window now, leaning on the sill, his hands widespread. His face was a bit indistinct, but it didn't matter, for she could recall it in minute detail, from the dark eyes, deep-set and piercing, to the long line of his jaw where muscles twitched when he was upset or impatient.

As he'd been tonight. Just before he'd kissed her.

He wanted her in his bed. She shivered as that thought lingered, tempting her beyond belief. What would await her there was a mystery, only one in a long line.

But the most tempting of them all.

Bernice Comstock had posed a question she could not answer. What if she had left family behind, in that mysterious place where she'd come from? What if part of that family included a husband? Had she ever done what Wes wanted of her? Would she know how to please him?

She closed her eyes as a flush crept up her throat. The image of Wesley Tanner flooded her mind, this time intent on fulfilling his promise. Her eyes blinked open and she shook her head, leaning forward, brushing the curtain aside to gain the breeze against her skin.

A motion caught her eye, and her gaze homed in on the man who watched. He lifted his hand in a salute she could not help but recognize as mocking. Her own hand rose, fingers clenched, as her fist brushed against her mouth. She bit at her knuckle, then allowed her fingertips to spread the width of her lips.

The curtain fell into place and she backed away from the window. Below, the music was raucous, one of the men pounding out a melody, the rest joining in to sing.

What if one of them came up the stairs? What had the sheriff said? *One good punch with a cowhand's heel.* She shuddered. The thought of a man in her room brought a chill to her flesh. And yet, her memory prodded, she'd been warmed by Wesley's presence.

Her sigh was deep. If she should need him, if she should scream, Wesley Tanner would hear her.

Wesley Tanner would hear her. She held that thought tightly.

And whispered his name as she slept.

Chapter Four

"Is breakfast comin' pretty soon?" The whiskey-soaked voice whined from behind Wes, and he grunted an unintelligible reply. The cell farthest from his desk was occupied, Duane Goody having been too drunk to climb aboard his horse when the Golden Slipper closed last night. Lest the man stumble into more trouble than he'd already managed to get into, Wes had trundled him off to a thin mattress and a single blanket at the far end of the jail.

"Sheriff?" The mournful cry, accompanied by the rattling of the cell door, pulled Wes from his thoughts, and he rose, keys in hand.

"Keep your pants on," he said, taking a deep breath before he entered the corridor. He caught a glimpse of Duane, both hands clutching the cell bars as if he were in dire need of their support.

"You got a mess to clean up before I let you out," Wes warned. "Get you a bucket of water and the mop and make that cell presentable." He unlocked the door and watched as Duane ambled from sight, snatching up an empty bucket before he headed toward the back door of the jail. A pump stood just outside, and Duane knew the routine.

In moments he was slinging the mop across the cell

floor, muttering beneath his breath. "If you'd left me be, I coulda made my mess in the street," he grumbled. Wes watched as the man walked past him with the bucket, aiming for the pump once more.

"I'll send you off with coffee," he offered. "Your horse is in the livery stable, and if you get a move on, I'll bet they've saved you something to eat back at the Richardson place."

"Damn woman can't cook for squat," Duane said with vehemence. "I've a mind to find someplace else to park my bedroll."

Privately, Wes thought the Richardson place would be well off if that were to come to pass. Still, tending to Duane gave him a reason to pin on his badge this morning. Some days it seemed like being the sheriff was about the easiest job in town.

He wondered if Oscar Rhinehold's days as sheriff had included tossing Nate Pender into a cell on occasion. Wes searched his memory, recalling nights when the man he'd called Father had not come home, in those days before Gabe and Rosemary Tanner had taken two children into their home. Nate's reputation as the town drunk had been well deserved, and Wes felt not a twinge of pity or remorse as he thought of the years that miserable specimen had spent in prison. No one here in Edgewood missed his presence, that was for certain.

Wes shook his head, dismissing the memories, and stepped to the doorway. He looked up and down the dusty street, nodding at a passing horseman. And then his gaze sharpened as the stranger drew up his mount in front of the bank, one hand resting for a moment on his gun.

The comforting weight of his own weapon resting against his thigh was a reminder that not every day was as peaceful as the past several had been. In less than a moment, the street before him could hold danger. In less time than that, a gun could be drawn and bullets fired. Life was uncertain at best, he reminded himself, stepping from the doorway to cross the street.

"Hey, Sheriff! Can I go now?" From behind him, Wes heard Duane's whine and he lifted a hand to bid the cowhand farewell. His mind was already focused on the man who'd pulled open the bank door, then stepped inside quickly.

From Phillipa's emporium, across the street and to his left, he caught sight of a woman, her hand on the beveled glass door as she moved onto the sidewalk. Her step was light, her golden hair gleaming in the morning sunlight, and his breath caught in his throat. Angel was out early, apparently. Maybe buying tea, he thought, remembering her slender fingers filling the silver tea ball she set such store by.

Well, whatever she was doing out and around this morning, she was about to walk past the bank at the wrong time. He stepped up on the sidewalk and moved quickly toward her.

"Miss Angel." His words were quiet, yet curt in his own ear, and he was not surprised when she looked up warily, clutching her purchases to her breast. "I'd appreciate it if you'd step back into Pip's store for a minute."

Blue eyes met his, then darted toward the lone horse tied to the hitching rail before the bank. "Is there a problem, Sheriff?"

He shook his head. "Probably not, ma'am. Just do as I ask."

Angel turned from him. "Yes, of course."

He watched as she slid inside the emporium, and then headed to the bank once more. The brass knob turned easily in his hand and he stepped inside the single room. It was spic and span, floor neatly swept and windows gleaming. Pace Frombert looked up from his desk, half hidden by the walnut barrier that separated the banker from his customers. One hand rose in a greeting, then fell back to his desk as Wes shook his head in a barely perceptible movement.

The stranger was before the single teller, speaking quietly, his manner that of a gentleman, and Wes allowed the hackles on his neck to settle into place. Probably no need to be concerned, he decided. Just a fella looking for a place to put his hard, cold cash.

With a murmured word, the stranger turned and headed for the door, meeting Wes's eyes with a narrowed gaze. "Morning," he said, nodding politely as he opened the door.

Wes turned to watch him go, alert to the appraising glance, the studied movements of the man. "Know that fella?" he asked Pace Frombert as the horse and rider trotted down the street.

"Nope, never saw him before. You got suspicions, Sheriff?" Pace asked, joining Wes at the doorway.

Wes shrugged. "Guess not. Just didn't like the looks of him for some reason. Kinda smelled like trouble, maybe." He grinned, dismissing his apprehension. "Besides, now that Duane Goody's on his way home, I've got an empty cell. Never know when you're gonna find a hardened criminal walkin' into the bank. Guess I need to earn my pay."

"You do that, Wes," Pace assured him, then turned to his teller, a young man with an earnest expression. "What did the gentleman want?"

"Just asked me about opening an account," Fred Hoskins answered quickly. "Seemed to be a nice enough man."

"What's his name?" Wes asked.

Fred shook his head. "Didn't say. Just told me he'd be back one of these days."

Wes reached for the doorknob. "Must be new around here. I didn't recognize him." He stepped onto the sidewalk and nodded at Pace. "Time for breakfast. Think I'll go over to the hotel and see what they're cookin' this morning."

"Same as always, like as not," Pace answered. He glanced past Wes, his eyes lighting up. "Now why don't you see if that young lady would fry up an egg for you, Sheriff. I'll warrant she could set a nice table."

Wes knew without turning who was behind him, and he felt a frown furrow his brow. "Maybe so, but not to my liking." And if that wasn't the biggest lie he'd told in a month of Sundays.

Pace backed into his bank and Wes drew in a deep breath, turning to face Angel. She hesitated, then halted beneath the overhanging porch of the newest shop in town, where a sign in the window announced the presence of a modiste, and hand-drawn sketches of fashionable dresses lined the lower sill.

"Good morning," he said laconically, one hand tilting his hat just a bit.

"What was that all about?" Angel asked, peering past him to where the rider was already on the fringes of town. "I thought surely I'd hear gunfire, or at least see you in hot pursuit, Sheriff. With all your precautions, I thought maybe the man was up to no good."

Wes shook his head. "Just checkin' him out, ma'am."

"And here I thought I'd get a chance to see you in action," Angelena said, her mouth twitching at one corner, as if she suppressed a smile.

"You almost got a chance at that last week, as I recall,"

Wes answered quietly, watching as his meaning sank in and Angel's cheeks turned a rosy hue.

"I beg your pardon," she said, her words cool, her eyes icy with what looked like contempt if he was any judge. She took a step forward. "I have work to do. I need to get back."

"You cookin' breakfast this morning?" Wes asked, stepping to her side, one hand clasping her elbow. "Maybe I'll join you."

She jerked against his hold, to no avail, then glared in earnest. "Please release me, Mr. Tanner. I have more to do than pass the time of day with you."

"I haven't seen you out and around lately," Wes said idly, ignoring her haughty demeanor. He set off in the direction of the saloon, his grip urging her to keep step.

Angelena's feet shuffled a bit as she attempted to keep up. "Did you ever think it might have been intentional? I could go for years without setting eyes on you, sir," she muttered, her head high as she stepped quickly, keeping pace with his long strides.

"Well, I sure as hell can't say the same," he growled, his voice as harsh as the grip he held on her arm. "We'll come to a meeting of minds yet."

"If you're thinking I'll ever be your doxy, you'll wait a long time," she said in a low voice. He glanced down, his look slanting over her face, noting the frown she wore. She bit at her lip then, and he recognized the flinch she could not suppress as his grip tightened again. Damn, he was hurting her, and that was the last thing he wanted to do.

He relaxed his hold and her eyes closed, her forehead once more smooth and unblemished. "Why didn't you tell me I was holdin' on too tight?" he asked, slowing his pace as he recognized her efforts to keep up with his long strides.

"Would it have done any good?" Her lips curved in a rueful smile, their lush fullness offering a invitation he was certain she was unaware of. And one that he itched to accept.

"Look." His feet felt leaden, his jaw tightened, and the urge to halt smack-dab in the middle of the sidewalk was right next door to being desperate. The woman was too much temptation by far, and all his good intentions were about to fly out the window. Reputation be damned! Even the sheriff was allowed to... He grimaced at that thought. Not in broad daylight, he wasn't.

The Golden Slipper was only feet away and he paused, unwilling to enter the swinging doors with her in tow. "You want to go ahead and I'll come around the back?"

She shook her head. "No, I'll go around the back. But I'd rather you didn't. I've not invited you for breakfast, Sheriff. Indeed, there is nothing between us that would call for such a visit to take place."

"Nothing? I don't agree with that, not one little bit, lady. But you can mark this down in your little book. Being my doxy is not what I have in mind for you."

"That was the impression I got the other night." Her voice was firm as she tore from his grasp. Her cheeks were pink, her nostrils flared, and that soft, alluring mouth formed a thin line. "Believe it or not, Sheriff, I want nothing to do with you."

His teeth gritted at her words of denial, and it was all he could do not to sweep her off her feet and tote her right through the damn doors and up the stairs. "We'll both go around the back," he announced, one long arm circling her waist as he hustled her around the far corner of the saloon and down the alleyway. She was reluctant, but aside from muttered words of protest, she allowed his dominance, waiting as he opened the back door of the saloon, then preceding him into the big kitchen. And there she took her stand.

One hand lifted, index finger extended, and she shook it in his face. The movement was so reminiscent of Rosemary, he bit his tongue to hold his laughter from erupting. Her words echoed in his ears, quiet, yet forceful. Damn if she hadn't gotten brave, all of a sudden.

"I told you I'm not cooking for you, Sheriff. In fact you'll be mightily embarrassed if you park your carcass here very much longer."

He leaned forward just a bit, sorely tempted to latch on to the tip of that gesturing finger. His mouth yearned to hold her captive, if only in this small way, but good sense prevented him from purposely angering her further. And yet her exasperated sigh told him he already had.

"It's about time for four ladies to come down those stairs, and when they do you might find yourself skedaddling out that door."

He blinked at her words of warning. "You mean they might be in a state of undress, ma'am? Wearin' their knickers, so to speak?" There was no help for it; his grin appeared, and a chuckle followed it.

"I don't see anything to laugh about," she said primly, turning from him to jerk her apron from its hook, then tying it in place. He almost expected her to sniff elegantly, somewhat like his Sunday school teacher back in the days when Rosemary'd dressed him up fit to kill and trotted him off to church. That female creature had often inhaled sharply as some of the more unwashed of his class entered the small, poorly ventilated room on Sunday mornings. Thankfully, he'd been a member of the Tanner household, exposed to soap and a tub full of hot water before being allowed to don his best pair of britches and a freshly ironed shirt.

Angelena favored him with a smoldering glance over her shoulder, her eyes holding more than a trace of aggravation. "You're crowding me, sir. The stove is hot." Pret' near as hot as she was, he thought privately, admiring the flush of anger she wore with such dignity, aware he was about to increase its intensity.

"Sorry, ma'am. Didn't mean to upset you."

He leaned closer, his words a growling whisper in her ear. "Hate to tell you otherwise, but the sight of a lady's drawers is not gonna cause me to faint dead away."

Her mouth twisted in a grimace as she turned to face him, and his hands were quick to tug her in his direction. "Don't want your apron strings to get all het up," he explained as he moved her from the stove. She looked about to explode, her hands trembling as she clenched them together.

"You are a rapscallion, Mr. Tanner. Obviously no one has taught you to speak nicely to a lady."

His brow rose in silent, mocking query as he absorbed the barb. "Are we talkin' about you, ma'am? The *lady* who makes her livin' in a saloon?" And wouldn't Rosemary blast him if she'd heard that remark?

As if someone had tossed her into a frigid stream, she began to tremble, her lips losing their color, her shoulders slumping. Worst of all, her eyelids fell to cover the brilliant blue eyes that had intrigued him with their fire and fury. His fingers slid to meet at her waistline and he drew her closer. She stumbled, as though her feet were glued to the floor, and a shivering sigh escaped her lips.

Head tilting back, the better to meet his gaze, she opened her eyes. The proud cast of her features was overshadowed by the glaze of sorrow as she watched him. One shoulder rose in a gesture that spoke of indecision, and then she pronounced her judgment.

"Just when I think there might be some small part of you I could like…" She shook her head and a smile twitched one corner of her mouth.

A sound behind him alerted him to listeners and he bent to speak in a low tone. "Don't be too angry with me, honey. My tongue tends to have a sharp edge when I'm out of sorts. Fact is, I'm just a needy soul, lookin' for a little sustenance."

Her shove was quick and effective, forcing her release from his hold. "Don't come looking here, Sheriff. I told you the other night. I have nothing to offer you."

And wasn't that a statement he'd give a whole lot to dispute.

His hands moved to clasp her shoulders, even as the four women reached the foot of the narrow stairway. He heard their whispers behind him, was aware of the smothered giggles they allowed to escape, and yet he could not leave her. His mouth touched hers softly and he inhaled the fragrance she wore. Lilacs, sure enough. He was causing enough gossip to flood the town six inches deep, should the wives get wind of it. But for this moment he cared little. The men who might hear of this encounter would not dare to repeat it to anyone, lest the sheriff of Edgewood find some reason to toss them in one of his jail cells.

He wanted Rosemary to see her. The thought emerged full-blown as his hands framed her face, uncaring of the audience behind him. Her blue eyes wore the guise of innocence, and for this moment her name was fitting. "Angel." His brow furrowed as he tasted the name on his tongue. "Angelena sounds better, doesn't it? Or maybe Lena? Anybody ever call you that?"

He watched as she shook her head, her lips compressed

as if she would hold back words, her eyes wide as she heard his questions.

"I don't think so. No, no one here, anyway," she said finally.

"I like it," he announced, aware that the shuffling footsteps behind him were retreating. "Especially if no one else…" It would be one small thing, branding her his own. *Lena.* His eyes drank in the pale beauty of her face, his ears heard only the soft sounds of her breathing, and his lungs filled with the aroma of fresh womanhood, mixed with the scent she favored. His fingers slid the length of her arms and he enclosed her trembling hands in his, drawing them to his mouth.

She closed her eyes again as he brushed his lips across her skin, opening his mouth to touch each knuckle with the tip of his tongue. "Look at me, honey," he said quietly, his gaze intent on the sweep of lashes as she obeyed. Now, this very moment, he could almost believe that Jason was right, that the cape of purity she wore was genuine, that beneath the beauty of form and figure lay a core of honesty and virtue.

"I'll see you later." It wasn't what he wanted to say, but the thought of an audience of giggling women overhearing his thoughts was off-putting. He waited a moment for her response, even if it was only a denial of his intent, but she was silent, still, as if some spell had overtaken her and left her frozen in place.

Wes backed from her, then, in three long strides was at the back door. He snatched his hat from the hook where he'd tossed it upon entering, and was gone. The alleyway held a clutch of boys, crouched around a circle drawn in the dirt. A marble squirted from one lad's fingers and rolled toward him, even as his presence was felt by the others.

Wes bent low, picked up the glass orb from the dirt and

examined it, holding it between two fingers. His eyes met those of the boy who had shot it in his direction, and he allowed a grin to curve his lips. "Nice shooter," he said, tossing the marble back.

"Thanks, Sheriff," the boy returned, snatching the aggie in midair. Red hair caught the sunlight as the lad stood facing him.

"Aren't you Dex Sawyer's boy?" Wes asked. "The oldest one?"

"Yes, sir, I sure enough am. My ma calls me Dexter." His chest puffed up a bit as he grinned widely. "My pa says he knew you when you was about my size."

Memories of his early years flashed through Wes's mind. Dex had been a champion when hope was all but gone. He walked past the circle of boys, aware of innocent blue eyes that met his with no hesitation. "Your pa's right, son. He was one of my heroes."

"Wow! Really? My pa?" If it were possible, his grin widened as Dexter Sawyer considered that fact; then he squatted once more, his importance established. An air of nonchalance sat on his shoulders as he accepted the honor due his father, and Wes heard the murmur of young voices speaking his name as he made his way down the alley.

He'd left her to face the firing squad. Answering the questions they were sure to ask was just about the equivalent of torture, Angelena decided. Making no attempt to hide their curiosity, the four women surrounded her.

"Did he kiss you?" Subtlety was not Sarah Jane's long suit, Angelena thought, even as she felt the hot sting of color travel to her cheeks.

"I haven't had a good kiss in ages," Jolene blurted. "Men don't hold with kissin'. They just like to get down to brass tacks."

Her cheeks burned anew as Angelena weighed the re-mark, and her stomach churned as she considered the brass tacks Jolene spoke of. "The sheriff was just being friendly. He walked me back from the emporium."

"I saw how friendly he was, with his hands all over you," Mary Ellen noted. "I'll just bet you he's gonna ask you to be available for visits."

"No, he's not!" Angelena turned away, lifting her hands to cover her face.

"Just cut it out, now," Lily said decisively. "We're about to lose our cook, girls, if you don't start behavin' yourselves here. Leave Angel be."

Jolene flounced to the table and settled herself in a chair. "Well, I've never seen Wes Tanner get so hot and both-ered about anybody else in this dump. Angel's gotta be givin' him a little something to keep him comin' around."

"That's enough!" Lily announced loudly. "Angel's doin' nothin' of the sort, and I oughta know." She looked around at the three women. "Seems like we could pitch in and help her this morning. She's a little behind, and Molly's gonna be here with our laundry any minute. Y'all got your bundles ready for her?"

Angelena pressed her lips together, thinking of the bas-ket in her room, where a week's worth of undergarments and her wash dresses waited. "I need to get mine ready, Lily. I forgot this morning."

"Well, you trot on up, and I'll put the coffee on while you're gone," Lily said, patting Angelena's shoulder, nudging her toward the stairway.

Knuckles rapped on the back door as Angelena ran si-lently up the stairs. "I'll bet that's Molly now," Lily said. "Go give her a hand, Sarah Jane."

Adjusting her belt, Sarah Jane sauntered to the door, swinging it open with a flourish. "Hope you got those stains out of my good red gown," she said, reaching to pick up a basket in the doorway.

A wide grin slashed Molly McCumbee's round face as she turned to her wagon and tugged at a second container. "You're sure enough a mess, Sarah Jane. Took me ten minutes scrubbin' with a piece of lamb's wool to clean that thing up. Thought you'd have a hole to mend before I got done with it. Next time you better get you a man that ain't so sloppy."

Sarah Jane shrugged. "Can't complain. He's a good tipper."

Molly plopped her heavy basket on the kitchen floor and removed the topmost wrapped bundle. "Well, one of you ladies has got herself a problem, if my calculations are right."

Lily stepped closer, keen eyes noting Molly's subdued look. "How's that?"

"This bundle's got no monthly rags in it. It's been more'n two months since the new gal's been here. Without a sign of her doin' her womanly thing. As a matter of fact, unless she's doin' her own washin' out in her room, she's headed for a mighty big problem." Molly looked over the four females before her. "You think she might be in the family way?"

Dead silence followed her query as the matter was considered. Then Mary Ellen spoke up. "Well, if she is, it didn't happen here. I'd bet my bottom dollar on that."

"You'd better tell Jason," Jolene told Lily, and her mouth curved in a smile. "Looks like our Angel ain't nearly as pure and innocent as Jason thought she was."

"That's enough," Lily said, her voice squelching Jolene's claim. "I'll take care of it. Not a word, you hear?" She looked around her, and three heads nodded a silent reply.

Molly shrugged. "It ain't none of my affair. I just thought somebody ought to know. Don't seem like that young'un's old enough to be let out of the nest, to my way of thinkin', and here she's maybe hidin' a secret under her skirts."

Angelena's voice echoed as she made her way down the steps. "I got it all together, Molly. Sorry I was so late." She reached the bottom of the stairs and halted, aware of four pair of eyes upon her. "Is something wrong?" she asked hastily.

"Nothin' I know of," Molly said with a cheerful smile. "I'll just gather up my load and be off. See you ladies next Wednesday, just like usual."

The women sorted out their own stacks of clean clothing, each bundle separated by a clean pillowcase within the baskets, and made their way up the stairs. In the corner of the kitchen, four pillowcases held Molly's work for the day, and Angelena lent a hand.

"I surely do appreciate you doing up my things, Molly. You remind me of the wardrobe lady—" Her eyes rounded as she spoke, and as quickly as it had made itself known, the vision of a woman carrying three fancy gowns across her arm vanished from her mind.

"Here, you're lookin' like a ghost," Molly said hastily, leading Angelena to a chair. "What's the matter, girl?"

"I just remembered something. A woman who used to do for me." Angelena closed her eyes, then opened them, blinking as a rush of heat enveloped her even as she shivered with a chill.

"You all right, honey?" Molly squatted before her, rubbing Angelena's hand briskly between her own. "You been feelin' poorly?"

"I'll tend to her." From the stairway, Lily spoke quietly. "She'll be all right, Molly."

A look of understanding passed between the two women, a glance not missed by Angelena. "I'm fine," she whispered, her mind awhirl with the black clouds of missing memories.

"Come on, sweetie," Lily told her with a smile. "I'll give you a hand here. We're all about to starve to death."

Angelena rose, seeking respite from the overwhelming sense of despair that sought once more to entangle her. "I'll be fine," she repeated. And as she busied herself with the everyday chores that made up her life in this place, the vision faded from her mind, and was all but forgotten.

"Look, Jason. I don't want to cause any trouble for the girl. Heaven knows she's got enough on her plate already, what with no memory and men sniffin' after her wherever she goes."

"Oh, yeah? Like who?"

Lily's eyes gleamed with humor as she faced the man across the bar. "You know damn well who I'm talkin' about. Wes Tanner can't keep his eyes off her, and half the men in the county are just itchin' to pay her a visit upstairs."

"Well, they're not gonna do it," Jason said stoutly. "I promised her she'd be safe here."

"Looks to me like somebody should have promised her that before she got here," Lily announced.

Jason leaned closer. "You really think she's..." He glanced around as if to guarantee their privacy. "I'm certain nobody's been up in her room since she got here. All but Wes Tanner, and he wasn't there long enough to cause this kind of a problem."

He shook his head. "Damn! I can't put the girl out on the street, but once she's showin', I can't have her up front on the stage. Why the hell didn't she say something when she hired on?''

Lily blotted at a drop of water on the bar, then snatched Jason's towel from his hand and rubbed it dry. ''I don't think she knows.'' She lifted her head, her shoulders hunching a bit as she leaned closer. ''She's about as innocent as they come, Jason. She pret' near upchucked in the kitchen this morning, and I've seen her reach for a chair, like she was dizzy, a couple of times, but I don't think she's got a notion in her head that she's gonna be hatchin' a chick one of these days.''

Jason inhaled deeply. ''Guess there's no help for it then. Keep a good eye on the bar for a while,'' Jason said, reaching across the wide, wooden expanse to brush a stray lock of hair from her cheek. ''I got me an idea. Let's see what I can do about it.''

''You checkin' on Duane Goody?'' Wes rose from his chair as Jason Stillwell entered the front door of the jail. ''I sent him home once he sobered up. He do any damage in your place?''

''Not enough to worry about,'' Jason said, halting before the battered walnut desk. ''You'd think the folks in Edgewood could buy you a decent piece of furniture for this office, Wes. That desk's 'bout as old as dirt.'' A chair behind him caught his eye and Jason gave it a second look. He occupied it, easing his body onto the seat, his legs straight before him, ankles crossed.

Wes eyed him warily. ''You never come callin' on me, Jason. What's the problem?''

Jason's brow lifted. ''There have to be a problem, son? You've paid me a couple of visits lately. Thought I'd return the favor.''

Wes's look was wry as he sat down. ''Reckon I'd better

settle back and wait for the fireworks to go off.'' He folded his hands against the broad expanse of his chest and watched his visitor.

Jason shifted in the chair, his grin barely visible, as if he hid a secret and only needed to be nudged a bit before he'd be willing to share it. ''Things are goin' good at the saloon,'' he began, eyeing the toe of his boot.

''You got a full crowd most every night,'' Wes agreed.

Jason shot a quick look across the desk. ''Can't hardly run those cowhands off, what with them wantin' to sniff around Angel.'' As if he pondered a length of fuse, he waited.

Dynamite, stifled by self-control, shone from Wes's eyes. His jaw tensed, crimson edged his cheekbones and his mouth formed a straight line, lips drawing back to expose gritted teeth. When he rose from his chair, Jason stiffened in his. When words of fury emerged from Wes's throat, Jason sidled toward the doorway. And when Wes allowed his anger to erupt in a curse word, the barkeep was across the threshold.

''Haul yourself back in here.'' Fit for a bear roused from his winter's nap, Wes's growl nailed Jason where he stood, and he hesitated for just a moment too long. ''You want to spend the night in a cell?''

His response to the threat might have been humorous had not Wes been so far beyond anger. As it was, the two men faced each other, one with fists clenched and body taut and ready for action, the other wishing he were anywhere on earth but smack-dab in front of Wes Tanner.

''Didn't mean to upset you, Sheriff,'' Jason managed to mutter.

''Didn't you?''

''Well,'' Jason began, tugging at his collar, ''I know you've been lookin' at the girl, but then so have half the men hereabouts. Thought you might like to know up front what's goin' on with her.''

"Spit it out," Wes said harshly, his hackles rising as a vague premonition scratched the surface of his mind.

"Well, I have a little problem. Maybe I'd better start off by sayin' that Angel has a little problem."

Wes moved around the desk, silent but with a deadly light in his eyes that would have frightened a lesser man. Jason spoke quickly, aware that his explanation must be terse and succinct. "Actually, we think Angel has a big problem. Well, maybe small now, but guaranteed to get bigger."

Wes halted in his tracks. "What the hell are you talkin' about?"

"No easy way to say it, Sheriff," Jason said quietly. "Lily tells me that Angel is in the family way. The tough part is that the child doesn't even know it herself."

As if a stake had been plunged into his chest, Wes felt the pain of betrayal. And wasn't that foolish? Angelena owed him nothing, not a pristine past, not a purity beyond belief, certainly not the semblance of virginity that her fragile, innocent façade promised. So why was he stricken with a sense of dismay?

"How can she not know?" he asked harshly.

Jason shrugged. "Lily says she's green as grass."

"Maybe she's married." And wouldn't that be a fine mess, Wesley Tanner all hot to trot over a woman who ought to be wearing a wedding ring.

"Doesn't seem likely. Lily says she don't seem to know the first thing about men. But—" he paused, shaking his head "—someone, somewhere, a couple of months ago made a real impression on the girl."

A knot in his stomach impelled Wes across the room, one hand rising to rest on the window frame as he stared unseeingly across the street. He'd been so tempted today, just hours ago, to make the woman an offer, to ignore her gibes about being his doxy. His laughter caught in his throat as he considered his own foolishness. There, for just a few minutes, he'd considered the idea of taking her home to Rosemary, thought of giving her a new beginning and a new name.

Jason shifted his stance and cleared his throat. "The girl needs a husband, Wes. I thought maybe—"

Wes turned on his heel to face his friend. "You want me to... *Me?* I'm supposed to play the part of *daddy* to a child from nowhere?" A lump formed in his throat as he shouted the words, and behind his eyes a cruel stinging sensation brought panic to the surface. Panic lest he should allow bitterness to flow from him and show himself to be vulnerable.

"Get out of here." One hand clenched tightly, he gripped his belt with the other, as if by curling his fingers in upon his palm, he could keep them from closing around Angelena's throat. That white, slender throat that contained music fit for the gods.

"Out!" With a final thrust of his jaw, he ordered the hapless barkeep from his office, then watched as the man hastened across the street to disappear within the swinging doors of his establishment.

One fist swung at the wall beside him; the other provided support for his forehead as he leaned against the door. "Damn...damn..." His words were impotent, helpless to stem the tide of anger. That he should once more be so stupid. That he'd allowed a woman like Angelena to creep beneath his skin was not to be tolerated.

He stood erect, examining the scuff marks on his knuckles where he'd hit the wall. He'd have her. By God he'd have her.

But on *his* terms.

Chapter Five

Lena. He wanted to call her Lena. And she'd as much as given her permission.

Had anyone named her as such, back in that life she could not recall? The syllables sounded strange, foreign to her ears, and she shook her head, denying their familiarity. Her image in the mirror was that of Angel, her hair long and curling past her shoulders and down her back, her eyes blue. A woman without a past, a saloon performer.

Would he have her be different? Perhaps she could change, could be that person for him, this man who filled her thoughts with emotions she could not contain.

He liked her. Beneath his cynicism and harshness, he more than *liked* her. She knew it, could feel it. In the heated gaze of narrowed eyes and the desperate hunger of his mouth when he kissed her, he'd given her a glimpse of the dark passion lurking within him. For just a moment she allowed herself to remember, hugging her waist as she recalled the possessive grip he'd taken on her arm. And then the moment when their lips had touched, and he'd inhaled, whisking away her breath and replacing it with his scent.

Her fears had been immersed in his kiss, her trembling

ceasing within the circle of his embrace. The curtain in her mind had seemed less murky. His presence spelled danger, and yet it was not of a deadly sort, like that she sensed in the avid glances some of the customers bestowed upon her. Wes was different.

He thought she was pretty, and that remembrance brought a certain amount of satisfaction. She eyed herself more closely in the mirror. It didn't hurt that her features were arranged in such a way that they brought admiring glances from the men who listened to her perform. And yet...

Her mama had said... She caught her breath as the thought crowded all else from her mind. As surely as she heard the birds singing outside her window, she heard her mother's words.

God gave you your voice and your pretty face. You can't take credit for either one, but only be thankful.

There was a glimpse, just a flash of golden hair and a sweet smile. And then it was gone.

"Mama." Her voice sobbed the single word, and a sense of desolation enveloped her as she sank to the floor, tears squeezing from tightly closed eyelids. Somewhere, sometime, she'd been a beloved daughter, and her heart ached as she mourned the loss of that memory.

Legs trembling, she rose from the floor and smoothed the wrinkles from her skirt. A few strokes of her hairbrush restored order, and she twisted the curling length against her nape, anchoring it with pins. The cool cloth she placed against her swollen eyes was welcome; and she leaned closer to the mirror, using a trace of powder to conceal the effects of her weeping. With luck, no one would notice, she decided. And who would she see, anyway, on this jaunt to visit with Pip and then on to the bank?

Wes Tanner, perhaps. Wes Tanner, probably, if her

hunch was correct. Some things she just *knew*. Even yesterday, she'd had a flash of knowledge, when the vision of a woman, Jane... Yes, Jane was her name. Jane, the woman who kept her costumes in order. Costumes? What costumes? Perhaps the dresses she wore when she sang. She shook her head. No, there was more to it, even more than the fancy clothing she'd brought with her, packed in her trunk.

A headache pierced her temple, sudden and absolute, as though her effort to break through the fog brought to mind a harsh pain that all but banished the memory. Jane... The woman's face was there again. And then was gone.

The headache eased as she set her room to rights. Before her open window, she bent to inhale deeply of the familiar scent of this town, a mixture of fresh air and dusty streets. That she scanned the length of the boardwalk across the street was only a habit, she told herself sternly. Her gaze traveled to the jailhouse, where the open door announced *his* presence within, and she felt the beat of her heart increase. Was it only yesterday she'd seen him last? When he'd been so arrogant, and yet, somehow different, softer, maybe.

Her reticule was on the dresser and she picked it up, opening it to count again the money she'd placed there. Jason Stillwell was a generous man. It was time to take her cache to the bank. She locked her door when she left.

In a matter of minutes, Angelena found herself on the sidewalk, then crossing the street and turning toward the bank, careful not to meet the eyes of those she passed. That several men watched her and whispered her name was a fact she could not change, and she wished mightily that her walk and demeanor might be that of an ordinary housewife.

It was not so. Her stylish clothing was beyond ordinary

and her presence here constituted a mystery. Wes Tanner's gaze made her aware of that fact, more than that of any other man on the sidewalk. He came out the open door to stand before the jailhouse, arms folded across his chest, leaning indolently against the door frame; and in his dark eyes there was a heated, measuring look that ventured beneath her taffeta dress. He tipped his hat, a slow, solemn movement, and she nodded her head in polite response.

And then he watched her approach. Not the smallest flicker of a smile curved his lips. Not the tiniest trace of good humor sparkled from his eyes. He might well have been a statue, so still, so silent he appeared.

Angelena faltered, then stumbled, her toes catching at a raised plank on the boardwalk. She caught herself abruptly, suddenly dizzy, then leaned against an upright post to gain her balance.

"You all right, honey?" his gravelly voice asked from behind her.

How had he moved so quickly?

Her nod was brief. "Yes, I'm fine."

"You need an arm to lean on?" He was next to her now, and she glanced up at him.

"No, I seem to be a little clumsy this morning, but I'm all right now." Her palms were damp as she considered how firm his forearm would be beneath her touch.

"I'd be happy to escort you, *Lena*." He drawled the name softly as his hand enclosed her elbow, each finger radiating heat that spun through her veins. "Are you going to see Pip?"

She shook her head, her mouth dry, the dizziness returning like a cloud of pesky mosquitoes to hover over her head. "I don't know." And then more forcefully, "Yes, I am."

As though her confusion spurred him to action, he propelled her along the sidewalk, aiming for the emporium; somehow she was tucked next to him, her arm drawn though his, her fingers clenching the muscles of his forearm.

"Feelin' better?" His low voice murmured the question in her ear, and her response was quick as she nodded her head. As if she could tell him that his very presence caused her head to spin, her legs to tremble beneath her? When on earth had she become such a weakling?

The door to the emporium opened before them, and Bernice Comstock stood just inside, her sharp eyes coming to rest on Angelena's face. "You look all wiped out, child. Come in where it's cool."

"She tripped a moment ago, and I think it jarred her," Wes said quietly, steering her past Bernice.

"I'm just fine, really," Angelena said, wishing for all the world that she were back in her room, where the wide expanse of her bed would be a welcome sight right now.

"Here, come and sit in the rocking chair," Pip called from behind the counter.

In moments, Angelena was shuffled from Wes's care to Pip's and then on to the padded seat. "I can't believe he's making such a fuss," she whispered to Pip. "Convince him, will you?"

Pip shot a quick look at the sheriff, then grinned at Angelena, her eyes crinkling as she revealed her amusement. "I think the man's smitten with you, honey. He's got his jaw all set." She leaned closer to whisper. "Looks like he's about fit to be tied."

"Ma'am?" Wes's deep voice demanded attention.

"Which ma'am you talkin' to, Sheriff?" Pip wanted to know, straightening to face him.

"You, I suspect," he said, snagging his hat from his

head. "What do you think?" His nod was in Angelena's direction, and Pip chuckled.

"Why don't you just leave me out of this and hunker down there and talk to the lady?" Her skirts swished around her ankles as she turned away, oblivious of the glare Angelena shot in her direction.

"Honey?" He squatted next to the rocking chair, one hand reaching to touch her knee. She gasped at his intimate gesture, and he snatched his fingers from their perch.

"Sorry. I wasn't thinking." His hand opened and closed indecisively and then reached for hers, scooping it from her lap. "I need to talk to you," he muttered gruffly.

"Now?" She blinked, wary of this tack.

"Well, I'd like a bit more privacy, but this will do, I reckon."

Angelena looked around the store. So far as she could tell, they were the only two inside these four walls, except for Pip, who was probably listening behind the curtain. "All right," she agreed carefully. Something was on his mind, and she'd better let him have his say.

"You sure you're feelin' some better?"

"Oh, for pity's sake!" she grumbled. "I only took a misstep. You're acting like I broke my leg or something. What do you want?"

"I want you to come over to the jailhouse and take a look at my rooms upstairs."

She felt the hot blush that climbed her cheeks at his announcement. "Whatever for? I'll be the talk of the town if I go there."

"Not when they find out you're gonna marry me, you won't."

She shut her eyes, suddenly certain this must be a bad dream. Surely when she opened her eyelids, the sun would be shining into her room and Wes Tanner would be where he belonged.

"Lena?" The name he had chosen for her whispered against her ear, and she was aware that he'd leaned over the arm of the rocker to speak. His mouth touched her cheek, leaving a damp spot behind, and then he spoke the syllables again. "Lena?"

This was no dream. She was smack-dab in the middle of the emporium with the sheriff on his knees beside her, whispering in a voice that made her think of things she'd never considered in her lifetime. At least, so far as she knew she'd never had knowledge of the carnal nature of men. And unless she missed her guess, that was the road he was traveling with his whispers and soft words.

"Why would you want to marry me?" Her husky tones matched his, the sound trembling on her lips. "I remember a night when you wanted to buy me, when you told me..." She swallowed, unable to speak the words. "Then, yesterday, you were barely decent, the way you acted."

He shook his head impatiently, and his voice was gruff. "Never mind that. Just tell me yes, and we'll settle this thing today."

Her eyes flew open. "Today? You want to marry me today? And I don't deserve to know why? I'm supposed to just say the word and you'll *settle this thing?*" Her voice rose on a current of anger.

Pip brushed past the curtain and bustled around the counter. "What's going on out here? Angelena, don't you answer him, you hear me?"

"Stay out of this, Pip." It was an order, direct and deliberate, and Wes glared in emphasis, ensuring there was no doubt it would be obeyed.

Angelena scooted back into the cushioned comfort of the chair, seeking a refuge. Above her, Pip simmered in silence, her cheeks tinged pink with anger, her eyes flashing as she stood her ground.

Wes rose to his feet, one hand outstretched to Angelena. "We'll talk somewhere else." His look dared Pip to interfere as he drew Angelena from the chair.

She rose reluctantly, casting one brief glance at Pip before she turned to face Wes. "I don't want to go anywhere with you, Sheriff, I don't know what you have in mind, but you can't seem to decide just what you want from me. One time I'm dirt, and then the next time around you think I should marry you. And I'm not about to make my vows with any man. I don't even know my name."

"You've got enough of a name to suit me." His fingers tightened their grip, and she pushed her free hand against his chest.

"Let go of me. I'm not going with you." A wave of nausea swept through her, saliva gathered in her mouth, and she inhaled deeply, wishing vainly for privacy, a commodity that seemed to be in short supply today.

"Sheriff, I think you'd better leave her be for now. She's not up to this." Pip stepped closer, her gaze intent on Angelena.

Wes looked down at the hand he held captive, then brought it to his lips, repeating the silent caress he had bestowed yesterday. His eyes scanned her face, and he nodded. "All right. I'll be back later."

It was a promise, and Angelena took it as such. She turned her head away, unable to bear his scrutiny, and he released her, then bent quickly to press his mouth gently against her cheek. Her hand was warm with the memory of his touch and she thrust it into the pocket of her dress, clenching her fingers tightly.

His boots vibrated against the wooden floor, then the bell sounded in her ears as he opened the door. It closed behind him, and she opened her eyes, catching sight of his tall figure outside the window, his strides long as he passed before her. Pip stood silent, perplexity and concern mixed in her gaze as she waited.

"I think I'm going to throw up," Angelena whispered after a moment.

"Well, I've got a good place for that," Pip said bluntly, "and it isn't in the middle of my store. Come on in back."

"Yes." She followed obediently, inhaling deeply as she fought the churning in her stomach, then leaned with relief over the bucket Pip provided. It was a small matter, since breakfast had consisted only of several bites of toast and a cup of tea. Pip provided a cool cloth and a chair, which Angelena promptly pulled over in front of the big desk. She swept aside the papers lying there into a pile and pressed her cheek against the cool surface.

"Any chance you might be in the family way, honey?" Pip asked quietly.

The question penetrated slowly, and Angelena frowned, unable to reply. Her shrug was eloquent, and Pip apparently understood the gesture. "Have you had your monthlies?" she asked.

Angelena lifted her head, squinting her eyes to focus on her friend. "I don't know." She thought a moment. The normal cycle of her body, her monthly session of womanhood was just one more detail she'd apparently locked away in the vault of lost memories. Now it sprang full-blown into her conscious mind.

"Not since I've been here." And how long was that? More than two months. Going on three, now. More than enough time to watch the moon wax and wane, a couple of times over, affecting her body in its usual fashion.

"Do you think you had a man in your life? Before you got here, I mean?" Pip asked, turning to rinse out the damp cloth. She stepped closer and pressed it against Angelena's cheeks, then wiped her forehead.

The familiar sensation of weightlessness swept over Angelena and she closed her eyes. "I'm in a fog, Pip. It's as though I'm looking into a tunnel and there's no light at the other end. Some things I just know, dumb stuff like how to dress and undress, things that come to me automatically. I can remember recipes when I get in the kitchen and lyrics when Dex plays an introduction, but when I try to see faces and places, I'm stumbling around in a mist."

Pip's hand was cool against her temple, her fingers brushing waves and curls into place. She pressed a tender kiss there, where her hand gave comfort, and her whisper was warm and encouraging. "Don't fret about it right now, honey. Won't do any good anyway. But if that's your problem, it puts a whole different color on things. We'll just have to wait and see, most likely."

Angelena's laugh was shrill in her own ears as she buried her face in her hands. "And won't the sheriff be surprised if he finds out he's asked a pregnant woman to marry him!"

Pip was silent for a moment, rinsing the cloth once more before she brushed Angelena's hair to one side, exposing the graceful line of her neck. She settled the cloth into place there. A bell sounded as the door at the front of the store opened, and Pip patted Angelena's shoulder. "We need to consider something, honey. Maybe he already knows."

Playing daddy to another man's child had never been cause for reflection before. Hell, playing daddy to his own child seemed far off in the future. But it looked as if he'd better think about it now. Somehow, he couldn't really fathom the idea that Angelena was in the family way. Slim, but rounded where it really mattered, she was a woman ready to bloom. Yet, if things were what they seemed, she'd already been plucked from the bush, so to speak, and that thought made his teeth clench. Could he handle those circumstances, knowing she'd belonged to another man?

Damn right he could, if it meant having her in his bed and wearing his name. How he'd gotten so entangled in her wiles so quickly was a question he couldn't answer. He only knew that if it took marriage to claim her, he'd go that route. There'd be time and plenty to consider the baby. Maybe months before the town knew she was having a child. And those months would enable him to set his house and wife in order.

For now, he needed to backtrack a bit, maybe refine his proposal a little. She'd looked pale and frazzled back at the emporium. Even more so when he'd sprung his idea on her. Aware of his blundering, he shook his head. He'd gone about it the wrong way. Of course she wouldn't want to see where he lived. In fact, he'd better be on the lookout for a house.

His sigh was deep. As proposals went, his had been less than illustrious.

Lifting his glass from his desk, he peered within. It was empty, and for the first time in years, he thirsted for the taste of Jason's whiskey. Water just wasn't gonna cut it today.

The interior of the Golden Slipper was dim and cool. Wes paused inside the swinging doors to gain his bearings, then headed for the bar. Jason eyed him warily. "You don't look so hot, son."

"Maybe I'll take you up on that offer you're always so fond of makin' me," Wes said bluntly, resting his elbows on the gleaming walnut surface.

"Uh-uh," Jason said, shaking his head. "I don't think so. Booze ain't gonna solve your problem."

Wes straightened, cutting a glance to the tables in the back of the room. "You're probably right. Just seemed like a good idea for a minute there." Four men around the farthest table played stoically, dealing cards and mumbling bets, as if their poker game had lasted more hours than their weary minds could deal with. The piano was silent, Dex nowhere in sight; and at the top of the stairs dust motes shimmered in the muted light from the end of the hallway.

"Pretty quiet," Wes said, turning back to Jason.

"She's upstairs." Jason's gaze was fixed on the bar as he swiped at a fingerprint with his shirtsleeve.

"I wasn't lookin' for her," Wes said abruptly.

"No?" Jason gave him a doubting look. "You just come to visit?"

Footsteps behind him alerted Wes and he turned to face Jolene, her smile coy, eyelashes fluttering as she approached. "You lookin' for company, Sheriff? I'm available. We can sit at a table and talk if you want to." Her skirt was short, revealing slender legs, and his gaze barely hesitated as he scanned her.

"Sorry, ma'am. I'm just havin' a word with Jason here. Reckon I'll be on my way."

Jason shook his head. "Go on now, Jolene. This is a sorta private conversation."

She cocked a pose, her lips pouting. "Don't say I didn't offer." Her skirt flounced as she turned, and she paused, looking back over her shoulder. "She's upstairs, Sheriff." Her curls bounced on her shoulders as she walked away, and Jason chuckled.

"That one's been after you for two years, Wes. Not your type?"

Wes shook his head. "I had my fill of saloon girls a long time ago. I learned young."

"Really? You never said," Jason murmured, reaching to pour a glass of soda water.

"What'd she mean by that last remark?" Wes growled, his brows lowering as he accepted the drink.

"Just what you think she means. The same thing I meant. Angel's close by if you want to see her."

Wes looked up. "Does everyone know, about...you know? Everybody, except for Angelena?"

"Well, I'm sure all the women do, and from the look on Angel's face when she came in here a while ago, I wouldn't be surprised if somebody hasn't let her in on the secret."

"She was upset?" The soda water tasted flat against his tongue and Wes placed it back on the bar. "I talked to her at Pip's place. She as much as turned me down flat."

"She turned you down flat," Jason repeated, and then grinned widely. "You asked her to marry you?"

"Yeah." He looked around, took a deep breath, and met Jason's look. "Not really. I just sorta sprung it on her."

Jason looked skeptical. "How'd you manage that?"

Wes slapped the bar with his palm. "Hell, I don't know! I just said she should marry me."

"Well, that's a dandy way to get her feathers ruffled, I'd say." Jason leaned closer. "I think you're supposed to sweet-talk a little first and then ask politely."

Wes looked over his shoulder, aware of the interested men at the back of the room. The poker game had slowed to a dead stop, and four pair of ears were tuned to more interesting things. "I think I botched it."

He glanced back at Jason. "You suppose Pip said something to her? Maybe she guessed something was going on.

Angelena tripped on the sidewalk and she was green around the gills and kinda shaky.''

Jason grinned, taking the soda water from Wes's hand.

"Hey, I was about to drink that," Wes growled.

"You need to rethink your approach, Sheriff," Jason said. "Here." He handed the glass back. "Drink up, and then get outta here. I don't want you upsettin' Miss Angel before she sings tonight. I'd just as leave she not see you if she comes downstairs early."

"Damn stuff is flat anyway," Wes grumbled, turning to the swinging doors. Behind him, the poker game resumed and he tossed a threatening look in that direction as he left, just to keep his hand in. What he really needed was a good fight or a cattle rustler to chase this afternoon. Something to occupy his mind and let him work off a little steam.

Muffled sounds from the next room began to set her teeth on edge, and Angelena knelt before the open window, leaning her arms atop the sill, seeking a breath of fresh air and a distraction from the activity she could no longer ignore. Most of the time she could accept the murmuring voices and the occasional male laughter from Jolene's room, but tonight the sounds had chased her from her bed, disturbing her slumber. She knew what went on in the beds on either side of the hallway. Somewhere in her mind, she acknowledged the acts of passion that united men and women, and yet, her own memory held no such recollection.

If Pip's suspicions were valid, she'd been involved in such things. Angelena shivered at the thought. Surely she'd remember, wouldn't she? The idea of offering her body, of giving herself to a man was beyond belief. But if it were true, if she was indeed carrying a babe within her, she must have known and loved a man.

Her hands met, spanning the flat width of her belly and her lashes feathered shut, as if in her mind's eye she could see within herself, identify that tiny being who even now might be taking sustenance from her. A thrill shot through her. And in its wake a dull sense of despair. Without a husband, she would be considered a fallen woman. Who would want her then?

"Wesley Tanner." The name sounded aloud, vibrating against her ears, and she recognized her own voice speaking the syllables. "He wants to marry me," she whispered. "But what will he say when I tell him?"

She lifted her head, looking across the street to where the jailhouse sat, shadowed and silent. The windows above were dark, one marked by the ghostly fluttering of a curtain, caught by the breeze, its hem lifting on a current of air.

He was there. As though his masculine presence spoke to her, she knew he waited, just beyond the boundaries of her gaze. She narrowed her eyes, to better see beyond the darkness that veiled his room, and as if she beckoned him, he appeared, one hand catching the curtain, holding it aside.

Through the wavy glass on the upper windowpane, she caught sight of his white shirt, saw his hand, wrapped in the curtain, as he rested it against the wooden frame. A match sparked, then flared and flickered. In the faint light he held it before his face, and a cigar glowed. He watched her, his gaze bathing her with heat, and she lifted her face to his scrutiny.

The cigar flared briefly as he drew its flavor into his lungs, and then he backed from the window, releasing the curtain to flutter as it would.

Her heartbeat was a noticeable presence in her breast as she peered intently at the front of the jail. When his tall figure appeared, moving from the narrow alley beside the building to cross the street, her reaction was audible, a gasp that seemed to draw his attention. He glanced upward and she backed from the window, almost falling to the floor in her haste. Then, stumbling to her feet, she sped to the door, checking the lock.

And with apprehension shivering the length of her spine, she waited.

Chapter Six

"Lena, open the door." Softly, yet underlaid with steely strength, his voice called her name, ordered her to do his will.

She shivered, leaning against the wall beside her window, and acknowledged his words. "What do you want?"

He was silent for a moment, and she tilted her head, listening for retreating footsteps. It was not to be. A key scraped against the lock, then penetrated the aperture and spun the tumblers. The handle turned silently and he swung the door open, just far enough to permit his entry.

Angelena pressed closer to the wall, wishing she might disappear through its plaster and lath and be borne far from this room, where the towering presence of Wes Tanner seemed to fill each nook and cranny. The faint scent of cigar smoke met her nostrils and she inhaled it, then closed her eyes as nausea swept from her stomach to her throat. One more reminder of her frailties, she thought with an almost silent laugh.

"I cannot abide cigar smoke, it seems," she whispered softly, uncertain whether she spoke to herself or the man who watched her.

"I left it in the street," he answered.

"It doesn't matter," she said. "The smell followed you."

"It didn't bother you before," he countered roughly. "I kissed you with it on my breath."

She closed her eyes at the memory, and winced. "That was a while ago. Things have changed."

His voice coaxed her. "Come with me. I'll put on a clean shirt, and we can talk."

Her eyes opened as she heard the brush of his boots against the carpet. He towered over her, his hand outstretched to grasp hers, and she felt the enveloping warmth of his fingers against her own. They bade her silently to obey and she nodded, stepping in his direction. "Outdoors, please," she murmured. "The shirt will be fine, but I need fresh air."

From below, men's voices rose in laughter, one of them trying his hand at the piano, the sound harsh in the background. Before them, a sole gaslight, flickering against the flocked wallpaper, lit the hallway. Quickly, they traveled its length, then down the back stairway to the kitchen, and out the door into the alleyway. Angelena inhaled deeply of the night air, catching a scent of dusty streets and the promise of rain in the overhanging clouds.

She tugged her fingers from his grip and stepped apart from him. "What do you want to talk about?" The nausea was easing and she caught another breath, thankful that she would not be mortified before him. It was bad enough that Pip had seen her at her worst, bent over a bucket and retching from the depths of her stomach. That Wes should watch such an exhibit would be unthinkable.

"I think you know, don't you?" he asked, allowing her to set the boundaries between them. "Come with me. We'll walk."

It was less than an invitation, the words edged with authority, and, too weary to quibble, she agreed with a nod. He set off, heading for the back street, where small houses nestled beneath tall elm trees, and lamplight cast its glow from narrow windows. His stride was short and she kept pace easily, ever aware of his imposing stature, his stern profile visible as she tilted her head.

She could walk forever, she thought, captivated by the night birds as they warbled from the trees overhead. The breeze carried a hint of wildflowers on its wings, and she wondered idly if their aroma would blend with the odor of his cigar and overcome its pungency. Her gaze lowered to the ground they trod, and she purposely matched her steps to his, stretching beyond her usual gait to keep up. "Where are we going?"

He bent his head, and his chuckle was ripe with amusement. "Well, wherever it is, you're sure in a hurry to get there, aren't you?" She'd stepped double time to keep in stride with him, even though he'd slowed his usual pace. And without complaint. She was rare, this small, fragile-seeming woman. The puzzle she presented gave him food for thought, and his mind tallied her attributes.

Far different from the usual saloon girl, she wore a façade of purity that warred with what he knew of her. No woman could remain unsullied for long by the atmosphere of Jason's upstairs rooms. Either she was deaf and blind, or she chose to ignore what went on up and down the hallway when the ladies entertained their clients nightly. All but Sunday. Even Jason could not ignore the blue laws that closed down his establishment on the day the churches in town did their best to reform its citizens.

"Sheriff?" Angelena peered up at him, frowning. "Could you slow down, just a little?" She skipped for two paces, glanced up to meet his gaze and stumbled over an exposed root. Her breath drew in with a hiss, and immediately she was held steady by his hand, clasping her arm with a firm grip.

"We've got all night, honey. I won't leave you behind," he murmured, his words silken with promise. He offered his arm and she slid her hand within the bend of his elbow, obediently matching his shortened stride.

Walking beyond the last house, they headed toward a grove of trees, where the road trailed off to a narrow path, then to a grassy verge. The tall trees beckoned, their branches offering privacy, and he led her there. Ducking beneath a low-hanging limb, they approached the base of an enormous oak, its trunk seeming to sprout from the velvet carpet beneath their feet. Just beyond the sanctuary he'd sought, the clouds moved restlessly, shifting and changing, lightning flashing above them, causing them to glow from within, their incandescent glory favoring the earth below.

"Will we get wet?" she asked, shivering as a low roll of thunder rumbled in the west.

He leaned against the tree and tugged her toward him. "I doubt it. It's not gonna rain for a while." His hands were firm, turning her to face him. Finally, without onlookers, he was able to gaze his fill. His embrace loose, lest he frighten her, he relaxed against the rough bark behind him.

She was prettier than Kitty, softer, more youthful, certainly more elusive. Kitty had been...what was the word? Alluring? Shrewd? Knowledgeable? All of those, but most of all, available. He felt a smile twist his lips at that thought. Kitty had been a whore of the first degree. Not much of a singer, but with other talents more to his liking. Aware of his youthful devotion, taking advantage of his generosity, she'd led him on, beguiling him with all her tricks of the trade, taking all he had to offer.

Then finally she'd laughed at the boy of nineteen he had been, when a cowhand with more hard, cold, available cash came along and ousted him from his position as Kitty's favorite customer.

He'd learned his lesson well. Had taken another look at the women who inhabited the saloons he'd frequented, and found they fit the same mold.

"Wes? Wes?" One small hand fisted against his chest and thumped, getting his attention. "What did you want to talk about?" Her words were breathless, her body rigid beneath his touch, and he mentally gave her points for the air of innocence she assumed with such ease.

Leaning forward, he pressed one long finger beneath her chin, tilting her head just so, then levered his palm to cup her jaw. His mouth mere inches away, he whispered the thoughts that stirred his desire, that would not remain subdued. "About you. And me. And finding a place with a little privacy, so I can unbutton your dress and untie that fancy bow that hangs down your back and moves every time you take a step."

His hand eased down the length of her slender neck and his nimble fingers released the button at her throat from its moorings. She bent her head to watch, aghast at his actions. Then, in a movement so rapid he was stunned into silence, she leaned back, and the palm of her right hand struck him with a force he was not prepared for. His head snapped to the side, and he felt his eyes widen with shock.

"What the hell was that for?"

Her hands clutched at his, halting the movement of his fingers. "I'm sure a smart man like you can figure that out, Sheriff." She inhaled sharply, her expression wary, as if she'd only now realized her position. She was without defense, a woman at the mercy of a man bent on his own satisfaction.

His words were harsh with barely suppressed anger. "Don't tell me this is a brand-new experience for you," he said mockingly. "We both know better than that, honey."

Her grip tightened, nails digging into the backs of his hands. "I will not allow you to disrobe me, sir." Her teeth clenched tightly, and she blinked, fighting the onset of tears. "I came with you because you said you wanted to talk to me. You're taking advantage of your superior strength, Sheriff."

He looked down, brows lifting as he studied her. "I'll warrant I haven't drawn blood, ma'am. Can't say the same for you, though." His fingers loosened their grip on her dress and he lifted his hands before her eyes. She peered at the eight half-moon indentations he bore. Indeed, fully half of them wore a thin line of blood where she had broken the skin.

"I suppose you expect an apology." Her voice trembled, and she cleared her throat. "You are not a gentleman, sir."

"Am I supposed to believe that you're a lady?" His tone was incredulous, his laughter without humor. "You're sleepin' every night right next door to a whore, Angel."

She winced at the thrust and then lifted her chin defensively. "At least she's honest about it. You hauled me out here tonight to *talk,* and then proceeded to put your hands on my body. Wasn't that about as dishonest as you can get?" She stepped back, and he allowed it, his hands moving to rest against his hips.

"I will not be treated that way, Wesley Tanner. I deserve better from you."

He watched her silently, his nostrils flaring as he filled his lungs with air. "Maybe. But if wantin' you in my bed is a sin, then I'm more than halfway to hell anyway, lady.

Let me tell you something." He leaned over her, his threat clothed in a velvet whisper.

"Mark my words, lady. You'll be in my bed by the end of the week."

She was mesmerized by him, by the shimmering intensity he exuded, his breath warm against her face, teeth clenched, eyes flaring with desire.

The smell of his cigar was almost gone, swept away by the breeze, leaving only the scent of man and horse and a musky aroma that spelled lust in no uncertain terms. Her heart clenched as she recognized the lure of unknown passion.

It wasn't fair! Somehow, for all his arrogant behavior and raw language, he drew her like a magnet. He'd more than insulted her, yet his touch was a temptation. Beneath that hard exterior and cynical mien was a man whose appeal could not be denied.

Though she yearned for the strength to turn away, to disallow him access to her heart, her honest soul would not allow the deception. Wes Tanner held her fate in his hands. Though she might be separated from her past by a dark curtain in her mind, her future loomed before her, and it was linked to this man. The knowledge was bone-deep, and it frightened her beyond belief. She was immutably drawn to him, knew a yearning to rest in his embrace.

And that fact was more frightening than the fury in his gaze.

She looked into his eyes. They were dark, with secrets she ached to explore. "Tell me why you brought me here."

"Lena, you know what I want." The sound was almost guttural, the words harsh and rasping. His hand cupped her cheek, his fingers taut against her flesh, lifting her face to meet his gaze. "I thought at first I could crawl into your bed and be satisfied, but that won't work now. There'll have to be a wedding."

"A wedding? You want to marry me?" Deep in her heart, she had known it would come to this. Knew that he could not maintain his position as sheriff with a doxy on the side. Especially not when that doxy was going to have a child. Not with the legendary Rosemary Tanner as his mother.

"Yeah, I'll marry you," he said quietly. "But on my terms. We both know you're not in a position to bargain, and I'm not willing to act the part of a courting swain. I'm ready to marry you and take care of things."

He paused, and his hand tightened on her chin. His shrug was arrogant, his eyes bold as she jerked her head to one side, dislodging his grip. Bowing his head mockingly, his mouth twisted into a parody of a smile.

"Mark my words, lady. It may be the best offer you're likely to get."

"You think me unworthy of a decent proposal?" And in her heart of hearts, she had to acknowledge the truth of it. The tears were balancing on her lower eyelids and she held back the urge to blink, knowing that salty drops would cascade down her cheeks.

He shook his head. "I'm *offering* a decent proposal. Your next best would be Avery Sims over at the bank, but I wouldn't hold out much hope for him takin' on another man's child."

She turned from him, uncaring now of the tears that fell. *He knew.* No wonder he thought her to be without honor. Her heart clenched, the pain of it almost beyond bearing as she heard his cruel words. *Another man's child.* "And you?" she asked, the words broken and wrapped in sadness. "You would take that responsibility?"

"I'd take on half an orphanage, honey, if that was what

I had to do to get you in my bed." Darkness tinged his declaration, and she drew in a sobbing breath.

"I won't know what to do when I get there," she whispered. "If I'm truly going to have a child, I need to tell you that I don't know what happened to bring me to this point." How to make him understand? "You must believe me. I can't remember what happened to me. I won't know what to do." She stopped, her head bowed, and felt his arm snake around her waist, knew the heat of his breath beneath her ear.

"We'll talk about all that later," he promised. "Whatever you don't know, I'll teach you. And if you can't remember the baby's father, that's all right with me, too." He laughed roughly, the sound rasping in her ears. "Probably better that way, now that I think about it. We'll start fresh."

"What will people say?" Her eyes were blurred with tears as she looked back at the town, at the houses gleaming with light.

"We'll make it quick," he answered, turning her to face him again. "No one will say a word, trust me. They can think what they like, but the sheriff carries a certain amount of clout in town. No one will say a word against his wife, so long as he holds her in high regard."

"And will you?" she asked, seeking in vain for some softening in his harsh features.

"I'll be as polite as can be," he said mockingly. "You won't be able to fault my actions, honey."

She swallowed, as if readying herself for what was to come. "And when we're alone? Do I need to fear you?"

"My mama taught me to respect ladies," he answered. "I've never raised my hand to a woman yet, Lena. I won't start with you."

"But the other—"

"Am I gonna make love to my wife?" His laughter was muffled as he drew her against his chest and buried his face in her hair. "You damn betcha I am, sugar. Every chance I get."

"Rosemary Tanner! I haven't seen you in ages," Pip said, her voice overlaid with good humor and affection. She skirted the end of the counter and met Rosemary head-on. Their embrace was a joint effort, with Rosemary dropping a quick kiss against Pip's rosy cheek.

"I seem to be getting good at making lists for you, don't I?" Rosemary said. "There's so much to do at home, I end up sending someone else to town."

Pip leaned back to look at her friend. "Well, it's about time you showed up." Her voice lowered, and she glanced around the store, as if she would avoid having anyone overhear her words. "You've been missing all the fun." Her eyes danced as she led Rosemary to where two chairs sat near the big front window. "Here, sit down with me."

"My husband says he's heard rumors about Wesley."

Pip grinned widely. "More than just rumors, to my way of thinking."

Rosemary leaned closer. "I think I need to meet the young lady. How do I go about it? Do I really have to visit the saloon to find her?"

Pip nodded toward the back room. "Nope. You just go through that curtain. Angelena's rocking the baby for me."

"Now? She's here?" Rosemary frowned, darting a glance to where the curtain hung in place. "You know, I'm wondering if this was really wise. I've been hoping he'd bring her out to the ranch to meet us. But if it's just a dalliance..." Rosemary sighed. "I'd hate to think of my Wesley in that sort of an association. I guarantee he'll be fit to kill if I take it on myself to speak with her."

Pip snorted. "Humph! He'd probably be surprised if you didn't. Right now, she's not in a very good state of mind, so don't expect much of her."

"What's wrong?" Rosemary whispered.

Pip shook her head. "I don't think I'd better tell you. It's something she needs to work on. At any rate, she needed some time to think, and it's always been my contention that rockin' a baby can do wonders for your disposition."

"I won't argue with that," Rosemary answered, her gaze lingering on the entrance to the back room. "Do you suppose she heard you speak my name when I came in?"

"Probably. Unless she was singin' one of her lullabies. That girl's got the most beautiful voice I've ever heard, Rosemary. I swear, she was rightly named."

"Angel?" Rosemary pondered that thought for a moment. "What does my son call her?"

Pip glanced at the curtain, then back at her friend. "I've heard him use her given name, Angelena. And then last time I saw him with her, he called her Lena, like he didn't like the *Angel* part."

Rosemary bit at her lip. "How does he treat her?"

Pip rose from her chair and paced to the counter and back, as if unwilling to give her opinion. She halted, her hips pressed against the walnut case behind her and shook her head. "I don't know how to explain it," she said in a low voice. "It's almost like he doesn't *want* to like her." The words ended in a whisper and Pip frowned. "And yet I know he does. But, then, there's reason for all of that, too, I suppose."

Rosemary stood abruptly, brushing her skirts down. "Well, now that you have me thoroughly confused, I believe I'll go introduce myself to the young lady." She patted her hair into place, twitched her skirts again, then made her way to the back room. "No need to come along, Pip," she said, waving a hand for emphasis.

Angelena looked up as the curtain was swept aside, expecting to see Pip's familiar face. Instead, she beheld a woman she'd never seen before, her hair dark but for a streak of silver against one temple, her eyes as blue as a summer sky. *Wes Tanner's mother.* Angelena's low, whispering song ended abruptly, the words trailing off.

"Are you his mother?" Her words rode upon a breath of air.

The woman nodded and then grinned. "We are talking about Wesley, aren't we?"

Speechless, Angelena inhaled the scent of fresh air and starched clothing, unable to do else but nod her agreement.

The blue eyes crinkled with humor, and Rosemary chuckled. "You're the girl they call Angel, aren't you? The one that's got my son all in an uproar, according to the latest gossip."

Angelena closed her eyes. "Folks are gossiping about me?"

"Might's well face it, honey," Rosemary said. "Anything the sheriff does is up for speculation. He sat next to a neighbor's daughter one Sunday in church and by Monday morning the ladies were planning a bridal shower."

Angelena's eyes opened at that. "I'll bet he was fit to be tied. I've noticed he has a bit of a temper."

Rosemary pursed her lips. "Has he given you a hard time again? I've taught him how to treat a lady, you know. If he's being ornery with you, he surely didn't learn it at home."

"Maybe it's because I sing in the saloon." The words were blurted out before Angelena had time to think. If Rosemary Tanner had any illusions about her, it was time to set her straight.

The blue eyes lingered on her, and Angelena lifted her chin, awaiting judgment. "I know you do." Rosemary's simple acknowledgment was accompanied by a smile. An abundance of understanding was implicit in her demeanor, as she touched her fingertips to Angelena's shoulder. "I've heard you sing like the angels."

"And you've wondered what I'm doing in the Golden Slipper, I'll bet." For the first time, Angelena felt a sense of shame wash over her. She'd not chosen her place of residence, or the means by which she earned her living, and up until now, it had not mattered. Not really. She saw little of the townspeople, except for the men who flocked to hear her music.

Now, facing this woman, who was far removed from the ladies she'd associated with over the past weeks, she wished fervently that her address was different.

Rosemary nodded. "I wonder even more, now that I've met you." Her eyes were kind, her voice soft as she bent lower. One hand reached to touch the baby's wispy curls, and Rosemary whispered, in deference to the sleeping child. "You don't look like you belong there, Angelena. I'm surprised that Jason Stillwell didn't send you to the parsonage instead of giving you a room next to his girls."

"They've been very good to me," Angelena said defensively. "I had nowhere to go, and Jason offered me sanctuary, and a job to boot."

"You can come home with me," Rosemary offered abruptly, standing erect as if she would take matters into her own hands this very minute.

Angelena felt a smile twitch at her lips. This woman was a force to be reckoned with, sure enough. No wonder Wes held her in awe. "I don't think that's a good idea, ma'am. I need to be at the Golden Slipper every evening except Sunday, and it seems like I'd be doing a lot of traveling during the night to get to your place.''

Rosemary shook her head. "If you come home with me, you'll not have to sing for Jason Stillwell any more.''

"It's what I do," Angelena whispered. "It's all I know.''

"My husband Gabe said he'd heard you have a loss of memory." Rosemary watched her closely and Angelena nodded her head. "You truly don't know who you are?''

"I know I'm a singer. I know a hundred songs, probably more. And I have all the trappings. You know, dresses and feathers and such. I just don't remember where I came from, or who I am.''

"If it's any comfort to you, honey, I'm a pretty good judge of character, and I've already decided about yours. Wherever it was and whoever you are, I'm about as sure as I can be that you're a good girl.''

Angelena felt the onset of tears. To be accepted so readily was beyond her fondest hopes. How sad that she must disillusion this woman. She looked down, aware of the tears staining the blanket she'd wrapped around the child in her arms.

"Apparently, I'm not," she managed to whisper, unable to meet Rosemary's gaze any longer.

Rosemary reached for the desk chair and hauled it across the floor, seating herself so that the two women were knee to knee. Her hand brushed Angelena's cheek and Angelena leaned into it, judging it the kindest, gentlest soul-easing touch ever bestowed upon a woman.

"Now, what's this all about?" Rosemary's tone was stern, brooking no excuses, and Angelena felt the impossible urge to giggle. No wonder Wes held this woman in such high regard. She hadn't given him a choice, with her balance of kindness and implacability, her softness and stern regard. And with that thought in mind, Angelena placed herself in Rosemary Tanner's hands.

"I'm going to have a baby. At least I think I am, and so do Lily and the washerwoman, Miss Molly."

Rosemary blinked and sat back in her chair, silent for a moment, as she assimilated this news. "You think?" She leaned forward suddenly. "Is Wesley the father?" Her eyes glittered now, like twin blue marbles in the sunlight.

Angelena shook her head. "Oh, no, ma'am. I've never...I don't know..." She stumbled into silence, unable to continue, her face hot with the flush of shame she could not control.

"You don't know." Rosemary was struck speechless, it seemed, and then she placed her palms on Angelena's knees, gripping firmly. "You don't know...what? Whether Wesley is the father?"

Angelena drew a deep breath. "I just don't know anything. I don't know how I got this way, or who...you know..." She lifted her head to look directly at the stunned expression on Rosemary's face. "I can't remember! I just don't know." Her tears fell in profusion. She wiped at them distractedly with the first thing that came to hand, but the edge of the blanket was totally inadequate to stem their flow. Her fingers fumbled in her pocket then, seeking the bit of linen and lace she had tucked there.

"Here, sweetie." Rosemary pulled a white cotton handkerchief from her reticule, ironed and folded, large enough to cover a bread pan, and stuffed it into Angelena's hand. "I make mine big enough to hold a full-blown crying fit."

"A tantrum? You?" Angelena mopped at her eyes, her tears subsiding as she considered the woman before her. "I can't imagine Wes's mama even shedding a tear."

"You've heard about me?" Rosemary asked, one eyebrow lifting.

"You made him apologize to me," Angelena said, recalling the incident. "It was the only time I've ever seen him blush."

"He did it, then? I've never known Wes not to follow through on something, but we didn't discuss that conversation again." Rosemary's mouth tilted in a smile, apparently immersed in memories of her own.

"He says he wants to marry me." Where the words had come from, Angelena didn't know. Only that she had blurted them out with no forethought, and now wished vainly that they could be recalled.

"Marry you? Wesley? He asked you to marry him?"

Angelena shook her head. "No, not really. He just sort of told me it was the best offer I was likely to get." She paused, remembering his words. "He's probably right, you know. If I'm truly in the family way, like everybody thinks—"

"Everybody? Who all knows about this?" Rosemary asked tersely.

"Jason and the ladies. Oh, and Miss Molly, the washerwoman. And Wes, of course."

Rosemary's brows lifted in unison. "You told him?"

"No." Angelena shook her head. "Actually, he told me. And then, when I thought about it for a minute, I had to agree with him." She felt the blush creep up her throat again as she thought of how the discovery of this whole thing had come about. "I feel so foolish, talking to you about this. I must seem a dunderhead, not knowing when, or how, or anything."

"You seem to me like a young woman who's caught up in a muddle," Rosemary told her. "If my son has had the good sense to come to your rescue, it's probably the smartest thing he's done in a long time."

"How can you say that?" Angelena whispered. "You don't even know me."

Rosemary shrugged. "No, but I've already made up my mind about you. Besides, Pip speaks well of you. That's good enough for me."

The baby Angelena held stirred, lifting his head to blink and peer at her, and she shifted him in her arms. "Are you done with your nap?" she asked softly, bending to kiss his rosy cheek. "He's a sweetie, isn't he?"

"Pip says you sing to him, Angel. I'd like to hear you sometime."

"Please don't call me that. It's what they've named me at the Golden Slipper, but it's not really me."

"You don't pretend to be a heavenly being? Well, I'm not surprised. There aren't too many of them living in this town, far as I know," Rosemary said placidly. "I'll call you Angelena, if that's all right."

"Yes, fine." The baby was squirming now, his gaze seeking the curtained doorway as he inhaled deeply, apparently looking for his mother. "I need to let Pip know he's awake," Angelena said, even as the baby uttered a first preliminary squawk.

Rosemary rose and shoved the chair beneath the desk once more. "I'm going by the jail and talk to my son."

Angelena felt her heartbeat increase as she considered what that occasion might bring about. She turned the babe against her shoulder, patting his back fervently. "Please don't say anything to him about me, about marrying me, I mean. I haven't even said yes. He thinks it's all set, but I haven't said I'd do it."

"I won't," Rosemary assured her, her voice containing laughter. "I'll just let him know I met you here. He can take care of the rest of it by himself. Now, I think I'd better get Pip in here before that child lets loose full blast."

* * *

"You did what?" Wes stood behind his desk, leaning forward to place his hands flat on its cluttered surface. "Tell me you didn't go to the Golden Slipper, Mother."

Rosemary shook her head, laughing aloud. "Of course not, silly. I went to Pip's and she happened to be there."

"She? Pip was there?"

Rosemary sighed patiently. "Angelena was rocking the baby in the back room, and I went back to meet her and we visited a while." And as if that was the most ordinary thing in the world to do, Rosemary stated her case and smiled at her son.

"What did she say?" Wes stood erect, vainly thinking his height might give him some advantage over the woman facing him.

Rosemary appeared to consider the question, her lips pouting a bit, one hand on her hip. "Well, we spoke of babies."

Wes felt a narrow line of sweat trickle down his spine. "Babies? What do you mean, babies?"

"She was rocking Pip's little one, Wesley. Has quite a hand with children, I'd say. I'm sure it will prove to be most beneficial when she meets a likely man and decides to get married."

"Get married?" He boomed the query. "She talked about getting married?"

Rosemary thought for a moment. "Well, now that you mention it, we did discuss the possibility." She leaned forward, her tone of voice lowering. "Women talk about such things, you know."

"And what did she say?" Bells went off in his ears as he spoke, his collar felt exceedingly tight and his nails cut into his palms. "Did she tell you?"

Rosemary was innocence personified, her eyes rounding as he spoke. "Tell me what, dear?"

"Damn!" The single word seared the air. "She told you, didn't she? She told you I'm going to marry her."

"I've taught you better than to swear, Wesley Tanner."

"Well?" The walls resounded with the single word.

"We discussed it." Rosemary looked down at her hand, inspecting her nails. "She did say she hadn't accepted yet."

"She's marrying me. She may not know it yet, but it *will* happen." As if he had sealed the fate of the woman in question, Wes shoved his desk chair into its kneehole and stalked across the room.

"Wesley?" It was her turn-around-and-look-at-me voice.

He obliged, stifling the urge to howl his dismay at this turn of events. Bad enough that he'd not been able to pin the girl down. Now his own mother was dissecting him like a gnat beneath a microscope. "Yes?" His voice sounded gruff, even to his own ears, and he cleared his throat. Not for the world would he be rude to Rosemary, even aggravating as she was today.

"I want you to bring her home for dinner." She considered for a moment. "Maybe it had better be tomorrow at noon. I'm thinking it's too late today, and supper isn't much to brag about tonight. Leftovers, mostly."

"Dinner?" He felt his eyebrows rise. "You want a saloon singer to come to the ranch and eat dinner with my little brothers? And Anna?"

"Your sister is more than twenty years old, Wesley. Surely she is old enough to be exposed to a young lady like Angelena."

"Lady?" Scorn heaped the word.

"We've talked about this before," Rosemary said quietly, her gaze narrowing as she looked at him. "I choose to think she's a lady, Wesley. I find no fault with her."

"No fault?" The woman was incredible. "You said you talked about babies, Rosemary. Are you aware that she is probably well on her way to having one of her own?"

Rosemary's eyes trapped his, their warmth replaced by a chill he recognized. It meant he was in deep trouble, and yet he could not back down. "Did she tell you?" he asked quietly.

"Yes, she told me. She told me a few other things, too, son. Things I chose to believe. And in the light of our conversation, I feel she is fit company for my family. I have yet to turn my back on a human being in need of a helping hand. I won't begin now."

His mind sped back to a day fifteen years in the past, when a young woman had approached a boy in dire need of help. Battered, bruised and bewildered by the hand life had dealt him, he'd been offered life and hope without measure. He nodded, bowing his head to bestow a kiss upon her cheek.

"I'll do anything you ask of me, Mother. You know that."

"Well, this time, I'm asking for the pleasure of Miss Angelena's company for dinner tomorrow. Will you oblige?"

He shrugged, a grin measuring his lips. "I'll ask. The rest is up to her."

Chapter Seven

"I'm still not sure this is a good idea."

Wes turned dark eyes on the woman beside him. "Neither am I. But my mama likes you, and she's determined to get you at her dinner table. Sorta puts the stamp of approval on you when she does that." His smile was quick, warming her, and for a moment Angelena saw a different man beside her. Without the cloak of cynicism he'd worn the other night.

"Approval?" She tasted the word on her tongue. Rosemary Tanner was prepared to accept her, but as what? Daughter-in-law? Friend? Perhaps both? That thought was most alluring, she decided, her apprehension lessening. "Who will be there?"

"The family." At his taciturn best once more, Wes snapped the reins over his mare's back and the buggy wheels rolled more rapidly. He slanted a glance in her direction and Angelena met it stoically, unwilling to be a penitent. "All right," he said, lifting a brow at her determined look. "I'm turning over a new leaf. I'll give you a rundown."

"Do you know that sometimes you are a royal pain in

the patoot?'' Her irritation was largely feigned, her smile hovering just a breath away.

He looked askance at her from the corner of his eye. ''What language! And my mama says you're a lady.'' His comeback was playful and she struggled to accept it as such.

''She may be right, you know.'' She turned in the seat, done with polite talk. ''I want to know about your family, Sheriff.''

Their knees almost touched, his right, her left, the skirts of her gown and petticoat brushing against his denim pants. She moved just a bit, shifting in the seat, until the tempting pressure of rough trousers against starched cotton was gone. It seemed so foolish, this urge to slide closer, to feel the warmth of his body.

You can't depend on men. They come and go like the wind. Her mother's voice spoke the words in her mind, and Angelena grasped desperately at the memory, her eyes closing, to better see the woman who spoke. Golden hair, like spiderwebs of sunlight, a slender form, but with no visible features, as though a blinding light cast its glow upon the woman's face.

''Lena? Are you listening?'' Wes's hand was on hers, his fingers strong and encompassing as he cradled it in his palm. ''Lena?'' Sharper now, his voice penetrated the vision she beheld, and she blinked as her eyelids lifted. A fine line of perspiration traced her upper lip, and a chill passed down the length of her spine.

Wes pulled the horse to a halt and turned to her, his hands gripping her shoulders as he drew her closer. She was limp, acquiescent in his grip, and he gathered her to his chest, wrapping her in warmth. His scent rose from the shirt he wore, and she recognized the aroma of Miss Molly's starch and soap. It was familiar and welcome, and she caught a sobbing breath as she inhaled its comfort. Her nose was buried against his throat, and she relished the warmth of skin, the scent of man. His shirt button was cool against her mouth and she touched it with the tip of her tongue, sorely tempted to undo it, yet more than hesitant.

Alive in her mind was the memory of his fingers at her throat, there beneath the oak tree, as he'd undone that one button on her dress. He'd been tempted, as she was now. Had her scent held him in thrall? Had he yearned to touch what lay beneath the crisp cotton of her dress? As she yearned now?

And for his efforts, she'd slapped him, scolded him and denied his touch.

"Lena?" Muffled against her hair, the lone word vibrated within her.

"I'm all right," she murmured. "I just—"

"You remembered something, didn't you?"

"Something my mother said to me." She lifted her head and looked into his eyes, recognized the sober measuring of his gaze. "I saw her, Wes. Not her face, but her hair and her form." She blinked, shaking her head. "I heard her in my mind, as if she were here, speaking aloud."

"What did she say?"

You can't depend on men.... Could she tell him? Ruin the day that had begun so well? "Just foolishness. I can't remember it, some phrase she used on occasion."

His look was dubious, but leaving well enough alone, he nodded. "You all right now?" Mouth softening, on the edge of a smile, he watched her, leaning closer. "Still want to hear about my family?"

It was the distraction she needed and she grasped it. "Yes, certainly. I need to know who I'll meet today."

His arms were gone in a moment, his warmth with them. He snapped the reins, making a clicking sound with his tongue and teeth, and the mare set off in a quick trot. "Well, there's my father, Gabe Tanner."

"I've seen him in town, twice I think. Pip pointed him out."

"My sister Anna still lives at home, but she's thinking about a position in Dallas, working with children. Then there's the younger boys, Adam, Seth and Daniel, and last, but not least by any means, Rosemary's crowning achievement, my sister Jenny." The glow of pleasure he'd worn faded as his gaze skimmed her face, and she smiled, knowing he sought her welfare in that single, swift glance.

She made an effort, sprinkling her voice with enthusiasm. "Jenny? She's special, isn't she? I can tell by the way you say her name." She watched his hands on the reins, grasping the leather with confidence. His fingers were long, hands sinewed, skin tanned by years in the sun. She was aware of his strength, had known its harnessed power, and yet it was balanced by tenderness, his voice alive with that quality as he spoke of his small sister.

"Special?" His chuckle was low and warm. "Yeah, I guess she is. We've all spoiled her rotten, Rosemary says." Shooting her a slanting grin, he shrugged. "It's pretty hard not to. You'll know what I mean when you meet her."

"Who does she look like?"

He was different now, speaking of his home and the family he loved. Softer, more approachable, his eyes warming as he considered Angelena's query. "Hmm. I don't know. Maybe mostly like Rosemary. Dark hair and bright-blue eyes. She kinda glows. You know what I mean?" His eyes were eager as they met hers.

"I'll bet you spoil her worst of all."

"Naw, I haven't been home for a lot of years. I'm kinda like her favorite uncle when I get there. She was born after I left."

This was news. Although she might have known that a man like Wes Tanner would not be bound by the acres of land his father owned, that he would reach beyond the confines of this small community to spread his wings. "Where did you go?"

"I'm not sure you want to hear my life story, Lena. I made my way across a couple of states and a territory, worked at a number of ranches and did a stint as a deputy sheriff. By that time, I was pretty sick of bedrolls and trail food. The thought of my mother's cooking made me head back in this direction."

"You moved in at the ranch?"

He shook his head. "That's where I was headed. Had all the best intentions in the world of working with Gabe. It didn't work out that way. I rode through town just as two cowhands decided to settle their quarrel with a gun-fight. Oscar Rhinehold was the sheriff then, an old coot who hated to turn in his badge, even though he was beyond the age of forming a posse or wanting to draw a gun on anybody."

"You rode into the middle of a gunfight? It's a wonder you weren't shot."

"Not a chance, sweetheart. I rode past Benjie Albertson and knocked his gun out of his hand, then drew my own against the hothead who was aiming to stake a claim on Sarah Jane. Next thing I knew, the mayor was askin' me if I wanted to be sheriff. And Sarah Jane was telling me I was a genuine hero, for keepin' Benjie alive."

"The Sarah Jane I know?" That two men should be willing to shoot each other over the favors of a woman was beyond consideration, she thought privately. "Surely those men didn't draw guns over a woman."

"I'd draw a gun on any man who looked crossways at you," he said firmly.

She sniffed and shook her head disbelievingly. "That seems a bit primitive to me."

"Hell, Lena. Men are primitive creatures. Didn't you know that? Once they stake a claim, a woman might as well get used to the idea that she's personal property."

"Back up a little," she said slowly. "Does all this amount to the same thing? That you've 'staked a claim' on me? And I should stand by while you act like an idiot?"

His laughter rang out. "You think I'm about to haul you around by the hair?" He shook his head, sliding one arm around her waist. "You might say I've put my brand on you though, Lena. By this time, everybody in town knows it. There's no point in wasting your breath arguing the fact. Taking care of you is my job, whether that requires protecting you or providing you with a home. Whatever it takes, I'll do it."

"You've put your brand on me? Like a newborn calf?" She glared at him. "Why don't I feel honored?"

"Well, actually the brand is called a wedding ring. And it's not on you yet, but you'd better start countin' the days. I told you by the end of the week, remember?"

"The end of the week? Friday? That's tomorrow." She stiffened, leaning from the pressure of his encircling arm. "I think you take a lot for granted. What if I decide not to say the right words when the time comes?"

"We've had this discussion, Lena. It's going to happen. I'm itching to get you out of that saloon, and away from all those men who goggle at you every night."

"Goggle? Wherever did you get that word? And just because people enjoy listening to me sing, you've decided I should leave the Golden Slipper?"

"It isn't the listening to you sing that I have a problem with. It's the way the men look at you," he grumbled, and she watched as a flush crept up from his throat to settle on his cheekbones.

"You look at me, too," she reminded him, amused at his embarrassment.

"That's different. I'm gonna marry you."

"So you say."

Irritation laced his words as he tightened his grip on the reins. "You're pretty brave today, aren't you? Startin' in a fuss just when we're about to see my family. I suppose you think I'll just back off and let you tell me how things are going to be."

"I wouldn't be that optimistic," she said with a short laugh.

He turned to her, amazement alive in his face. "I've never heard you laugh before. Not even halfheartedly."

She looked across a pasture that was alive with cattle, most of them with heads bent to the grass. "I guess I haven't done much of it lately. I've been too bound up in trying to figure out who I am and what I've left behind."

"You may never know those answers, Lena. And in case you've wondered, I don't care who you were before you got to Edgewood, Texas. I told you before, I'm not interested in your past. Only your future."

She turned to face him. "So you did. I'd almost forgotten that. I just didn't think you were considering marriage."

"I knew I wanted you. One way or another, I figured you'd belong to me."

"I thought we'd put the idea of my being your property into cold storage."

"Once that ring's on your finger, you're mine," he said bluntly. "As good as branded."

"I'll bet you that Rosemary doesn't consider herself a

branded woman. Did Gabe Tanner ever stake a claim on her?''

"Yeah, he surely did."

If she were any judge, the expression on Wes's face gave the word *smug* a new meaning. "You really mean to marry me, don't you?"

His glance was startled. "What the hell do you think we've been talkin' about? I told you that the other night. Haven't changed my mind since. In fact, I talked to the preacher this morning."

"And what did he say? Was he leery of my being a saloon singer?"

Wes shook his head. "Not for a minute. Seems you have a better reputation in town than I gave you credit for. The good reverend thinks you don't belong in the Golden Slipper."

"And what do you think?" Angelena asked quietly.

"I think you belong with me. I've got a line on a house just outside of town. About half a mile south. It needs some work done on it, but the price isn't bad."

She was stunned. "You're going to buy a house? We won't live over the jail?"

"Now, do you really like the idea of two rooms in the middle of town?" He favored her with a grin. "I'd prefer a bit more privacy than that."

"I guess I didn't think about you buying a place." And that said a lot about his sincerity, she decided privately. "You're willing to do that for me?"

"No, for both of us. About time I settled down anyway. This just got me moving in that direction."

And if that didn't put a pin in her balloon, nothing would, she thought. He was going to settle down, and she was a convenient prospect. It was enough to make a woman lose her pride. If she had a whole lot to start with.

"Look, there's the ranch house." He nudged her, invading her thoughts as he pointed off to the north. A long lane beckoned them and he turned the mare's nose from the road to follow where it led. Less than quarter of a mile away, surrounded by trees and greenery, a big house with porches surrounding it welcomed them.

"It's beautiful." Angelena sighed. "No wonder Rosemary married your father. This house is enough incentive all by itself, let alone loving the man."

"Well, when she agreed to come here to live, she sure enough wasn't in love with him." Wes laughed aloud, as if it were a story worth hearing.

"Really?" Angelena's interest was piqued by the oblique statement, and she determined to hear Rosemary's version of the tale.

The tabletop was covered by platters and bowls of food, more than Angelena could remember having seen in one place in her life. Rosemary moved between stove, cupboard and table with economical movements that were daunting to the uneducated. Angelena watched in awe. As a cook, her experience was limited to the kitchen behind Jason's saloon. Putting together a meal for a dozen people seemed a chore beyond her talents.

Somewhere, she'd learned how to put a meal together, but the memory of when and where eluded her. Only the ability to heap ingredients into kettles or bowls had remained within her sphere of knowledge. The recipes swam to the surface of her mind when needed, a pinch of this, a cup of that, and she was ever amazed at the hidden treasures held captive inside her head.

"Check those biscuits in the oven, will you, Angelena?" Rosemary sliced a huge ham with swift slashing movements, her mind apparently capable of sorting out the meal and issuing orders at the same time.

"Get another chair from the dining room, Daniel," she said to a dark-haired youngster who watched from his place in a big rocking chair.

"Yes, ma'am," the boy answered with a fleeting smile at Angelena as he slid to the floor and hastened out of the kitchen.

In the backyard, sounds of youthful laughter and the deeper tones of a man's voice caught her attention, and Angelena glanced through the open window. Wes pumped water for two young boys and they splashed noisily as they washed in the trough. Three tanned faces wore grins, and if she wasn't mistaken, Wesley Tanner was in his element, teasing his younger brothers.

She turned away reluctantly, aware that she watched a side of the man he had not exposed to her view. The oven was hot, and her cheeks burned as she hastily checked the big pan where Rosemary's biscuits had taken on a golden hue. "These are ready to come out," she said, closing the oven door against the invasive heat. "Where do I find a potholder?"

"You'll need two," Rosemary told her. "That pan's heavy." She tossed a pair in Angelena's direction. "Use the basket on the buffet."

"I'll get it, Mama." Elfin looks and a quick smile bestowed beauty on the child who flitted across the floor, her feet seeming to barely touch the wide boards. Jenny, the object of Wes Tanner's affection. She rose on tiptoe to reach the basket, securing it in both hands before she turned to Angelena.

"Are you Angelena?" she asked, no shyness evident in the sparkling eyes and wide grin.

Why Wes was so taken with the child was easy to understand. She was lovely, her whole being promising a glimpse of the beauty to come when she was grown. "Yes, I'm Angelena. And you're Jenny, I suspect."

The girl nodded. "Does my Wesley like you lots?" The basket clutched to her chest, she waited for an answer.

"Yeah, your Wesley likes her lots," came a resounding reply from outside the screen door. It was pulled open, Wes ducking his head in an automatic motion as he stepped inside. Jenny exploded into movement, shoving the basket in Angelena's direction as she flung herself with abandon at her big brother.

"Oh, Wesley! It's been s-o-o-o long since I've seen you!" Exaggerating her words and gesturing dramatically, Jenny clung to Wes's neck and buried her face against his shoulder.

He hugged her, a look of such adoration painting his features, Angelena had to look away. Her eyes filled with tears as she opened the oven again, removing the pan of biscuits. She bent her head, transferring biscuits to the basket, thankful for the small task that hid her from his observation. But not for long, it seemed.

"I see you put Lena to work," Wes said, stepping across the kitchen, pausing to drop a kiss on Rosemary's cheek. "I figured she'd come in handy."

"Well, she knows her way around a kitchen," Rosemary returned smartly. She glanced sharply at Wes. "Put that child down and ring the dinner bell. Jenny has silverware to arrange and napkins to put in place."

"He was just huggin' me, Mama," Jenny said, chortling as her brother poked her gently in the ribs. "I'll do my work." She pulled at Wesley's ear and her whisper was easy to overhear. "Put me down, Wes, before Mama scolds you."

He pulled a mock frown, turning his mouth down at the

corners as he lowered the child to the floor. A quick swat that ruffled the back of her skirts sent her on her way and he turned to Angelena. "See how I'm treated around here?" His breath was warm against her ear as he spoke his complaint.

She relished the grin he wore, her eyes capturing the carefree expression that tilted his mouth, crinkled his eyes and brought a tenderness into being within their depths. "Poor baby," she whispered mockingly. "I find it hard to feel very much sympathy, I fear." She turned, biscuits in hand and he stepped back, allowing her a clear path to the table. The basket in place, her fingers twitched at the checkered tablecloth, smoothing a wrinkle. "You look different here," she whispered. "I've never seen you look so happy before."

"This is where I belong. It's my home." His words were abrupt, and she glanced up at his stern profile as he stepped to the door, then out onto the porch. His back was straight, shoulders wide, and his hand firm on the bell rope, tugging it three times so that the bell clanged out its message with six peals, then subsided with a small flurry of discord. She watched as he turned back to the kitchen door, and their eyes met through the screen.

Perhaps this was the real Wesley Tanner. If so, it boded well for her future with him. If just once he looked at her with the same expression he bestowed on his small sister... She yearned for that, and at the same time held out little hope that it would come to pass. Wes looked at Jenny with tenderness. His eyes held little of that emotion when he turned them on *Angel*. But, there'd been glimpses of warmth, of good humor, and with that she might have to make do.

Her lips curved in a smile as she watched the menfolk of the ranch file through the back door, two small boys at the end of the line. Daniel, who'd hauled in a big chair for her benefit, gravely held it as she sat at one corner of the table. The family took their places, Jenny vying for the seat next to the visitor, Wes on her other side at the end of the long table. She was offered a hand on either side, and she bowed her head as Gabe Tanner uttered several sentences, thanking the Almighty for the food Rosemary had prepared.

The warmth of Jenny's hand was gone the instant a low "Amen" was spoken, and the child shook out her napkin, tucking it inside her collar. "Are you hungry, Miss Angelena?" she asked, wiggling in her chair.

"Oh, yes," Angelena answered, waiting as Wes helped himself to a chicken leg before passing the platter into her hands. "Do you like white meat or dark?" she asked Jenny, then watched in delight as the girl hesitated, clearly in a quandary as to which piece suited her fancy.

"A wing, I think," Jenny said after a moment. "That way I really get two pieces, if I break it apart."

Angelena subdued the grin that fought for expression. Not for the world would she want the child to think she laughed at her sober calculations. She speared a wing for Jenny's plate and a piece of breast meat for herself, then passed the platter on to the ranch hand sitting beyond Jenny. He looked a bit familiar, and she smiled.

He grinned in return, slanting her a look of recognition and his face flamed as he served himself. His eyes touched her face again and he bent in her direction. "I heard you sing, ma'am. The prettiest thing I've ever been privileged to listen to, and that's a fact. All the men say the same thing."

"I didn't know you could sing, Miss Angelena," Jenny said, her eyes widening. "Will you sing for me, too?"

Anna, the older sister, smoothing her dress beneath her

as she joined the group, perked up at that. "I'd be interested to hear you, too, Miss Angelena." She bent her head toward Rosemary, and spoke softly. "I'm sorry I'm late, Mama." With a flip of the fabric, she placed her napkin in her lap, then turned back to Angelena. "Maybe after dinner? There's a piano in the parlor. Do you play?"

The single word from the man at the end of the table was whispered, but potent in its anger. *"Damn."* Wes glared at the hapless ranch hand sitting beside Jenny, ignored both of his sisters, then offered Angelena a look of warning.

She placed her fork on her plate, folding her hands in her lap. Jenny awaited an answer, looking up at Angelena expectantly, and her lips quivered as she forced a smile.

"Maybe another time, sweetie," she whispered, bending over the dark hair to deliver her message into the child's ear. She met Anna's look of inquiry with a small shake of her head, and received a nod of understanding in return.

Rosemary said nothing, watching from across the table, but Wes was the recipient of her sharp glance. "Good chicken, Mother," he said, covering his lapse of temper quickly, nodding in her direction. "I always said you were the best cook in Texas."

The others picked up threads of conversation, the men discussing the chores scheduled for the afternoon. Apparently, the ranch hands all ate their noon meal in this kitchen every day, and Angelena was glad for their preoccupation with the work they would accomplish before the day was done. At her left, Wes ate without speaking further, his eyes slanting a look in her direction, as if he cautioned her.

Whether he had resented Jenny's attachment to her, or the youthful ranch hand's attention, she could not say. But something had displeased him. Deliberately, she opened a biscuit and spread it with jam, then bit into its tender texture. Her lashes lifted and she cast a quick look at Wes, noting the muscles of his jaw as he stoically chewed his food. He met her gaze, his eyes measuring, and she deliberately turned away.

Whatever his problem, she would not allow him to take it out on her in such a rude manner. She picked up her fork, determined to enjoy what she could of the meal Rosemary had prepared. To do less would be an insult, and she would not sink to such an exhibit of poor manners. Wes Tanner be hanged. He could be as ornery as he liked, but she refused to follow his example.

Her voice was low as she bent to speak to the child beside her. "Jenny, how about if you and I sit on the porch after dinner dishes are done, and I'll teach you a song?" she asked, her voice purposely light, her expression coaxing.

Wes's fork clattered against his plate, once more drawing her attention. Angelena lifted her brows and sent a look of inquiry in his direction, secretly pleased at his scowl. If the man didn't want her to form an attachment to his little sister, he should not have brought her here to the ranch. If Rosemary thought she was good enough to meet his family, surely he would have to agree. Wouldn't he? And whether he did or not, she would act the part of a lady, no matter what he thought.

Purposely, she smiled at him, her lips parting, her eyes wide, as if seeking his good humor. For a moment his mouth turned down, and then, with a cocky half salute, he allowed his lips to curve. The message was clear and she read it easily.

We'll talk about this later.

"I didn't help with dinner, so I'll clear up," Anna said as she rose from the table.

"I'll get my mending together then, if you don't mind," Rosemary announced, heading for the doorway. "The light in here is good this time of day."

"I'll talk Wes into helping, Mama," Anna called after her, then turned to Jenny. "Why don't you take Miss Angelena out on the porch swing? I'll bet she knows a song you could learn in jig time."

Jenny's step was eager as she led the unprotesting woman from the kitchen, and Wes watched them leave, Angelena's slender form moving gracefully as she followed the small child out the door. The woman did have a way of moving that drew his eye, he had to admit. He stepped closer to the window, watching the proceedings.

"Come on over here, ma'am," Jenny instructed, her words wafting back through the screen door. "Now, be careful how you do this. You must sit carefully so the swing doesn't move back and forth and hit the house." Jenny's voice was stern, as though she had done that very thing more than once and knew the consequences.

"I'll try," Angelena said, her movements deliberate as she tucked her skirts beneath her and placed herself gingerly on one corner of the wooden seat. "Now, I'll sit still while you get on," she offered.

Jenny wiggled her small bottom onto the slats, her feet sticking straight out before her. She clasped her hands in her lap and grinned. "Now you can let us just swing back and forth. Push a little bit with your toe." Leaning forward, she nodded approvingly. "That's right, you're doing just fine."

He couldn't help it. His grin was automatic as the child gave her instructions in a pseudoadult voice, probably copying Rosemary's tones. Yet there was within him a surge of jealousy once more, as Jenny beamed her delight with the visitor. He stood erect, feeling diminished by the emotion that swept through him. Angelena, though considered by some to be a woman of dubious virtue, had proved to be gracious, her manners beyond reproach, and his family had taken to her wholeheartedly.

And he was pouting over it. He grunted his dissatisfaction, turning from the window. She was as welcome here as he, and after all, what had he expected?

"You're not very nice to her," Anna said quietly. She stood at the sink, nearly up to her elbows in dishwater, rattling silverware in the big kettle she used to wash the dishes. "If you're going to marry the woman, you at least ought to treat her as if you like her."

"I like her," he answered quickly, walking to the dresser to retrieve a dish towel.

"You don't act like it." Anna rinsed the handful of silverware she held and placed it on the sinkboard. "In fact, I wouldn't think it was wise to marry her unless you love her."

"Love? As if you know about such things." Wes's voice rumbled as he muttered the words.

"Maybe not on a personal level," Anna said quietly. "But I've seen love in action every day of my life since we came to this house, Wesley. And so have you," she reminded him subtly. "There's never been a man and wife so in love as Mother and Father."

He picked up several forks and dried them methodically. "I'm not marrying her for love," he said quietly. "And how did you know about my plans?"

"Mother told me." She picked up a plate and washed it slowly, her smile teasing. "I've heard things in town anyway."

"You'd ought to know better than to listen to gossip."

She laughed with good humor. "Women thrive on gossip. I thought you knew that. When's the big day?"

"Tomorrow." The single word was terse, brooking no discussion.

"You're getting married tomorrow?" Her whisper was harsh, her eyes filled with stunned surprise. "And you're not having your family there?"

He shrugged as if the thought had not occurred to him. "If you want to come, you can. We're going to the parsonage in the late afternoon."

"Does Mother know?"

He shook his head. "Hell, now that I think about it, Angelena doesn't even know. I told her it would be by the end of the week, though, so she shouldn't be too surprised."

Anna closed her eyes, exasperation filling each word she spoke. "I can't believe my own brother could be so dense." She turned to him, waving the sopping wet dishrag in the air, water spattering his shirtfront. "You've made all the plans, and haven't included your bride-to-be?"

He stepped back, brushing at the water spots. "Watch what you're doing! This is my best shirt."

"Well, at least you thought enough of her to put on a clean one," Anna spouted. "I can't believe you're such an idiot."

"What are you two fighting over now?" Rosemary stood in the doorway, watching her eldest children with amusement.

"You won't believe what this dunderhead is planning for tomorrow," Anna said, her whisper filled with aggravation. She glanced out the kitchen window to the porch, where the swing moved to and fro and a faint melody could be heard through the screen. "He's going to marry Angelena in the afternoon, and he hasn't even let her in on the secret."

"Wesley!" Rosemary's eyes were piercing as she spoke his name, and he felt a reluctant urge to apologize.

"You can come if you want to," he said hastily. "I just didn't think it was a good idea to make a big fuss over it."

"Well, I do," Rosemary muttered, her voice low in deference to the open window. "Your family will be there. You may not want our support, but I'm thinking Miss Angelena will need it, if what I saw at the dinner table is anything to go by."

His eyes narrowed as her words penetrated. "I've treated her nicely," he said harshly. " And she's not complaining. In fact, you should hear the way she talked to me on the way out here."

The soft voices on the porch were silent. The swing had come to a halt, and then it rocked wildly, and one end hit the siding on the house as Angelena stood abruptly.

"Now see what you've done," Wes said, his words an accusation as he glared at his sister.

"Me? I didn't do anything but try to set you straight." Her face flushed, and he eyed her with surprise. Anna was never angry, and yet, unless he was mistaken, she was downright put out with him now. What with waving her wet dishrag at him and scolding him to beat the band, his sister was hell-bent on defending Angelena. Matter of fact, his whole family and half the ranch hands seemed to have taken to her in a big way, even Gabe himself welcoming her with a glad hand.

"I think you need to mend some fences," Rosemary told him. "Take her home and get your plans in order. We'll all be in town tomorrow afternoon. What time is the ceremony?"

Wes looked down at her, aware that Rosemary in a snit was a force to be reckoned with. "About four o'clock. I was gonna take her to the hotel for dinner, once I get all her stuff cleared out of the Golden Slipper.''

"Well, do that first, and we'll have dinner with you," Rosemary said quietly. "She will not become a member of this family without some sort of celebration, and that's that.''

"Sheriff?" Angelena's voice was a welcome distraction. "I need to head back to town now." Her attention went to Rosemary, with a quick smile in Anna's direction. "I appreciate the wonderful dinner, Mrs. Tanner. Thank you so much for asking me. It was lovely meeting you, Anna."

"Do you hafta go?" Jenny's wail of disappointment sounded from behind her, and Angelena turned, crouching before the child.

"I was just about remembering all the words, Miss Angelena. Now I'll forget them before I see you the next time." Her mouth curved down at the corners, and big tears hovered on the edge of her lashes.

"I'll bring her back again, Jenny," Wes said, pushing the screen door open. "You'll be seeing a lot of her. We're getting married tomorrow, and Rosemary is bringing you and the whole family to the wedding."

Chapter Eight

Wes lifted Angelena's slight weight, his hands around her waist. That she could have climbed into the buggy on her own was obvious. And that was probably exactly what she wanted to do. But his hands itched to touch her, and with his family watching, he figured she was pretty much obliged to put on a smile and put up with his fingers wrapped around her middle. Her right foot touched the step and she hoisted herself. With little effort, he placed her on the seat, receiving no audible thanks for his effort.

"You're welcome, ma'am," he said softly, slanting a look at her set features. She was stewing, that was a certainty. How long she could keep it under control was the question that increased his pace as he loosened his mare from the hitching post and climbed atop the buggy seat.

Wes snapped the reins and the mare set off with a flourish, her tail flying, her hooves lifting high as she broke into a trot. Beside him, Angelena drew in a deep breath. He took the opportunity to slide in a remark he thought might cool her anger a bit.

"I was going to tell you on the way out here, but you were fussin' at me and I couldn't get a word in edgewise,

Lena. Besides," he said self-righteously, "that's what you get for listening in on a private conversation."

She sputtered. She absolutely sputtered, and while he couldn't help but be amused at the sounds she emitted, he recognized her anger as a thing to be respected. Angelena about had Rosemary beat when it came to looking like an avenging angel. And unless he missed his guess, she was well on her way to having a genuine temper fit, right here and now. He'd seen it coming, and thus had put wings on their departure. It would not do for his family to hear what she had to say when she finally got her breath and started in on him.

Her glare cut to the heart of the matter, her words giving it a fine edge. "You had no such intention in mind, Wesley Tanner. You were going to spring it on me tomorrow. You planned to hustle me over to the parsonage and get this thing done with, without any fuss or bother." Her voice rose, and her eyes snapped the fury she made no attempt to conceal. "You knew I was outside that window. How could I help but listen, especially when I realized you were having a set-to with Anna?

"And another thing. You didn't even plan on telling your family, did you?" Without a pause, her words flowed over him. "Don't try to cover it up, Sheriff. I've got your number."

It wasn't going to work. She was bound and determined to be mad, and there wasn't a damn thing he could do about it. His shoulders hunched as he settled into the seat, ready for the next barrage. It was not to come.

She was silent, looking away from him, as though the sight of his face would only serve to make her ill. Her hands twisted in her lap, one of them glistening, a scattering of moisture dotting its back. Moisture? *Damn, those were tears.* Lena was crying and too mad to even holler at him anymore.

The road to town was deserted, and he pulled his mare beneath overhanging branches on the edge of a grove of trees. The reins taken care of, he turned to the woman beside him.

"Lena. Look at me." His hands firm against her shoulders, he tried to turn her to face him, but her resistance was more than he'd bargained for. She shrugged from his touch and slid from the buggy, stumbling as her feet touched the ground. Pulling herself erect, she walked away, beyond the first stand of maples, to where a stream glistened in the sunlight.

"Hey, wait a minute!" He jumped from the buggy, lowering the weight he carried over the side to keep the horse from wandering. In half a dozen steps, he'd tramped his way down the path she made, keeping her in sight. "Lena! Wait for me," he shouted, only to see her hasten her steps as she walked through the tall grass.

Damn, she could run into a snake or who knew what else, and then he would be in a fix. Ducking beneath a tree limb, he stepped up his pace.

He called out again, his voice strident with the worry he could not conceal. "Lena? Come on back here. We need to talk."

A squirrel overhead chattered his opinion of the man below, and Wes darted a look upward, to where the noisy creature perched. Reminded him of the woman he was chasing after, he decided, sassy as all get-out.

A line of weeping willow trees swept the ground, and through the low-hanging branches the stream of water appeared. Before him, Lena's shoes had stepped lightly, but several bent stems and crushed wildflowers mapped her route to his discerning eye, and Wes followed her in silent pursuit. Ahead, another enormous willow grew, branches swaying with the breeze and he bent to peer beneath them, seeking the telltale sight of Angelena's dress.

A flash of color gave her away and he halted, then swept aside the branches and entered the leafy bower. She stepped from behind the trunk to face him, pale and breathless as if she recognized his anger, yet would not be cowed by his presence.

"I can walk home, Sheriff. It's not that far from here."

"Like hell," he growled. "I don't intend to have you come draggin' into town, and folks talkin' a mile a minute about you. You'll get back in that buggy and ride with me."

She shook her head, her jaw set firmly. "I'm so angry with you, I can't imagine sitting beside you for another minute."

"Well, startin' tomorrow, you'll be spendin' a lot of time with me, lady. You'd better get used to the idea."

"I'll marry one of the cowhands before I promise to love, honor and obey a man who can't even allow me to choose the time and place for my own wedding." Her words were short, staccato bursts of sound, and her eyes filled with angry tears as she faced him down.

He couldn't stand it. Mad or not, he couldn't stand to see her so distraught, so small and fragile, yet brave to a fault. "Aw, hell, Lena. Come over here, will you?" He held out his arms and she hesitated. "Please." His feet moved one step closer, and she shook her head.

"I'm not willing to give in so easily," she told him, her firm jaw warning him off. "I didn't like the way you treated me at your mother's house. You acted like a spoiled child, just because your family welcomed me."

"Dusty was flirtin' up a storm and you let him," he said harshly.

"Who?" The word was unbelieving, her eyes widening at his accusation.

"That damned cowhand who told you how wonderful you are," he grumbled.

"And you were jealous?" Her tone softened, her mouth twitching.

He glared at her. "Hell, no! I just thought you could have... I don't know what I thought," he conceded after a moment. "I guess it bothered me that Jenny took to you so quick, and Anna was all set to roll out the red carpet." He drew in a deep breath. "You acted like you liked them more than you do me."

Her stance softened, her tears already drying on her cheeks, and she shook her head. "I want them to like me, especially if we're going to be married, like you say. But you're family, Wes. They love you."

Her words warmed him, the message one he was aware of, yet more than welcome from her lips. "I guess you're right there," he said haltingly. "They want to come to town for the wedding. Rosemary said they'd be there."

"All of them? Tomorrow?"

"Yeah, tomorrow. You'll agree to that? No more fussin'?"

Angelena considered his words. "Do you like me, Wes? As well as they do?"

He took another step and his hands gripped her shoulders. "Do I like you? Hell, you've been drivin' me to distraction ever since the first time I laid eyes on you, Lena." He tugged her forward and his hands slid across her back, pressing her against his long, hard body. "Do I like you? That's a pretty puny word for what I feel, sweetheart. All I can think of right now is how soft and warm you are, and how sweet you smell."

She turned astonished eyes upward, her head tilting to

one side as she examined his face. "All of that? Soft, warm and sweet?"

"No," he murmured. "There's more than just soft, warm and sweet. A whole lot more, but I don't think you want to hear it right now. I'm gonna need a bed and more time than we've got to finish this conversation." His hands moved to press her hips forward and she allowed it, her eyes widening a bit as he moved against her.

"I'm not sure...." she began, hesitating as if the words were difficult to speak.

"You don't have to be." He felt his mouth curve, watched as her eyes scanned his face, finally meeting his gaze. "I'm sure enough for both of us." He ducked his head, catching her unaware, her eyes widening as she sensed his intent.

Then their lips touched, his arms wrapping her in an embrace that lifted her against him, pressing her breasts against his chest, even as she lifted her arms to wind them around his neck. His mouth softened as he recognized her surrender, and he caught her bottom lip between his teeth, suckling it for a moment. Her murmur of surprise pleased him, and he chuckled, deep in his throat, his tongue moving on the soft surface. His teeth released his prize and his lips opened against hers. He tasted her flavor, relishing the soft sounds she made and the tension of her fingers against the back of his head.

Reluctantly, he moved on, the warmth of cheek and temple luring him to explore. A pattern of damp kisses marked his path and he brushed her lashes with the tip of his tongue, pleased with the shiver he engendered. His mouth whispered words against her eyelids, and she was unmoving, breathing in short shallow inhalations, as though straining to hear the syllables he spoke.

Wes pressed her close with one long arm, the other hand

rising to cradle her cheek. Her eyes opened, their blue depths shimmering with desire, and she caught a deep, shuddering breath. He drew back, watching her, taut with the tingling awareness that spun between them, bathing them in its passionate force. Angelena clung to him, a faint flush rising from her throat, her nostrils flaring as she drew his scent deeply into her lungs. Beneath her ear a rapid pulse beat a swift cadence, and he bent his head, touching his tongue to the spot where her lifeblood flowed. He inhaled the faint aroma of some elusive fragrance and his mind tried in vain to place its origin.

His head lifted, and he felt his nostrils flare as he gazed his fill at the woman he held. Damn, she was pretty, her skin as soft as the rose petals on his mother's prized bushes. There wasn't a bit of waste to her, all sleek and slender as she was, and yet soft in the right places, with a lush, rounding bosom that made his hands curve in anticipation.

Her lashes spread shadows against rosy cheeks, and as he watched she inhaled, the edges of her teeth showing. It was more than he could resist.

His lips covered hers, his tongue barely touching the moist entry. From one side to the other, the tip of his tongue explored, rising, then dipping to touch the front of her teeth, urging without words for the opening he sought. She shook her head, the minutest amount, resisting his approach further.

"Wes?" Her lips formed around the tip of his tongue as she whispered his name, and he murmured a sound of encouragement in his throat, to no avail. She could not be persuaded further to join the game he'd begun. At least he'd escaped the flat of her hand with this venture, he thought, a chuckle rising from his depths. With a muffled sigh he reluctantly allowed her withdrawal, scattering countless damp kisses on the glowing countenance before him. And yet, she clung, burying her nose in the hollow of his throat.

Her murmur of pleasure encouraged him and he urged her closer, forming her soft curves to his needy groin, at once fearful that the obvious evidence of his burgeoning manhood would frighten her, yet willing to risk her outrage. As if oblivious to the throbbing pressure against her belly, she turned her mouth to his, breathlessly seeking the pressure of his lips once more. He acceded to her silent demand, his mouth taking hers with all the pent-up need of a man hungry for the taste of the woman he desires.

Limp in his arms, she murmured his name softly, and he turned his head, shivering as her warm breath freely offered the message he'd tried his best to pry from her only moments past.

"I'll marry you tomorrow, Wes Tanner. Truth to tell, I don't see any way out of it, and I'm smart enough to know that I don't have much of a choice anyway."

It wasn't exactly what he'd had in mind, but she'd surrendered the fight, and he didn't intend to push her any further. "We'll do fine together, Lena." He pressed her head against his shoulder, his big hand brushing the hair from her forehead and cheek. "Who will you ask to stand with you?"

She was silent for a moment. "I hadn't thought about that. Maybe Pip? Or Anna? Do you think either of them would do it?"

"I suspect they'd both be pleased to be asked," he said. "You'll have to think about it and make up your mind before morning."

"I don't have a wedding dress," she whispered.

"Would you wear the white gown you had on, that first time I saw you?"

She considered for a moment, and her whispered reply was dubious. "You don't think it's cut too low?"

He thought of the flimsy costumes the rest of the women at Jason's place wore, comparing them to the quality of Angelena's wardrobe, and shook his head. "No, it's fine. We just need to have Pip find a piece of veil for you to pin on your head."

Her eyes lost their luster, and she turned her face from him. "I can't wear a veil, Wes. That privilege is reserved for a virgin bride. Since our reason for a wedding has to do with my being in the family way, I don't think I deserve that right."

"I didn't know a veil had any significance, Lena. Anyway," he announced firmly, "it doesn't matter in this case. We're gettin' married early on, and folks will just think you're havin' your baby a little ahead of time."

She hesitated and he gritted his teeth, preparing himself for her argument. To his surprise and relief, she nodded slowly. "I'll ask Pip and see what she thinks about it."

Now all he had to do was get to Pip first and put a bug in her ear.

"You're getting married tomorrow? And you want me to stand up with you? Really?" Pip's eyes glittered with tears as she responded to Angelena's request. Delivered in a halting manner, it had nevertheless been warmly received, and Angelena felt relief sweep over her.

"I couldn't decide between you and Anna, but I've known you for weeks, and only just met Wes's sister today. I've felt almost like you're mothering me sometimes," she confided. And then her eyes widened, as if she reconsidered her words. "Not that you're old enough to be my mother. I know that. It's just that you've looked out for me."

"I'd think I could easily be your mother's age, sweetie. I doubt you're more than nineteen or twenty."

Angelena shrugged. "That's something I'll likely never know, at least at the rate I'm going. And there's another thing. Wes says I need to have a veil. Oh, and one more thing. I have to have a last name to put on the marriage certificate, don't I?" Never had she felt so lost, so bereft as in this moment, she decided, watching as Pip considered her problem.

"I'll tell you what," Pip said, her words slow, as if she considered at great length what she was about to propose. "Why don't we just do a kind of unofficial adoption here, and Dex and I will give you our name. How does Angelena Sawyer sound?" Her mouth widened in a grin as she spoke, and she reached for Angelena, hugging her tightly. "I'd be proud to own you as a daughter, sweetie, and unless I miss my guess, Dex is of the same mind."

"It won't be legal," Angelena reminded her. "Do you think the preacher will let us do that?"

"I suspect he'll figure that Sawyer is better than no name at all." She released Angelena from her embrace, bustling around the end of the long walnut counter. Lifting a stack of yard goods from the shelf behind her, she placed them on the counter. "Now that that's settled, we'll solve your other problem. This is all the odds and ends that I don't sell very much of," she told Angelena, sorting through the bolts with purpose. "I know I have just the thing here somewhere."

She chose quickly, flipping a bolt from the center of the stack with a practiced hand. The rest she replaced on the shelf. Angelena watched as Pip unrolled yards of soft, white veiling.

"Oh, I won't need nearly so much, Pip," she whispered, aghast at the amount of fine tulle piled on the counter. Her fingers yearned to touch the cloud of white, and she allowed her right hand to venture forth.

"Here," Pip said quickly, lifting a length and draping it over Angelena's arm. "Isn't it pretty? I usually only get a call for it when one of the girls hereabouts gets married."

Angelena turned to the front window, looking through the fine veiling. The front door opened and she turned, her eyes widening as Wes stood in the doorway. The sunlight behind him cast his face in shadow, and through the white cloud he was cast in the role of a stranger, resembling a man she'd seen once, in front of the theater.

In front of the theater. Her mouth went dry, as if a desert wind took her breath and left her throat parched and rasping. She dropped the veiling, her eyes closing.

"Lena!" He'd somehow crossed the floor, and his arms were around her. "What's wrong, honey?" He lifted her, and crossed to the rocking chair. She felt herself lowered to its seat and then his fingers loosened the button at her throat. "Pip, can you get her a drink of water?" he asked.

From her other side, Pip answered quickly. "I'll be right back, Wes."

Angelena opened her eyes, her gaze seeking his. "When I saw you in the doorway, you looked like a man I saw in front of the theater one day."

"What theater, honey? Who was he?" Wes leaned toward her and held both of her hands in his.

She shook her head. "I don't know." The words burst forth in a sob, and she struggled to halt the tears accompanying it. "It wasn't here, of course, and I don't know who the man was. You just looked like him, I guess, and it was as if a window opened and closed, and he was gone."

Pip was there, offering the glass of water, and Angelena accepted it gratefully. "You all right, sweetie?" Her brow furrowed as she considered the young woman. "You looked like you were about to faint on us. Like to scared me to death."

"She remembered something," Wes murmured. "It's gone now."

The front door opened and Bernice Comstock entered the store. Pip hurried to greet her, attempting to turn her attention from Angelena. With little success.

Bernice eyed the proceedings with an eagle eye. "Miss Angelena not feeling well?" she asked briskly. "There's a lot of summer colds going around, I hear, some of them carryin' a touch of dysentery."

Wes stood, offering an easy grin. "No, she's just a little excited today. We're plannin' a wedding, ma'am."

Angelena felt her cheeks redden and swallowed another mouthful of water. Now the fat was in the fire. Bernice Comstock was probably the nicest lady in town, Pip aside, but once she had wind of a bit of gossip, it might as well go up on a signboard for everyone to read. She smothered her groan with another swallow of water, and lifted her head.

"I'm fine, Mrs. Comstock."

The woman bustled closer, her bright eyes raking Angelena's slender form. "You're going to marry the sheriff?" she asked. "Right soon?"

Angelena caught a whiff of aggravation in Wes's obliging reply. "Tomorrow, as a matter of fact, ma'am." He lowered his voice and stepped closer to the liveryman's wife. "I'd sure appreciate it if you could keep it under your hat for a day, though. We'd like it to have just our family present."

"Your family, Sheriff? I understand that Miss Angelena doesn't have anyone here in town." Her words were kindly, but the truth was still hurtful, and Angelena was pierced by the knowledge that so far as she knew, there was no one she could call her own.

"Mr. Sawyer and I will be there for Angelena," Pip put in quickly. "As a matter of fact, I'll be doing the honors as her attendant. Dex will give her away."

Bernice's face glowed with delight. "Well, isn't that fine? No bride should walk down the aisle alone."

Dex will give her away. The words sang in her mind, and Angelena nodded her agreement. Surely he would be willing, and if by chance he dragged his feet, Pip would put it right.

"Well, I'm needing some yard goods, Phillipa. You just go on with what you're doing and I'll look around a bit," Bernice said brightly. She looked back at Angelena. "I'm pleased for you, young lady. You couldn't find a better man than our sheriff, here." Turning on her heel, she made her way to the far counter, where bolts of fabric awaited her inspection.

"I'll take care of this," Pip said in a low voice, gathering up the yards of veiling she'd unrolled. She straightened the bolt on the counter and using her shears, she cut the tulle she held free from its moorings. Holding it by the edges, she found the center and allowed the folds to fall in a pristine cloud.

"We'll just weave in a wreath of flowers here," she announced, letting the rest fall over her arm in dainty profusion. "My mock orange bushes are blooming to beat the band. I'll cut me some and use a length of wire to fix it up. Won't take but a few minutes."

"How much is the tulle?" Angelena asked softly, wishing she had carried a bit of money with her.

"It'll be part of my gift to you," Pip told her, her stern look brooking no interference with the plan. "I'd better get

Dex over here to watch the store while I make sure his good shirt and his suit don't need pressing.''

"I'll stop and tell him," Wes offered. "I think I'd better walk Lena on over to Jason's place to get her things in order."

"I'll have to leave my things there for tonight," Angelena said.

"You're not singin' one more time at that saloon." Wes turned to look at her and his eyes were stormy, his jaw taut.

"I have an obligation to Jason," Angelena told him quietly. "I'll move out in the morning, but for tonight, I still have a performance to give. Two of them, as a matter of fact." Her gaze was unwavering as she met his eyes. "He's been very kind to me, Wes, and I won't go back on our agreement. Tomorrow, you can probably get away with giving me orders. Today, you can't."

He nodded shortly, offering his arm as she rose from the chair. "Whatever you say. You know I'll be there, don't you?"

"At the Golden Slipper? You're going to spend the evening there?"

"Yeah, that's what I said. I told you, I'm responsible for you now, Lena. I'm gonna tuck you inside that room of yours for the last time tonight. I want to hear the lock snap in place, and I want to see you at the window, so I know you're all right when I get back to my place."

"You want me at the window? I'm supposed to just stand there and wait for you to show up?" She couldn't resist the urge to tease him, and his mouth twitched as he recognized her thrust.

"Yeah, I want to see you at that window." His pause was long and she waited for him to continue, knowing he intended to better her teasing. "I'll be thinking about you sharing my room tomorrow night," he said, bending to whisper the words in her ear. A tendril of anticipation, blended with a fear of the unknown, sent a chill down her spine, and she gripped his arm with tense fingers. "Take me home, please," she whispered, knowing her voice would not sustain more than that small sound.

"Yes, ma'am," he replied. "Whatever you say. For now."

They left the store, Angelena aware of interested looks in their direction as a few scattered passersby looked their way. Head held high, she marched at his side, looking neither right nor left, until they reached the back door of the Golden Slipper.

"This is the last time you'll be goin' in this place." His words spoke the end of her time with the women who had taken her in and looked after her for the past weeks, and Angelena felt a shiver of fear as she considered leaving the only home she remembered, the place where she had been accepted without question.

"I know," she said, lifting her chin as she met his stony gaze. "I'll tell them all goodbye in the morning. They don't know yet…about the wedding, I mean."

"I wouldn't count on that, if I were you," he drawled, opening the door for her entry. "I'll be surprised if you aren't the talk of the town before the hour is out."

"You think so?" she asked.

"I suspect by the time your audience shows up anyway."

She watched his mouth, those lips that had possessed hers with such force and fervor only hours ago. Tomorrow night he would repeat those kisses. Now his mouth was set firmly, his lips thinning to a flat line even as she watched. Her heart raced as she considered the knowledge she possessed, recalling the pleasure Wes Tanner's lips were capable of bestowing.

"You goin' in?" he asked, and she blinked at his words, then nodded, brushing past him into the kitchen. "Let's go up and get you packed," he said quietly. "I'll carry your things over before you have to get ready for your first show."

"No." The word was firm, and she turned to face him. If he went up with her, held her again, if those hands pressed her against that long, hard body... Her heart thumped as she remembered their encounter, and she shook her head. "I'll pack my trunk, but it will stay here until morning. I'd just as soon not cause any more tongues to wag than necessary tonight."

His shoulders lifted in a negligible movement. "Whatever you say, ma'am." He watched as she walked to the narrow back stairway, grasped the railing and climbed the stairs. She knew it, knew that his dark eyes were pinned on her, even before she turned at the top of the stairs to look back down at him.

He lifted one hand in a familiar half salute, and his smile was dark and without humor, as if he warned her that this was the last time she would defy his wishes. And if that were to be true, she might as well add sauce to the pudding, she decided.

Her own hand lifted in a mocking gesture, blowing a kiss in his direction. Before his reaction could set in, she turned away and walked down the hallway to her room, closing the door behind her. The lock snapped into place, and she moved across to the window, looking out upon the wagons and horsemen who peppered the length of town. The sidewalk was sparsely populated, most folks having already headed for home for supper.

A familiar form stepped onto the road and she watched

as he jammed his hat in place, her eyes intent on him as he crossed to the jailhouse and entered the door. It closed behind him with an audible sound and she smiled, satisfied that she had had the last word in this set-to.

Then her gaze moved up to the windows above. The curtains hung limply inside the closed panes, and she pondered what might lie beyond their filmy boundaries.

Tomorrow night she would know.

Chapter Nine

The Reverend James Worth was a pleasant man, his children almost full grown, a definite blessing to the community, according to Rosemary's whispered asides to Angelena upon entering the vestibule of the church. Truly a dedicated man of God. Yet, she approached him with a total lack of diffidence, and Angelena silently admired her aplomb, thankful for her presence.

"I'd like you to meet my son's bride, Pastor Worth, and welcome her to the church." Her eyes beckoned Angelena forward with a glance, and even as she moved to obey the silent request, Angelena began to understand Wes's respect for the woman who had raised him from boyhood. Rosemary was small, but mighty, he'd said, and with a single glimpse into the woman's eyes, she understood that statement.

Nodding her head in respect for the minister's position in the community, she placed her hand in his. He was neat as a pin, with gleaming white cuffs emerging from a fine wool worsted suit, and he spoke her name in respectful tones.

"I'm pleased to meet you, Miss Angelena. I understand you come to us under strange circumstances, and someday

I would spend time with you in order to hear your story. But for today, we will disregard all of that and give you a fresh page, an honorable beginning with our Sheriff Tanner.'' He leaned closer and whispered, "Now, I must join him and his father. They're waiting for me by the side door. We'll see you at the altar in a short while.'' His smile was encouraging, and Angelena grasped at it.

And if she'd heard right, he'd been rather gracious. Didn't his greeting to her sound like he was offering to ignore her rough edges and the sullied past she brought with her from her days at the Golden Slipper? He had welcomed her nicely, and that was all that really mattered. She watched as he left her, exiting the front door of the church to walk around the outside to where Wes and his father waited.

Rosemary took Angelena's hands and leaned to drop a quick kiss on her cheek. "I'd best take my seat, dear. Once Pip and Dex arrive, we'll be ready to begin.'' Her blue eyes held just a bit of moisture as she smiled. "Welcome to the family, Angelena.'' She whisked through the door from the vestibule into the church and pulled it half-shut behind herself, leaving Angelena in relative privacy.

Within seconds, the outer doors opened and Dex appeared at her side, offering his arm and a lush bouquet of mock orange blossoms, their slender branches trailing in lush profusion down the front of her dress. Matching, fragrant blooms formed a circle upon the crown of her head, and Dex's elegant hands were careful as he rearranged her veil before her face.

"You're beautiful, Miss Angel,'' he whispered, his eyes laden with kindness and affection she could not fail to recognize. "It was a fortunate day for all of us when you strolled down the street in this town. Wes is one lucky man.''

Tears welled in her eyes, and Dex shook his head. "You're not allowed to cry, or Pip will think I've said something dreadful to upset you." His smile was sweet, and she was overwhelmed with love for this man who had supported her with his talents and given unstinting respect when it was exactly what she needed in order to survive.

"Come, we'll wait by the doors for Pip. She won't be long," he said, his smile urging her to join him as he extended his arm. He was quite dapper, she decided, admiring the fabric of his suit, her fingers brushing it lightly.

Again, a door opened and closed in her mind as she recognized the feel of cashmere, and she felt a small spurt of glee as she recognized another glimpse into her past. Maybe, just maybe, her memory was returning. Only one tiny fragment at a time, but those bits and pieces might eventually weave themselves into a forgotten past, and she would be whole.

She tightened her fingers and Dex's arm was firm beneath them, the muscled forearm of a pianist. She gripped its strength, thankful for his presence on this day that was bound to change her life in limitless degree. Anticipation, blended with a sense of apprehension, flooded her being, and she sensed a trembling from her throat to the tips of her toes. Surely she would not be able to repeat the vows as instructed. Certainly she would never be able to walk the length of the aisle to the front of the church.

All was silent within the sanctuary as she peeked through the partially open door before her. From within the foyer, where they stood, the front of the church was visible, with an arrangement of flowers on the communion table, and a small cluster of people sitting in the front pews. Their clothing of Sunday-best quality, she barely recognized the backs of Wes's brothers, hair gleaming damply, as they fidgeted in their seats. Jenny peered over her shoulder, and her eyes lit with glee as she spotted Angelena through the doorway. One hand rising to wave a sedate greeting, she smiled with unconcealed joy.

"I'm almost late, aren't I?" Pip slipped through the outside doors and stepped close to Angelena. "I had to drop the baby off at the parsonage. Mrs. Worth agreed to watch him for an hour." She stepped back a pace and scanned Angelena, her eyes gleaming with delight.

"You look beautiful, child. The wreath came out well, didn't it?" Her fingers twitched at the veil as she adjusted it to suit herself. And then she subsided, hands clasped before her. "I wish you were truly our own, Angelena. For today, will you allow me to pretend that I gave you birth?"

"Oh, yes, I'd like that." It was going to be difficult not to stumble down the aisle if her eyes kept filling with tears she could not blink out of existence.

Pip turned away abruptly, probably hiding emotion of her own, Angelena suspected. "Where is my bouquet?" she blustered, searching the foyer for the arrangement she had put together. "Ah!" Her whisper was triumphant as she picked it up from a bench just inside the door. "I think we're ready."

The organ swelled with the first notes of a hymn, and a door opened on the right side of the church, the Reverend Worth entering with Wes and Gabe Tanner close behind. Angelena watched through the partially open door as the men made their way to the center of the church, then stepped back as Pip prepared herself for the business of a wedding.

"Don't set out until I'm almost there," she whispered, opening the doors fully, so that she was framed in the center of the aisle. The music boomed in recognition of her presence, and she glided with precision down the aisle. Dex watched his wife, beaming as though she were the central figure in this celebration, then turned to look down at Angelena.

"Are you ready, honey?" Patiently, he waited for her nod of assent before he led her into the sanctuary. Their march was unhurried, as though Dex wanted the groom to get a good look at the girl he was about to marry.

A part of Angelena wanted him to hurry along, another yearned to press this moment in her sparsely populated book of memories, making it last as long as possible. Marrying Wes Tanner had not been her first choice. But then, she really didn't have a first choice, after all, and Wes had a knack for making her yearn for him. That was something to be thankful for. It would make living with him palatable.

Perhaps even more than that. If only she weren't so frightened of him sometimes. No, she thought pensively, as she shot a quick glance at his somber visage, not of him, but of what he made her feel.

He was before her now, and her heart reacted in its usual way to his presence, thumping in a swift cadence beneath her breastbone. Almost, she met his gaze, her eyes meeting his, then lowering to the floor. One glimpse was enough. There was a measuring quality in his scrutiny of her. Dark and penetrating, his eyes scanned her, and she felt their heat.

Purposefully, she lifted her gaze, allowing it to touch the minister's solemn face. Unerringly, she glanced at Wes once more and then looked quickly away, directly into the eyes of Gabe Tanner. He smiled at her, his harshly handsome face looking more kindly today than yesterday when they'd first met, and she worked up the courage to smile at him.

Although Pip had told her that they were not related by blood, the two men were strangely alike, both muscular specimens of good health and clean living. Dark hair and eyes, blended with height and an innate touch of arrogance gave them the distinct look of men who would always attract their share of women. And yet, there was not a word of scandal aimed at either of them.

They stood side by side, hands behind their backs, watching her intently as she paused just one step from the altar. Then, as one, they turned to face the minister and waited for his instructions.

"Who gives this woman to be married to this man?" James Worth intoned.

Dex cleared his throat and drew Angelena's hand from his arm, offering it into Wes Tanner's care. "I do," he said quietly, then turned to Angelena and with great care lifted her veil over her head, allowing it to drift over her shoulders. He bent his head and brushed his lips across her cheek, and she smiled up at him, aware that never before had they shared such an affectionate moment.

The words she spoke seemed a role she must play, new and unfamiliar. Yet the knowledge of watching such a ceremony seemed a part of her memory. Wes slid a ring on her finger, and she looked down in surprise. She hadn't known, had not expected him to purchase a ring for her. Probably Pip's doing. Yet it didn't look new, but burnished with time. He turned it in place and she saw delicate carvings on the surface, their edges blurred by wear and tear.

"I now pronounce you man and wife." James Worth said with a deeply resonant phrasing that sent a shiver down the length of her spine. "You may kiss your bride."

Wes released her hand, his palms cupping her face, his mouth parted ever so slightly as he bent to her. "Hello, Mrs. Tanner," he whispered, his breath warm against her lips. His kiss was brief but thorough, and she yielded to it, closing her eyes and tilting her face to one side just a bit more, the better to receive his caress. She tasted moisture on her mouth as he straightened, and their eyes met, his dark with a smoldering emotion she hesitated to explore. The tip of his tongue skimmed his upper lip, and one corner of his mouth quirked.

The message was unmistakable, and, recognizing it, she felt a flutter of misgiving in the pit of her stomach. There was no escape from the night to come. Indeed, she was not sure she sought one. And yet, a shroud of mystery hung before her, dark and impenetrable, with no prior knowledge to draw upon.

She took his arm, they turned toward his family, and were immediately surrounded by an outpouring of affection, marked by the appearance of hankies that mopped up tears at an amazing rate. Rosemary's nose turned pink as she attempted to curtail her emotions, and Gabe took her in hand, holding her tightly against his side without a shred of compunction. Anna hugged her brother unreservedly and then turned the full force of her smiles upon Angelena.

"I'm so pleased he was smart enough to marry you," Anna blurted emphatically. "I couldn't have asked for a better sister."

"How about me?" Jenny asked plaintively. "I'm your sister, too."

Anna bent, picking the child up quickly. "Of course you are, sweetheart. And Angelena is your sister, too. It's just that we're *big* sisters, and you're our little sister."

Jenny appeared to consider that thought for a moment, then leaned to enclose Angelena in a hug that became a three-way embrace, effectively welcoming the newcomer with a full measure of affection.

"Well," Gabe said, scanning the sanctuary, "I think our sons have hightailed it out the door, Rosemary, and unless you plan on taking a bunch of ragtag hooligans into the hotel for dinner, we'd better catch up with them."

James Worth halted Wes with a light touch on his shoulder. "Sheriff, perhaps you and your bride would like to sign the marriage certificate now."

"Yes, certainly," Wes said, then turned to his family. "We'll meet the rest of you in a few minutes. We won't be long."

In but a moment Angelena held the pen in her hand, careful lest she spatter ink and blot the document. *Angelena Sawyer,* each letter carefully drawn, the surname written for the first time. Beside her, Wes was silent, but his look in her direction held an unspoken question.

"I don't have a last name. Well, I do, but I don't know what it is," she told him quietly, "and Pip offered hers."

Wes took the pen from her hand and bent over the desk to write his own signature. "You may not have known your last name before today, Mrs. Tanner. But there won't be any doubt in your mind from now on, will there?" He shot her a look from beneath lowered brows. "You'd better start practicing. You'll be signing from now on as Angelena Tanner." A smile of grim satisfaction twisted his mouth as he handed the pen back to the minister. "On second thought, you'd better make that Mrs. Wesley Tanner."

She'd made it to the first step when she realized she was climbing the stairs behind the jailhouse alone. "Go on up, Lena. I'll be there in ten minutes." Wes stood on the ground behind her, offering her these few moments by herself.

"Is the door unlocked?" she asked, turning to look to the second floor, where his living quarters offered privacy. Her feet carried her upward even as he answered her query, and she moved quickly, as if she sought any degree of solitude she could manage to acquire.

"I'm not sure the lock works. I've never used the key," he told her. "There's a lamp on the table if you think you'll need it."

Wondrous hues of pink and violet marked the western sky as the sun neared the horizon, and Angelena nodded. "I'll need the light to find my things."

"Ten minutes," he warned quietly.

She reached the top of the stairs and turned the doorknob. A last glance over her shoulder did little to bolster her courage, for, if the look on his face was any indication, Wes Tanner was impatient for his wedding night to begin.

She entered his quarters and closed the door behind herself, leaning against it as she surveyed the room. Against one wall a table had been set with two places, and several covered dishes gave promise of a late meal. Pip's doing, no doubt. A couch and overstuffed chair sat on either side of a library table, and it was there that Angelena found the lamp Wes had mentioned. Beside it, a box of matches waited, and she lit the wick, lowering the globe into place.

The room was sufficient for a man living alone, but it bore no evidence of cooking equipment, nor anywhere to store food. Most likely, he ate at the hotel or had his meals brought in. She shook her head wonderingly. How did the man expect her to cook? Before her, an open door led into another room and she crossed to its threshold. A bed took up the majority of space, with a tall chest of drawers on one side and a mirrored dresser between the two windows.

She crossed to look out from the nearest one, lifting her hand to brush aside the filmy curtain. Her eyes were drawn to the saloon across the way, where the upstairs rooms were dark, their occupants already busy circulating among their customers in the big room below. One window in particular held her interest, and she gazed intently at it, wondering how she had appeared to him, those nights that he'd watched her from this vantage point. He'd stood, just so, the curtain held to one side, his image dark and holding a trace of menace.

Then he was there on the street below her, a movement drawing him to her presence, and she stepped back, a useless gesture, since he'd already caught her gaze. As she looked down at him, he took his timepiece from his watch pocket and made a production out of opening it, then replacing it.

Offering her a look of warning, he stepped to a nearby storefront and leaned with casual ease against an upright post. One finger tilted his hat back, and he again tugged his watch from its place. He polished the cover against his vest, then opened it with a gesture of nonchalance, and scanned its crystal. As if he would make the time pass more quickly by keeping close track of the passing of her ten-minute deadline, he held it in his hand and looked up once more to where she waited and watched.

She backed from the window, turning to the bed. Surely there weren't more than five or six minutes left of the time allotted her. Her small valise sat atop the quilt, and she bent to open it. Her nightgown and slippers were inside, along with a change of underthings for the morning. The rest of her belongings, except for personal items, were in the trunk he'd placed against the wall by the doorway.

A carefully folded garment, laid on one of the pillows, drew her eye. She picked it up, and it fell from its folds, draping across her hands as if it were made of gossamer stuff, with lace encircling the neckline and the edges of its cuffs. Of fine white lawn, it was handmade, sewn with dainty stitches, tiny mother-of-pearl buttons set inside delicately framed buttonholes. She shook it out and the fullness of its long skirt wrapped around her, blending with the white gown she wore until they seemed as one.

Pip must have brought it, while the rest of them dawdled around the table in the hotel restaurant and spoke of days long past, when Wes and Anna had been younger and newly welcomed members of the Tanner family. It had been an hour of enlightenment for Angelena, as Rosemary told of her initiation as mother, and Anna had chimed in with a tale of eating her first cookies ever at the big table in the ranch house. She'd listened avidly, aware of Wes's eyes on her the whole time. And then Gabe had broken in somewhat reluctantly, with the suggestion that it was time to head for home where the chores awaited his attention.

Goodbyes had been hurried, and amid the bustle of their departure she'd barely missed the presence of Pip and Dex. She'd hardly given them her thanks for their help with the celebration, and now her heart was touched by the evidence of Pip's gesture. If she could have chosen a mother to take the place of the one who was but a dimly seen vision in her past, Pip would have been her first option.

Angelena held the gown to her breasts and closed her eyes. Wes would expect her to be garbed in her night-clothes when he arrived, and unless she missed her guess, he was probably checking his pocket watch for the fourth or fifth time by now. She stepped across the room to where a curtain hung to one side of the open doorway into the parlor. She shook it from its moorings, allowing it to drape across the opening. It provided her with a certain amount of privacy, and she viewed it with satisfaction. Should Wes appear before she was able to disrobe and don the new gown, she would be hidden from sight when he opened the door at the top of the stairs.

Now the room was shadowed, the glow of the lamp not able to penetrate the door covering, and she undressed quickly, hanging her dress in the wardrobe where Wes stored his clothing. She stripped quickly from her stockings and underwear, folding them neatly before she placed them in an empty dresser drawer. In the mirror, her image was blurred, and she bent forward to peer at herself. With a quick flick of her wrist, she released the pins binding her hair, and it flowed over her shoulders and down her back in an unruly, pale cloud.

What would he think of her? Would she be more or less than he had bargained for when first he'd proposed this marriage? She was slender, but above her waist her bosom was full and rounded, and she winced as she viewed the abundance of her breasts. Perhaps she was too full, too... But perhaps not.

She shook her head. It mattered little. He'd looked her over more than once and still had said he wanted her. And whatever that entailed, it was a certainty that she'd soon be enlightened as to his plans.

He'd given her ten minutes and more. Damn, she'd been a temptation, looking down at him from his window. He'd swallowed his inclination to trot right across the street and climb those stairs. But he'd given his word, and though he fidgeted, he waited, the minute hand on his watch moving slowly, marking the time he'd promised her.

And then his strides were long as he crossed the street and made his way to the back of the jailhouse, where he took the steps two at a time. The door at the top opened silently, and he stepped across the threshold. Lamplight illuminated the empty parlor, and across the room the curtain hung in the doorway.

She waited there, where the close proximity of the bed made this wedding night a reality. A curved hook by the door received his hat and he sat down on the straight chair to remove his boots. Perhaps she wondered why he waited, why the curtain had not moved to admit him to his bedroom.

That was fine with him. Let her stew a bit. The memory of her mouth forming a silent kiss as she wafted it on the palm of her hand still rankled. She'd turned those big, blue eyes in his direction and they'd sparkled with mischief as her final salute was tossed in his direction. Was that just last night? Or was it a lifetime ago?

Today had passed as a series of slow-motion images, his impatience growing by leaps and bounds as he watched her. Every movement of those elegant hands, each twitch of her mobile mouth as she smiled and spoke, had fascinated his vision throughout the past hours.

But most of all, the scent of her, that elusive aroma that he intended to fill his nostrils with the livelong night, had kept him on the very edge of arousal since the moment he'd kissed her at the end of the wedding ceremony.

He, who had not intended to take a wife for years to come, who was content in his bachelorhood for the most part, had done the unthinkable. And in so doing, had most likely set the town on its ear. All because he could not visualize his future without the presence of a small, golden-haired woman with the voice of an angel. And at that thought, he yanked his stockings from his feet and tucked them inside his boots.

Rising, he slid from his coat and draped it over the back of his chair, then reached up to undo his tie, a simple task, since it only required tugging on one end of the soft strip of fabric and pulling it from beneath his collar.

Beside him, the table was set, with food waiting, and he glanced with an upraised brow toward the bedroom, where Lena had gone instead of taking the opportunity to spend time here at the table. He doubted that she was anywhere near as ready as he was to crawl into his soft, wide bed, but right this minute he didn't plan on giving her a whole lot of choice.

His shirt was undone by the time he reached the curtain and he pulled it from his arms, the sleeves inside out, and tossed it on the chair just inside his bedroom door. The room was almost full dark when the curtain fell back in place, and he pushed it to one side, anchoring it with the chair. He planned on taking advantage of the lamp on the table. In fact, if he thought he could get away with it, he'd have brought it into the bedroom with him. His mouth curved wryly at that thought and dismissed it. Fat chance that Lena would tolerate such close scrutiny.

In fact, from the looks of her, she'd like to slide under the carpet. She sat immobile on the side of the bed, clad in a filmy white gown that clung in all the right places and bore lace around her neck. Her fingers twitched, and as he watched one hand lifted to brush her hair back over her shoulder, revealing a circle of wide lace on the cuff. Someone had put out a pretty penny for that little beauty, he figured, and unless he missed his guess it wasn't Lena. She'd probably rather be stuffed into a flannel gown and wrapped in a quilt.

"Has it been ten minutes?" she asked, her eyes wary as her gaze swept over his naked chest.

"Longer than that," he announced, tugging his watch from its resting place. "I about wore the lid out, just openin' and closin' it while I waited." He flipped it open again and nodded. "Seventeen minutes, on the dot." His glance encompassed her. "I'm glad you're ready for bed."

"Yes, well, I thought we might eat first. I'm sure it was Pip, but whoever it was, they left us a meal." Her hands still trembled visibly and she clasped them firmly in her lap, underscoring the note of pleading in her words.

His yawn was feigned, and she winced as he covered

his mouth with his palm. "I don't think I want to eat right now, honey. It's been a long day, and I'm in need of a little rest on that nice soft mattress of mine."

She stood quickly, looking hopeful. "Well, maybe I'll have a bite to eat while you take a quick nap." Stepping around the end of the bed, she eased her way to where he stood and smiled with a valiant effort as she looked up at him.

His hand snaked out and he grasped her wrist, tugging her into his arms. The front of his trousers was undone and his arousal was becoming more evident by the second. Pulling her against his warmth, he looped one arm around her hips, the other behind her shoulders, and then he dipped his head, brushing his mouth across hers.

"I was hopin' you'd take a nap with me, honey," he murmured, his teeth nipping at her lips in lazy increments.

"I thought we'd eat first, Wes," she whispered, her hopeful gaze meeting his head-on.

He chuckled, and it was a low sound of amusement as he bent just a bit farther, breathing a heated message in her ear.

"Tell you what, honey, we'll eat a little later. In fact, give me an hour or so and I guarantee I'll help you work up a real good appetite."

Chapter Ten

Angelena winced, more at the words he spoke than the all-enveloping hold he subjected her to. She was well and truly pinned tightly against his length, every inch of her aware of the sinewy strength of the man she'd married. Her breasts ached, flattened against the rigid muscles of his wide, heavy chest. Strong arms contained her in an embrace she stood no chance of escaping, and against her belly, his arousal throbbed with an intensity she could not mistake.

He was a man set on a mission, and for all her lack of knowledge, there lingered an innate awareness of his intent, a frightening certainty that she would not escape from this encounter unscathed. He was tall and powerful, magnificently masculine in ways she was certain she could not cope with. His size alone was enough to put her at a disadvantage, not even taking into consideration his legal right to do as he would with her. And that right included his openmouthed seduction of her senses, his lips and teeth playing havoc, discovering with ease the measure of her face and neck and ears.

She had agreed to this, had spoken her vows without coercion, even though those few moments before the altar were but a dim memory. Somehow, she'd lost herself in a daze as the wedding took place, conscious only of the man beside her, enormously aware of his presence. From the first, he'd overpowered her, and she'd been too weak-willed to fight his dominion.

Now he was demanding his due, the payment she'd agreed upon for the use of his name and his protection for the child she seemed fated to bear. A sudden thought reverberated through her mind. What if...what if she were not pregnant? What if this was all a mistake, and she had married him without just cause?

What proof did she have that such a thing was true? The word of a woman who sold herself for a living? A man who admittedly wanted her in his bed? Unexpected panic swelled within her breast, and she heard a whimper escape her lips, followed by a moan of despair.

"Lena." He spoke her name with a dark, guttural sound, as if it were forced from his chest. He tilted his head back, and she forced her eyes open to behold a mask of masculine desire, dreadful in its intensity. Somewhere she'd seen that look, that intense, driven veneer of passion, and a fleeting vision brought fear to dwell where only apprehension had existed.

"Don't hurt me." She cringed as the words passed her lips and closed her eyes, ashamed of the child she must appear to be. Yet the terror would not be dispelled, the horror would not vanish, and she shivered in his grasp.

He lifted her from her feet, his embrace hoisting her so that their faces were on a level. "Open your eyes, Lena." He waited and she bit at her lower lip, unwilling to meet his gaze, knowing that it would blaze with emotion she could not match. "Come on, Angel," he taunted. "I've waited like a gentleman, even yesterday when I could have had you beneath that weeping willow tree. Remember?"

"No," she whispered, her denial fierce. "I won't let you treat me this way, Wesley Tanner."

"How?" he asked, his whisper harsh. "Like a wife? That's what you are, honey. I said all the right words and kissed you nicely for the preacher." His mouth sealed hers in a kiss she was not prepared for, his tongue invading between her teeth without warning. She felt herself shrivel within her skin, her heart beating with a harsh rhythm, her breath escaping as a sense of inertia surrounded her and her arms and legs hung limp and without substance.

"Damn!" He lowered her to the floor, his arms a cradle now, holding her erect, one hand shifting its hold to brush at the tendrils of hair that flowed over her cheek. "I won't hurt you. You'd ought to know better than that. You've had me hornier than a penned-up stallion all day, Lena, but I'd never cause you pain."

Her eyes flickered open and she peered at him, relieved at his glare of frustration. "My chest—" she wheezed out the words, and he looked down in perplexity.

"What the hell's wrong with your chest?"

"You were holding me so tightly, I couldn't breathe." The words were wispy and she hated the tremor in her voice, knew that tears were imminent.

His hand stilled against her face. "Let's start over. I was wrong to snatch you that way. I'm havin' a hard time keepin' my hands to myself as it is, and havin' you next to me at the table in the hotel, and watchin' you laugh and seein' the way your breasts fill out that white dress."

He shook his head. "Ah, shoot, Lena. On top of all that, I just keep thinkin' about whoever it was who got you into this mess, and wonderin' why you're tryin' so hard to play this game with me."

She stiffened, her legs achieving a stability that pleased

her. "I told you I don't know who it was, and until a moment ago, I didn't remember anything that happened."

His eyes fastened on hers and his hands withdrew from her, settling against his hips as he surveyed her from eyes that could have been formed from ebony. "What did you remember a moment ago?" A slash of crimson painted his cheekbones. "I did something that reminded you of another man?"

She nodded. "When you kissed me...*that* way. When your tongue—" She shook her head, a violent movement. "I don't think anyone ever did that to me. At least, I don't remember if..." Her voice trailed off and she ventured a return of his appraisal.

He was like a statue before her. "I don't want to do anything that reminds you of another man. Do you understand, Lena?"

"You never have, before now. At least I don't think so."

His jaw tensed, and she knew his teeth were clenched. She'd pricked his pride, had turned away from his kisses and declared his touch unpalatable. "It wasn't you," she said tentatively. "Truly it wasn't. Just for a moment—" Her body convulsed in a shudder she knew he had to be aware of.

His hands moved swiftly, circling her waist. "You all right?" he asked gruffly. "Do you need to sit down, Lena?"

"No, I'm fine," she told him. "Maybe just a glass of water, if you don't mind."

"How about a shot of whisky?" he asked, then shook his head as he noted her wrinkled nose and pursed lips. "Guess not." His shoulders shrugged and he glanced back into the parlor. "Tell you what, I've got a nice bottle of wine. Never been opened. Jason got it in by mistake and gave it to me. His customers kinda lean toward the hard stuff.''

"No, I don't need anything but water," she said firmly. And unless he had a sink hidden under the table, she didn't know where he'd get it from. Maybe, just maybe, he'd have to go downstairs and search out a pump somewhere.

"Right." He turned on his heel and passed through the doorway, crossing the room in several long strides. "Hang on right there," he said over his shoulder, opening the door to the stairway and closing it firmly behind him.

If the key had been in the lock, she'd have been sorely tempted to turn it in place and keep him on the other side of that door for the night. But a quick glance put paid to that notion, and she went back to sit on the side of the bed. The parlor was too brightly lit, and her nightgown was too fine to allow her to brave the parlor's illumination, the fabric clinging to her breasts like a second skin.

In less time than it took her to form her thoughts into a coherent pattern, he returned. His bare feet gave her no warning, and when the door swung open to allow his entry, she leaned forward just a bit, peering toward the far side of the parlor. He filled the outer doorway, his dark head only a couple of inches beneath the lintel, and his eyes scanned the parlor as he entered. One hand held a jug, the other a water glass, and his foot pushed the door closed behind himself. Silently, he crossed the room, limned in the lamplight, then, as he passed through into the bedroom, he became more specter than substance. Angelena caught her breath, vainly holding fast to whatever courage she had, only to feel it dissipate as his long shadow engulfed her.

"Brought you a whole jug. Enough to last until morning," he announced cheerfully, shattering the image of menace she'd attributed to his appearance. Rounding the bed, he bent to place the jug on the table beside her, then, pouring the glass half full, he handed it to her from his perch on the edge of the mattress. "You feelin' better now?"

She nodded, placing the empty glass on the table. His narrowed eyes pinned her in place, and he settled his big palm on one of her feet, grinning as his thumb rubbed the tips of her toes where they peeked beneath the hem of her gown. Pushing the fabric up a few inches, he tugged at her ankle, his smile widening as she uttered a wordless protest.

"Come on, honey. We've got to start somewhere," he said, his words and tone teasing her into a trembling smile. One long finger trailed down the center of her sole and she jerked away. "Ticklish?" he asked, releasing his grip. "I'll have to remember that."

He stood, his fingers quickly unbuttoning the front of his trousers, and she watched in unabashed wonder as he slid from them, bending to pick them up and fold them with a surprising amount of concentration. It was her first glimpse of a man clad only in his drawers, and the tight-fitting garment hugged his flesh from waist to ankles, providing her with an immediate education as to the conformation of a man's private parts.

Her face was hot, as if she'd been exposed to an open oven door for several minutes, and she knew without lifting a hand to investigate that her skin was burning with embarrassment. She turned aside, looking toward the windows, and he chuckled deep in his throat, the sound irritating her beyond measure.

"You might as well look, Lena. You're gonna be livin' with me for a lot of years, and I doubt I'll be walkin' around on eggshells, lest you see me without my clothes on."

"I've never seen—" She could not say the words, knowing that deep in his heart he probably doubted her veracity. He'd been struggling for weeks with the issue of her memory loss, and her past.

"No?" He cleared his throat, setting off on another tack. "Let's not fuss over that, honey," he said soothingly, and from the corner of her eye she saw his underwear begin a downward slide as his fingers undid the buttons holding them in place. He eased them down his legs and kicked them to one side, then stood in place, motionless, his silence a message she could not help but attend.

"Look at me, Lena. This is the man you've married. I've got all the equipment I was born with. I've got scars and blemishes, and I'm horny as hell right this minute, but you're stuck with me. Either you turn your head this way and accept me, just the way I am, with what I've got to offer, or I'll have to strip that pretty little outfit off you and do this on my own."

She gasped at his words, her hands clutching the neckline of her gown, and of its own volition, her head turned, her eyes fearfully focusing on his chest. "I won't allow you to take my nightgown off," she said, aware that her protest was not going to amount to a hill of beans if Wesley Tanner decided otherwise.

"Put your head on that pillow, Angelena," he said, his words a growl in his throat.

She scooted down from her perch, her bottom ruffling the yards of material she wore, until her legs were exposed to the knee. "Drat!" she muttered, lifting to pull the skirt down, wrapping it around her calves to provide a degree of modesty. Evading his gaze, she concentrated on the ceiling, yet she was only too aware of his magnificent form as he strolled to the other side of the bed.

He lowered himself to the mattress, and she turned her head toward him as he rolled to face her, wishing fervently that the lamp in the parlor would run out of kerosene. His face was in shadow, but there was no doubt as to the width of his shoulders or the length of his legs as he lounged on his side. He leaned on his elbow and his hand ventured forth, causing a lump to rise in her throat as she contemplated the movement of those long fingers.

His index finger brushed against her cheek, then across her parted lips, and an insane impulse urged her to snatch that wandering digit into her mouth. She shivered, considering what it might taste like, dismissing the idle notion as quickly as it formed. Her skin tingled where he touched, her lips almost vibrating from the gentle caress. And then his palm cupped, forming itself to her cheek, turning her head, tilting it a bit upward, as though seeking the proper angle. Bending his head forward, he dipped in a lazy movement, until her mouth was but a hairbreadth from his.

Her breath was indrawn with an audible sound, and he halted, his thumb tracing a small circle on her jaw. "I'm gonna kiss you, Mrs. Tanner." It was a statement of intent, and she accepted it as such. Her eyelids closed and she waited.

"The only thing is, you have to kiss me back, honey," he murmured, and she felt the brush of his mouth and heard the amusement in his voice as he spoke. His lips were damp, moving against hers, nibbling, and suckling, each movement slow and unhurried. She felt the rough edges of his teeth as they captured her lower lip, pressing lightly as his tongue laved the inner surface.

Deep inside, in that part of her that had only ever responded to this man, a heated flame blossomed. It rose within her, welling up in a hunger that threatened to overwhelm her with its urgency. Her teeth parted, her tongue venturing forth to whisper its message of acceptance against the surface of his.

He moaned, the sound muffled against her mouth, and met her challenge, gentle in his taking of the ripe freshness she offered. Within the dark cavern of her mouth, he explored each nook and cranny, tangling his tongue with hers, tender as he relished the significance of this virgin territory. It was a tentative compliance she bestowed, but delivered with such sweetness, such hesitancy, he could only honor it as such. And so he dallied, urging her to join him, delighted when she accepted his mouth as a part of their play.

And then it was too much, his body reminding him of the abstinence he had endured for the past months. "Lena." He eased from her, his murmur rasping, his hands moving to encase her slender form, then slipping to rest against the curve of her hips. She moved against him, a subtle tensing of her muscles sending a message he could not ignore. "Lena," he repeated, "look at me."

She murmured, deep within her throat, and slowly, in languid increments, her lashes rose and he was bathed in the warmth of her desire, her eyes heavy-lidded, seeking his with a silent message. He slid one hand to her gown, his fingers deft as he released the buttons, and she allowed it.

Bending his head to the warmth he had uncovered, he brushed a caress across her throat, then beneath her ear, where his teeth tested the resiliency of her flesh. He bathed the hollow of her throat with his tongue, and then he moved lower, his cheeks brushing aside the soft fabric that kept him from the firm, rounding temptation of her breasts.

She flinched, just a bit, as he nuzzled the crevice between the equally inviting treasures he held. "Shh...." His whisper, intended to ease her embarrassment, if that were the problem, instead caused her to shiver. Delighted with the results of that involuntary spasm, he brushed his thumbs across the rapidly tightening bits of flesh he nurtured.

Ah, she liked that, he decided, as her leg moved restlessly, only to nudge his knee. He slid his hand down, lifting her lower leg, easing it over his hip, until it fit nicely in the shallow dip of his waistline. His hand caressed her thigh, fingers smoothing the length of it, barely able to think clearly as he recognized her surrender to his will.

She clutched the back of his neck, fingers thrusting into his hair and gripping with a firm hold, as if she must anchor herself in place. A sound of urgency deep in her throat encouraged him, and he explored further, sensing her hesitation, yet delighted with her acceptance of his venturing fingers. His mouth opened against the soft surface of her breast and she gasped, an almost silent sound, her movements halting abruptly, as though she must be still and silent in order to focus on the sensations his caresses brought to bear.

"Lena?" He lifted from her and she murmured, her hand urging him back.

"Wes?" Her voice trembled, barely audible. "I feel so strange, as if wires are tugging inside of me. I think I'm burning up."

"You're just fine, honey," he whispered, his caress tender, his fingertips pressing and moving with gentle persuasion, and she jolted in his arms, her indrawn breath turning to a groan of pleasure. His mouth returned to her breasts, and his lips circled one dark crest, drawing the pebbled surface into his mouth, his teeth exerting careful pressure. She twitched, gasped and gripped his head with amazing strength.

He'd not expected such response, indeed had thought to coax her for a while, perhaps provide her a degree of satisfaction before he sought his own. That she should be so warm, so pliable in his hands, was a revelation he gloried in. Turning her beneath him, he pulled her gown to her waist, then fit himself between her thighs, his aroused manhood all but surging against her tender flesh. With slow increments, he pressed within. She'd begged him not to hurt her, and above all, he was determined that pain would never be allowed to be a part of what they shared.

Her eyes opened, surprise lighting their depths as she was stretched by the pressure of his arousal, and in the light from the parlor, he watched as her passion became fear, as the flush of desire turned to pallor.

"What are you doing?" In a voice that trembled, she whispered words that chilled him to the bone. "Why are you doing this to me?" A sob ripped through the frightened query, and her eyes became glazed with horror. Her body shuddered beneath him, and her head fell to one side.

Damn. He'd killed her. An overwhelming dread seized him, rendering him shaken and dismayed beyond measure. He rolled, taking her with him, one hand lifting quickly to hold her head. "Lena! Sweetheart! Look at me!" He rocked with her in his arms, his heart pounding at an appalling rate, sweat breaking out on his forehead and down the length of his back.

She stirred, whispering words he couldn't understand, but that was of no matter. She was alive, breathing; the pallor had lifted and her cheeks took on their natural color. He brushed at her hair, propping himself up on his elbow to better see her face. And then her eyes opened. She blinked, her gaze vacant, seeking and bewildered.

"Was he here?" And then she shook her head. "No, of course not." Her eyelids fluttered shut and she spoke his name. "Wes?"

"I'm here, Lena. I won't hurt you, sweetheart." His kiss

was one of reassurance, and he relished the return pressure of her mouth. "What happened, honey?"

She looked at him then, and her eyes were lucid, clear and trusting. "I don't know." Her hand lifted to touch his cheek. "I'm so sorry, Wes." Sitting up, she looked around the room, as if seeking a figure lurking in the shadows. "I thought I was on the train, and that man, you know, the one who helped me with my trunk..." Her pause was lengthy.

"No, of course you don't know about him." Her head bent and she lifted her hands to cover her cheeks. "I only just remembered him myself, didn't I?"

"What happened to you, Lena?" he asked, his chest hurting as he contemplated what she would tell him. There could be only one answer to the puzzle of her pregnancy. As sorely as she would be hurt, as painful as the memory must be, he must hear it from her, and for her own well-being, she must speak the awful circumstances aloud.

"He knocked on my compartment door, and I recognized his voice, because he had helped me with my trunk." Her look was startled, and then she frowned. "I was in St. Louis, Wes. That's where I saw him, and then later we spoke in the dining car." Her frown lifted, and a flash of fear returned to her eyes.

"I opened the door to him and he came inside and shut the door, and he just looked at me. It was as if he were another man altogether, Wes. He smiled, and his teeth showed, but his lips were pulled back, and...he frightened me." She sobbed silently, one hand covering her mouth.

"What happened, Lena?" Even to his own ears, his voice was calm, his words almost soothing, yet within his breast raged a beast named anger, fed by the look of hopelessness in his wife's eyes.

"He twisted my arm and pushed me down on my

berth.'' Her breathing was heavy, her eyes glazing in horror, and he wondered if even now she was reliving the events of that day. He'd wanted her to remember, had thought it would be well if her memory returned. Now, in this moment of revelation, he rued the day he'd wished for such a thing to take place.

He pulled her into his embrace, and his voice was urgent. ''You don't have to tell me, Lena. Forget it, honey.'' His hand tangled in her hair and he bent to press a kiss against her trembling lips.

''No!'' The single word was a shriek and she pushed at him. Tears flowed afresh and she blinked them away, to no avail. ''Wes, I'm sorry,'' she whispered. ''It isn't you. I swear it.''

His heart heavy with the weight of her despair, he nodded. Utter frustration gripped him as he watched, until finally their eyes meshed and she returned his tentative smile.

''I want you to know. And then I don't ever want to talk about it again. I remember he pushed my dress up and opened my drawers and he pushed himself into me. I tried to fight him, and we rolled from the berth to the floor. And that's all I remember until I woke up the next morning.'' Her hand lifted to touch her head, and she rubbed her fingers reflexively against a spot just above her temple.

''I suppose I hit my head on something. All I remember thinking is that I must have started my monthly time early.'' Her cheeks flushed at this disclosure, and he nodded. ''I had some blood on my drawers and legs, and I was sore, but I swear to you, Wes Tanner, I didn't remember what had happened. Not that day, not ever, until just now.''

''I believe you, honey,'' he said softly. ''Do you remember his name?'' And if she did, if she could recall any vital piece of information about the demon who had brutalized her that night... He bowed his head, aware that he, who upheld the law, would be capable of killing such a creature without remorse.

She shook her head, then lay back beside him. "Wes, will you ever want to do that again?"

"Do what?" Shifting her slender form, he enclosed her in his embrace, his hands circumspect, lest she be repulsed by his nearness. And he could hardly expect her not to be, given what she'd been through in the past minutes.

She shot a glance at him. "You know, what you were doing. What he did to me in the train." Her breath caught and she turned her head, looking fully in his face. "That's how it happened. That's why I'm going to have a baby, isn't it?"

Wes nodded. Whether she carried another man's child or not, whether he could ever truly accept such a child as his own, he didn't know. What he did know was that Angelena, whoever she was, was his wife, and his hopes for a wedding night were about as far from being realized as they could be.

"Not tonight, I guess, honey. I don't think you're up to it." And neither was he, if the truth were known. He held her loosely, but she would not have it. Her arm circled his neck, and she nestled her head against his chest.

"I need to turn out the lamp," he said after a moment. But there was no reply, and he slid from the bed carefully and quietly, pacing to the parlor where he made short work of his task then returned to his bed. He looked down at his sleeping wife for a moment, then walked to the window.

Across the street, the saloon was well lit, two of the upstairs rooms aglow with lamps or candles. His eyes sought the darkened room where Angelena had slept since arriving in Edgewood. Tonight it looked empty, forlorn, and he smiled at his fanciful thoughts. His own bed would never be empty again, and at that thought he looked over his shoulder, his gaze encountering the woman he'd married. She slept soundly, one arm flung over her head, her breasts visible in the moonlight, the sheet at her waist.

She was beautiful, his Angel. He might never speak that name aloud, but here, in this moment, she was his Angel, and he wished fervently that he might hold fast to the memory of this hour. For it was certain that doubts would assail and the past would intrude, and his masculine pride would find it difficult to accept what must be.

He turned back to the window, casting one last look at the length of the street, where only the light streaming from the doorway to the saloon called to passersby. A rider approached from the east, and Wes noted the weary slouch of the figure in the saddle, the slow pace of the horse. Pausing in the ray of light just in front of the Golden Slipper, the rider leaned forward, peering over the tops of the swinging doors, then slid to the ground. He tied his horse at the hitching post and stepped onto the sidewalk.

His profile was in full view, and Wes leaned closer, his hands gripping the windowsill. A familiarity he could not deny brought him to the edge of panic. It could not be. Surely it was the dim light, the distance across the way. Certainly, he would have heard if...

And then the man turned to look at the jailhouse, and tilted his head to peer through the night, his gaze aimed at the window where Wes stood. The moonlight illuminated his face, and a shiver of revulsion shot through Wes. At once, he was a boy of twelve years, bruised and battered by the man he most hated in the world. The man Rosemary Tanner had rescued him from on that day, fifteen long years ago.

It was his father. Nate Pender had returned.

Chapter Eleven

"Lena? Are you awake?" His whisper brushed her ear, and Angelena squeezed her eyes tightly shut. Only a few moments since, she had wakened and faced the memory of last night, spinning through her mind like a carousel gone mad. The sound of the outer door opening had alerted her to his presence. With deliberate deception she'd closed her eyes, her arm hiding them from his view should her eyelids flutter and reveal her subterfuge.

"I don't know how to make tea. Do you like coffee, even a little bit?" he asked hopefully, and immediately she felt a clenching in the pit of her stomach. The scent of coffee had sent her to the slop jar more than once during the past weeks, and even her beloved green tea did not always agree with her. Perhaps this would pass before long, but for today she could only shiver and wave her hand.

She sat up in bed, feeling at a disadvantage, pulling the sheet up to her throat. He towered over her, fully dressed and ready for the day, while she lay naked as the day she was born beneath a sheet. A *sheet,* for pity's sake. He watched her closely, his eyes sauntering from stem to stern, and as he paused to scan her breasts, she folded her arms over the sheet to cover them.

His grin was immediate, and he sat on the bed beside her, long fingers reaching to tug at the sheet she'd managed to anchor in place. ''Lemme see,'' he murmured, bending over to kiss her forehead.

''No!'' Scandalized by his suggestion, she clutched the sheet tighter, and he laughed aloud.

''I let you see me last night.'' His reminder of that moment when he'd stood before her, buck naked, brought her heartbeat to a thundering pace, and she flopped back on the pillow, pulling the sheet over her face.

''Was it that bad?'' he asked, just a hint of hesitation marring his words.

She shook her head. ''I'm feeling very mortified this morning,'' she muttered from beneath the dubious protection of a linen sheet. ''Please go away and let me get dressed.''

His sigh was enormous, and she pulled the sheet from her face, peering from over the hem. His eyes were reddened, his mouth drawn, and she felt a spasm of concern. ''Are you worried about something?''

He shook his head, a little too quickly, she thought. ''No, of course not.''

''You don't look like you slept well.'' The sheet fell lower, her fingers gripping it to her breasts as she sat upright.

He smiled, and the lines of his mouth formed into a more familiar pattern. ''I'm plannin' on sleepin' better tonight.'' He bent and kissed her, his mouth undemanding. The touch was sweet, inviting, and had her on the verge of abandoning the concealment of her sheet. She felt the sting of disappointment as he drew away and stood beside the bed. ''I need to get downstairs, Mrs. Tanner. I've got some checkin' up to do this morning. If you're hungry, I've told

Sam Westcott, over at the hotel, to put your breakfast bill on my tab.''

Her stomach growled at his words, and she thought of the food in the parlor. Perhaps there was something there she could make a meal of. Surely Pip had left bread with whatever food she'd fixed for their supper. "I'll not starve," she said, wishing he would lean over once more and kiss her with even half the enthusiasm he'd shown last evening. But then, what was bound to happen next was better suited for nighttime and darkness. Perhaps she'd be better able to do as he wanted tonight.

Wes turned from her, only to pause at the doorway and look back. "I may not be around much today, Lena. I've got something I need to do. Can you keep busy?"

She nodded. "Of course I can. I'll stop by to see Pip and give her a hand with the baby if she needs me. And I'll redd up in here a little."

He lingered, and she sensed a hesitancy in his manner that was not in accord with his usual behavior. "Is there something wrong?" She slid to the edge of the bed, taking the sheet with her, bending to pick up the nightgown he had managed to rid her of last night.

His eyes narrowed at her movement, and he was silent, watching her with the narrowed gaze of a predator. "There will be in about one minute," he muttered darkly, "if you don't wrap that sheet around your backside."

She looked down at herself, then over her shoulder, and her cheeks burned with chagrin. Clutching the sheet to her bosom had not taken into account the view she was offering from the rear. He stepped toward her and she whirled to face him, tangling her feet in the length of linen. Her sense of balance shattered, she fell to the bed, and before she could draw another breath, he was there beside her, his mouth hot and damp as he claimed her lips in exactly the manner she'd wished for only moments ago.

His hands tangled in her hair, lifting her to meet the all-consuming heat of his caress, and she responded as she had the night before, only too aware now of the potency of his mouth and lips. "I may never earn another minute's pay in this town, Mrs. Tanner," he murmured.

"Wesley Tanner, you need to be doing your job, not lying in bed," she managed to say after a moment. The urge to ruffle his carefully combed hair and the yearning to draw him against her, to feel the long, hard length of his masculine body form a protective covering for her vulnerable self, was almost irresistible. Instead, she combed her fingers carefully through his dark locks, smoothing the shorter hairs at his temples into place. "Go on, now," she whispered. "I'll see you at suppertime. Maybe Pip will let me cook in her kitchen and I can bring a covered dish back here."

He rose from the bed, tucking his shirt in neatly, watching her intently. "Get anything you need at Pip's place and tell her I'll make it right with her." Reluctantly, he left the room, as if the temptation of her barely covered body might be too much for him to resist, should he linger.

Angelena scurried to the window, watching as he came around the front of the jailhouse, standing away from the open frame, the better to hide from any passersby. He had settled his hat atop his head, and his stride was long as he crossed the street, heading for the Golden Slipper Saloon. Apparently, Jason Stillwell was the man he needed to check in with this morning.

"Morning, Sheriff," Jason said, rather cheerfully, Wes decided, for so early in the day. "Thought you might be sleepin' in today."

"It's another workday," Wes told him, leaning one elbow on the polished bar. "I saw something from my window last night." He glanced around the empty room. "You all alone here?"

Jason nodded. "I expect so, lessen there's a drunk hidin' under a table." He swiped his cloth over a forbidden smudge on the glossy wood, then glanced up at Wes. "You saw your pa." It was a statement of fact, plainly put.

"Yeah, he rode up out in front, and I watched him come in here," Wes said. "You talk to him?"

Jason snorted. "Not on your life. He wanted whiskey, and Benny took care of him. Benny told him it was cash on the barrelhead, and old Nate came up with the money."

"Did he drink all night?"

"Naw," Jason drawled. "Drank his whiskey and talked to a couple of cowhands. Tried to come on to Jolene, but she let him know he wasn't her type."

"You don't know what he's doin' here, any more than I do, then." Wes took the soda water Jason handed him and checked the perimeter of the open room again. He tipped his head back and drank deeply, wiping his mouth with the back of his hand. "I guess I never expected to see him again. After they nailed him for horse stealin', I thought sure they'd keep him in the coop till he kicked the bucket."

"Did he see you?"

Wes shook his head. "No, I was in my rooms." He met Jason's gaze with his cynicism in full sway. "The old man probably wouldn't recognize me anyway. I was twelve years old when Gabe Tanner took me in, and then had Nate put in jail. I suspect I've changed some since then." And in more ways than one, he thought ruefully, remembering the youth who had survived Nate Pender's cruelties.

"Well, you're a man now, Wes. Rosemary and Gabe made sure you had a decent life."

"Ain't that the truth." A flutter from the balcony caught his eye, and he scanned the upstairs hallway. Probably one of the girls, up early.

"What are you gonna do?" Jason asked, leaning on the bar, his voice low.

"Keep an eye on him, I reckon. Can't really chase him out of town without due cause." His laugh was harsh. "'Course, him just drawin' breath into that miserable body ought to be reason enough for me to send him on his way." He drank again from his soda water. "He's never been any good to anybody, Jason. Never will be, far as I can see."

"Can't argue with you, son. You've got more reason than anyone to hate his guts, lessen it's that sister of yours. She looked like a pale imitation of a child before Rosemary Tanner got hold of her."

Wes straightened, tightening his gun belt. "I don't suppose you know where he went."

Jason grinned. "Well, I can tell you one place he didn't go, and that's upstairs with any one of my ladies. Other than that, who knows. Maybe he slept in a stall at the livery stable. The man has to have a place to stable his horse. Go check with Bates Comstock, see what he has to say."

"Yeah, might's well. I'd just as soon he doesn't get a gander at Angelena, Jason. In fact, I'd just as leave boot him out of town. Or maybe persuade him to go on his own. The sooner the better."

Jason nodded and leaned over the bar, speaking softly. "It's a shame when a man's own kids don't want to set eyes on him."

Wes stared hard at the barkeep, unsure of the man's meaning. "If you want to see scars, I can pull up my shirt, Jason. My memory's pretty damn good, and if I laid into the bastard, I'd never quit, I'm afraid. He came right close to sellin' me, and Anna, too, for money to buy his booze with."

Jason held up a hand. "I know, I know, Wes. I remember how bad you had it. Seemed like everybody knew, but nobody did anything about it."

"Rosemary did," Wes stated. "She took us home with her and cleaned us up and set us straight."

"She came in here once, a long time ago," Jason said slowly, his smile reminiscent. "Banged on my back door and asked for a job. Told me she'd do my books. That was right before she married Gabe."

"I walked her home to the parsonage that night," Wes told him. "It was the first time I talked to her. Felt like I was keepin' company with an angel." He stiffened. "Speaking of Angel, I don't want her runnin' into Nate today. Think I'll go tell her to stay put this morning."

"You're too late," Jason told him. "She went by across the street just a minute ago. Looked like she was crossin' over to the emporium."

Wes headed for the door, waving a hand in hasty farewell. The swinging doors bounced back and forth several times behind him, and he headed for Pip's establishment at a fast walk.

"I thought I'd help you out this morning," Angelena said, taking the baby from Pip's arms. "Has he been fussy?"

Pip gave him over without protest. "I've been up half the night, what with him cuttin' teeth and Dex walkin' back and forth, makin' a rut in the bedroom floor. If I'd been smart, I'd have given him the baby to tote while he paced."

"Why didn't you?" Angelena asked with a chuckle. "You might have gotten a little sleep."

"He's frettin' about something," Pip answered. "I don't know what it is, but he's been stewin' for the past couple of weeks."

"Is he home cooking dinner?" Angelena settled herself into the big rocking chair by the window, the baby peering over her shoulder at his mother's movements.

Pip scooted behind the counter to pick up her order board. She kept a running tab on the merchandise she ordered from the city, and Angelena knew that today was the day she needed to run it down to the stationmaster to be put in the mailbag before the noon train came through.

Her pencil busy, Pip kept up a conversation, and Angelena watched and listened, as always, amazed at the woman's concentration and ability to do two things at once. "Does Dex have a family back east?" She'd wondered about the man often. His easy manner, his remarkable talent, seemingly gone to waste in this small town near the Texas border, and his devotion to the woman he'd married were only parts of the whole man. She'd thought at first that perhaps a man like Dex might come along one day, a man she could love. And then there'd been Wes Tanner.

"Family?" Pip repeated, jolting Angelena from her meandering thoughts. "I don't think so. He's told me about his folks, but I don't think he left anyone behind back east. He was pretty young when he came here, along about fifteen years ago. Just before Wes and Anna went to live with Rosemary, in fact."

"Wes doesn't talk about any other folks than Rosemary and Gabe," Angelena said slowly, patting the baby's back in time with the rocking of her chair.

Pip turned to look at her. "Give him time, honey. He's

had a tough row to hoe. Even after he spent all those years with the Tanners, he had to set out on his own, like he needed to prove himself.'' She walked closer, her eyes tender as she watched the child Angelena held. ''He was gone—'' Her brow furrowed. ''Oh, maybe four, five years. Showed up one day, kinda weary and with a look like he'd seen and heard more than a boy should. Same day he got the job as sheriff, matter of fact.''

''He told me a little about that,'' Angelena said. ''I just get bits and pieces.''

''Well,'' Pip said, motioning to the big plate-glass window. ''Take a gander at who's peekin' in at us.''

Angelena's gaze connected with dark eyes, and she quickly scanned the tall man who watched her from outside the store. ''He's probably just checking up on me,'' she said, her smile involuntary as she nodded at Wes. He tipped his hat at both women, and with a final glance in Angelena's direction, continued down the sidewalk. She felt a flush climb her cheeks as she recalled her intimate knowledge of what lay beneath his formfitting pants and the gray shirt he wore. Life as she knew it had changed considerably over the past couple of days.

Pip watched her closely. ''You all right this morning, honey? You're lookin' kinda rosy cheeked.''

Angelena met her gaze, nodding a silent reply.

''He didn't…you sure you're all right?'' Pip flushed, her fair skin being prey to embarrassment easily. ''I'm not prying, you understand. I just wanted to be sure he didn't push you too hard. Wes Tanner's a hard man sometimes, with more in his past than any of us know about. I'm really hopin' you'll smooth off his rough edges.''

Angelena bent to kiss soft curls, her nose catching the baby scent of the small boy she held. ''I'm fine, Pip. I remembered something last night,'' she whispered, almost unwilling to divulge the horror of that moment she'd recalled. "A man on the train—" Her eyes closed as the remembrance of harsh hands and brutal touches flooded her mind.

Pip's hand clutched Angelena's shoulder. "Do you know who it was?"

"No, not even his name. He hurt me, Pip, and apparently it's his child I'm going to bear."

"Did you tell Wes?"

Angelena nodded. "All I could remember. It's like a bad dream, but…" Her laughter was shaky, her lips trembling. "I've got the proof, haven't I?"

"Wes didn't—" Pip broke off, biting her lip. "He didn't *do* anything, did he? I mean, he didn't make you…you know."

"No, I really *don't* know. I kinda fell apart and he just put his arms around me, and we talked a little. I must have gone to sleep, because the next thing I knew he was offering to get me some coffee from downstairs."

"You haven't had breakfast yet?" Pip demanded.

Angelena nodded quickly. "Oh, no. I ate some of the bread you left for us last night, and the green beans."

"Green beans for breakfast?" Pip's eyes widened as she considered that thought. "Dex will be bringing dinner over in a couple of hours, and you're stayin' right here to get some decent food in you." She walked away, stepping through the curtained doorway to the back room, and then poked her head through again. "You didn't eat last night?"

Angelena shook her head. "No, I don't think Wes was hungry. And once I'd put on that nightgown you gave me, I wasn't about to come out into the parlor."

"We'll find you a wrapper of some sort," Pip decreed. "I keep forgetting you don't have a whole lot of everyday things to wear. Now that you're the sheriff's wife, you'll need some new clothes."

The sheriff's wife. Such a mundane designation to wear, Angelena thought. Unless one considered just who the sheriff was. Wesley Tanner was about as far from mundane as a man could get. He was a puzzle she had yet to solve, a complex, masculine creature with whom she'd vowed to share her life. A man who had set her aglow with kisses and caresses only hours past, and who was no doubt planning on more of the same before the sun rose tomorrow.

The livery stable was as it had been in the days of his boyhood, Wes decided, eyeing the long line of stalls, the buggy and surrey Bates rented out on occasion, and the latest in a long string of youths who were adept at using a pitchfork.

"You lookin' for Bates?" the boy asked, pausing to speak with a degree of respect.

"He around?" Wes asked, scanning the farthest door, which opened up into a large corral. A flash of movement caught his eye as a horse pranced into sight, Bates's hold firm upon the bridle as they appeared in the doorway.

"Yeah, he's gettin' ready to go out to your pa's place, Sheriff," the boy said.

"Sheriff!" Bates Comstock hailed Wes with an upraised hand. "Heard tell Gabe has a couple of horses he's willin' to part with. Headin' out that way now. You need me for something?" He approached, the horse he led kicking up her heels.

"Looks like you got your hands full," Wes allowed, grinning as he admired the sorrel mare. "She broke to saddle?"

Bates shook his head. "No, I use her for my buggy. If I bring back stock from your pa's place, I'll just tie them to the back.'' The mare nickered loudly, butting Bates's shoulder with familiarity. He reached up to stroke her muzzle. ''This one's spoiled rotten,'' he admitted. ''Kinda a favorite of mine.''

Wes stepped closer, his voice low. ''Heard tell you might have a stranger hereabouts.''

Bates snorted. ''Stranger, hell. And you know it, Sheriff. Old Nate Pender slept in a stall last night, and groused 'cause I charged him for it.'' He flapped a hand at the youth who hovered nearby. ''Go on, Lenny. You can finish up in here after I leave.'' The boy nodded, his steps slow as he hung up his pitchfork and headed for the street out front.

''What's he want, Wes?'' Bates's genial smile faded as he posed the question.

''Hell, I don't know. Saw him from my window pretty late last night. Jason said he'd headed here.''

Bates's shrug was noncommittal. ''You got me. He told me he'd be back, said he was lookin' for work.''

''Well, if that ain't just what I need!'' Wes blurted out. ''He's trouble, Bates, and we both know it. I don't want his greedy eyes on Anna, that's for sure. And I'd just as soon get his miserable butt out of here before he knows I've married Angelena.''

Bates grinned. ''Yeah, I heard about that. Only heard her sing once myself. Bernice isn't real fond of me goin' to the saloon.'' He lifted an eyebrow and chuckled. ''Funny thing is, she's pretty taken with the girl. Thinks she's just gotten herself in a bad spot.''

''Well, she's out of it now,'' Wes said briskly.

''Say,'' Bates said, snapping his fingers. ''Heard tell you're interested in the old Murphy place north of town.

''Homer Pagan said those folks got on the mornin' train to Shreveport, gonna live with some of their young'uns.

Put everythin' in Pace Frombert's hands. Homer says they're about willin' to give the place away, just to get out from under it.''

And that might be the best news he'd heard in a month of Sundays, Wes thought. It came close to overshadowing the sight of his father last night, in fact. "I'll check with Pace Frombert when I go past the bank later," he said, his mind awhirl with possibilities. "In the meantime, if you see Nate, give me a holler. I'll keep an eye on him. Much as I hate to, I'm gonna have to talk to the man and find out what's goin' on in that wretched mind of his.''

He turned away, Bates on his heels as they headed back to where a buggy waited. "Damn, I didn't expect he'd ever turn up here again. And who in hell's gonna hire him on anyway? Hasn't got an ambitious bone in his body, nor a decent word in his mouth.''

Bates considered that thought. "Might be somebody outside of town, newcomers maybe, folks who don't know about him." He slid the bit into his mare's mouth and straightened the reins. "He's probably been off the bottle in prison, Wes. Maybe he'll stay sober.''

"Yeah, and maybe it'll snow in August, too.'' Wes kicked at a stone in the doorway, watching as it flew through the air. Looking for the man who'd sired him was a chore he'd as soon not have to tackle, but there wasn't much of a choice. He couldn't have him running around town without having to do a hell of a lot of explaining to Lena. He'd only given her the top layer of his childhood to mull over. The bottom of the barrel was murky water, and he'd as soon not soil her ears with all the details.

The walk back to the other end of town was quick, and Wes made sure that several men knew he would be on the lookout for Nate Pender. That he received a number of sidelong glances was to be expected. Probably half the town would be talking by tomorrow, wondering what trouble the old man's arrival would set into motion.

Angelena had gone to Pip's house to cook her supper, and it was waiting in the warming oven for her to call for it later. Now she headed back to the emporium, intent on helping with Toby, her interest in the child more intent than ever. Perhaps it was the fact of her own approaching motherhood that drew her to the child. It mattered not, Angelena decided. He was a dear, and it was the least she could do to lend a hand in Pip's behalf.

His clear, rippling laughter reached her as she opened the door, and she spotted him sitting on the floor, a basket of spools before him. Pip was busy with a grocery list in her hand, and she cast a grateful glance as Angelena joined the baby in the sunlight from the big front window.

"Sweetie, did you miss me?" Angelena sang in the baby's ear. She picked him up, holding him on her lap as she helped him stack the empty thread spools. She'd managed to pile four of them in place before he swatted at them with his plump fingers and sent them sailing. Their laughter blended, and Angelena began another arrangement, singing in his ear as she amused the child. He yawned, leaning against her breast, looking up into her face with such confidence she felt near to bursting with love for the boy. A smile showed small white teeth, and as she sang, his thumb slid between them and he snuggled lower in her arms.

"You might as well use the rocking chair," Pip said from behind the counter. "Looks like he's about to close his eyes."

"It's not too close to suppertime, is it?" Angelena asked, her query blending with the melody she sang.

Pip shook her head. "No, I like to keep him up in the

evenings. Gives Dex and me a chance to play with him. Besides, I think he's about to drop off anyway. Those eyes are pretty near closed.'' Her smile warmed Angelena's heart as she felt the heartfelt approval of the woman who had befriended her.

She rose and settled into the chair, looking beyond the window glass to where women scurried past, probably heading for home to fix the evening meal for their families, she thought. A task she would be taking on as a regular duty, now that she was the wife of the sheriff. Her heart bounded within her breast at that thought, and the unexpected joy she felt brought music to her lips once more.

It was a lullaby, one she'd sung to Toby over the past weeks, a melody that brought a familiar sense of security to her when it passed her lips and into the child's hearing. Strange that it should possess the ability to offer a benediction of sorts, a blessing, as if comfort were bestowed upon her heart. She shrugged off the sensation of past knowledge. The words came easily, slipping past the barrier in her mind, blending with her melody, her gift to this blessed child as she eased him into slumber.

"Baby mine, sleep well tonight.
Angels watch while stars shine bright…"

She did not hear the door open and close, her attention fully on the child in her arms. She bent to touch her lips to his rosy cheek, then her index fingers traced a line from brow to chin, smoothing the baby-fine skin, her smile loving and filled with the sense of happiness he brought to her heart.

Dex stood behind her, his jaw clenched, face pale, his gaze disbelieving as he listened to the melody she sang. Her voice was low, but each note hung in the air as if angels had created it. He was silent, rapt, caught up in the music of her gentle voice and the melody that invited heavenly beings to watch over his child.

Pip stood behind the counter, her eyes narrowed as she watched him. And then she lifted her hand, motioning him closer. He nodded, stepping quietly across the floor until he stood before her.

"What's wrong?" she asked, her words subdued so as not to be overheard.

He licked his lower lips, closing his eyes for just a moment, and then his gaze met hers. His nostrils flared with the effort of his breathing, and he quietly cleared his throat.

"That song...I know that song," he whispered, his voice hoarse, each syllable strained.

Pip reached for him, uncaring of watching eyes. Geraldine Frombert glanced up, then went back to her shopping, fingering a length of yard goods, then holding it up to the light. Beyond her, a rancher's wife helped her two children choose candy from a jar on the far end of the counter. And in the early evening sunlight streaming through the window, Angelena sang a melody that pierced Dex's soul to its depth.

"Are you telling me you recognize the lullaby she's singing? I've never heard it before, except for these past few days when she's rocked Toby to sleep." Pip's fingers gripped his arm. "Dex, what's wrong? You're trembling." A frown puckered her brow and she shivered, as though fear clutched at her heart.

Dex turned to his wife, his eyes closing as he murmured the melody in tune with Angelena. "I wrote that song," he told Pip in an agonized whisper. "How could she know the music I wrote?"

"You wrote a lullaby?" Pip asked in wonderment.

"No." He shook his head. "It was a ballad, a love song to a woman I loved…long ago, in another time and place."

Pip's features pinched as if pain struck within her breast. "Another woman?" Her pause was long, but Dex paid no mind, lost in his thoughts.

"Who?" she asked finally. "What other woman?"

He flinched at her words, and his mouth trembled. "It was long before you came into my life, Phillipa Sawyer. Long before I met you and discovered what loving was all about."

"Who?" she asked stoically. "Who was she?" And even as she asked, a puzzle began to unfold in her mind. An unbelievable, tangled web, bringing to mind sleepless nights and a man walking the floor as he silently regretted his past.

"A woman in St. Louis," he said quietly. "A woman who sang like the angels. A woman with golden hair and no love to give, except to her music."

"You wrote the song Angelena is singing?" Pip asked, and knew, even as he nodded his head, that the words he spoke were true, and would break her heart. In all their years together, Dex had weaned himself from his music, as if he must put it behind him. Only when Angelena's need for an accompanist reached his ears had he once more taken joy in the melodies that filled his past.

"How long ago was that?" Pip asked.

"A long time…maybe twenty years." He lifted despairing eyes to his wife. "She was the toast of theaters in St. Louis. Olivia Marie Jordan. I played for her and loved her from afar. Until the time she took me into her life."

"And into her bed?" Pip asked calmly.

His gaze was unfaltering. "And into her bed," he repeated quietly. "I loved her, Pip. At least I thought I did." He laughed quietly, a humorless sound. "Now that I look back, I know it was a love for her music, her voice, that possessed me." His gaze rested on Angelena, her arms filled with the child of his heart.

"I have no proof, Pip. I only know that there is a tie that binds me to that young woman. I need to find out, honey. If it takes going to St. Louis, to search the records, then that's what I'll do.

"If my heart tells me aright, that girl may be my daughter. If she is…if she is—"

"Dex?" Angelena turned to where the room fell in shadows, where the sun no longer shone. "I didn't see you come in. Look here," she said in a soft, soothing voice. "He's asleep. I needn't have sung for so long." Her gaze tangled with the man who watched her, and her smile faltered, then faded.

"Dex? Are you all right? Is something wrong?" She rose quickly, the child heavy in her arms, and Dex stepped forward to take the baby's weight.

"No, Angelena, nothing's wrong," he said, his voice tight with emotion. "I was just admiring the song you sang to Toby."

She laughed, and the sound was golden. "Oh, that. My mother used to sing it to me every night when she put me into my bed. She kept a cot for me in her dressing room. She brushed my hair and tucked me in and sang to me."

"Her dressing room?" Dex repeated. "You didn't have your own bedroom?"

Angelena laughed again, shaking her head. "No, I mean in the theater, where she sang." Her words halted, the last a whisper, and her eyes widened in a face gone white.

"My mother! My mother sang." Her forehead wrinkled and she gave over Toby without hesitation, looking to Pip. "I remember my mother," she whispered, hands against her cheeks. "She sang, Pip. Like I do. Only better, of course. Her name was up in lights on the marquee. I can almost see it now." She closed her eyes and was silent, her body poised as if for flight, should the name speak itself to her mind.

And then her eyes opened and she turned away from the man and woman watching her. "I can almost see it," she repeated, hugging herself, her form visible in the darkening windowpane, as the sun went down in the west.

Chapter Twelve

The door slammed behind him as Wes entered his parlor. "What's wrong?" he asked tightly, stalking to where Angelena sat curled against the sofa cushions. The room was dusky with twilight and he wished for lamplight, the better to see her face.

She looked up at him, her eyes sheeting with fresh tears as he crouched before her. "Nothing. Nothing's wrong," she told him. "In fact, something may well be right, finally. I've remembered my mother, Wes. Not her name yet, but I can see her in my mind."

His arms circled her, and he leaned his forehead against her temple. "I went by the emporium to find you, and Pip said you were upset, honey. I came right home when she told me."

"You've been gone too long, Wes. I brought a dish of beef stew from Pip's, but it's almost cold."

He shook his head. "That's no matter. Supper's the last thing on my mind right now. I just want to be sure you're all right." His mouth touched her cheek, and she turned her face to accept his kiss. "Lena, come with me," he murmured against her lips, and she nodded, her arms circling his neck.

Wes rose to his feet, lifting her slight weight against his chest, then strode through the doorway into his bedroom. The bed was made, the pillows plumped beneath the quilt, and he paused only long enough to throw the coverlet back before he deposited her against the sheets. In one smooth motion, he slid to her side, once more enclosing her in the comfort of his embrace.

"Now, tell me about it," he said, the quiet words more than a request. If he must wait for the moon to rise and the night birds to sing, he would be patient. But it seemed the woman he held in his arms was not reluctant to speak the words he waited to hear. Apparently, her past did not pain her, as did his, or perhaps the evening shadows gave her courage, for she whispered the words he waited to hear against the taut lines of his throat.

He listened, hearing the despair in her tone as she struggled to recall the name of the woman who had borne her. He kissed her tenderly as she breathed the words of the song first heard at her mother's side, and he grieved with her for the lost memories she could not summon to mind. And in all of his care and concern, he was ever aware of the slender, pliant warmth of her.

No matter that he yearned to console her, that his arms held her with comfort and tenderness. Underlying his concern lay the throbbing evidence of his desire for the woman in his embrace. His mouth sought hers, again and again, murmuring words of compassion, assuring her of his presence. His hands caressed the line of her back, from shoulder to hip, his fingers tensing against the soft curves.

And she responded. Slowly, with an uncertain air of innocence he could only accept as valid, she returned his kiss, her mouth flowering beneath his, opening to the touch of his tongue, accepting its presence within her mouth. He baited her, teasing the inside of her cheek, tracing the edge of her teeth, and bathing the lush surface of her lower lip.

Murmured words he could not decipher sounded from low in her throat, a melody that encouraged his pursuit, and he responded readily. Her clothing was held together with an assortment of buttons and strings, and he silently cursed his clumsy fingers as he pulled buttons from their moorings and tangled strings from place. Bowing to his demands, she lifted one arm, then the other, shifting on the bed, obeying his bidding.

She reached for him, straining upward, her mouth seeking his, and he teased her with small, biting kisses over her throat and ears, then longer, damp caresses against her brow and the line of her cheek. Until at last he returned to the treasure of warm breath and sweet-scented skin. She tugged him closer, as though she feared losing contact with the heated promise of fulfillment he bestowed.

Her dress lay beneath her, her arms free of its binding sleeves, and the neckline of her chemise no longer hid the rise of her breasts. He lifted above her to admire the shadowed beauty beneath him. On his forearms, his weight holding her in place, he examined the softly rounded curves, one long finger pushing the fine fabric aside. Beneath his gaze the rosy crest puckered, her breast firming to his touch. He bent, his tongue barely brushing the skin that surrounded that crumpled bit of flesh, laving it, aware of the faintly salty taste, and the scent of lilac her clothing bore.

Beneath him, she shivered, and her hands rose to clasp his head, her fingers threading through the dark locks, pressing him to her breast. A sound that might have been satisfaction whispered from her lips, and he caught the tempting morsel she offered between his lips, suckling gently, aware of the movement of her body beneath him.

"Wesley—" Her tone held an urgency he could not ignore and he released her breast from his possession, only to move higher, his mouth at her ear.

"What is it? Did I hurt you?" The memory of her plaintive cry the night before haunted him, and he renewed his vow to cause her no pain, no regret for what would pass between them.

She shook her head, a quick gesture, and touched his cheek with her palm, turning his face, lifting it into the faint light from the windows. "No, you haven't hurt me." She looked deeply into his eyes, and he felt exposed, certain that the need for her that rode him must be apparent. Sweat dewed his brow, and his arousal swelled anew as he pressed its length against her.

She brushed her fingers across the width of his mouth, pressing against his lips, and, as if he answered a request for admission, he suckled her index finger, drawing it into the heat of his mouth. She drew in her breath audibly as he bit carefully at her flesh, and he held it captive there. "I'm sorry I was so cowardly last night," she whispered. "It wasn't the wedding night you wanted. I know that." Her smile was tremulous, and he bowed to it, releasing her finger, only to take his pleasure in the damp texture of her lips.

She returned the pressure of his kiss and sighed, her words solemn, yet filled with promise. "I want to be a good wife to you, Wes. I don't know how to begin, and I fear I'll disappoint you. But I'll try."

"Now, bein' disappointed's about the furthest thing from my mind," he told her, a chuckle escaping as he thought of the joy of teaching such a willing pupil. "We'll muddle along somehow," he said, "and before you know it, you'll be the sheriff's wife in every way there is to imagine."

She nodded agreement and then whispered a request, her words hesitant. "Can I take off your shirt?" He nodded, and her fingers did his bidding, aggressive, eager instruments working at the task. More adept than he at the business of unbuttoning, she opened his shirt in seconds, then lifted the undershirt beneath it, her hands spreading against the width of his chest. One finger touched his flat nipple and he inhaled sharply, then moved agreeably so that she could repeat the stroking of her fingertips against those sensitive buttons. Her touch was gentle, exploring slowly, exclaiming softly over each new discovery, and he absorbed her warmth, his flesh tingling with each whispering caress. Yet it was not enough.

She'd already been privy to all of his physical secrets, knew the contours of his body. If her eagerness now was anything to go by, she would not be offended if he revealed the full extent of his readiness to her now. And he would surely explode if she did not include that most masculine portion in her discoveries.

With a shrug, he slid from the anchorage of sleeves, easing from his garments, then rising, he made short work of trousers and boots. She watched, her eyes following each movement, her hands at either side of her head, her lips opening to accommodate the shuddering breaths she drew.

His heart churned within his chest as he stood over her, his pulse pounding to the ends of his fingers and down the length of his body, his manhood surging with the urgency of his need for this woman. And yet, in her eyes, no trace of fear existed, even though her gaze examined him in eager increments. Instead, she lifted one slender hand to him, her invitation implicit, and he nodded, bending to her.

His hands lifted her, his fingers snagged the fabric she lay upon, and in moments only the linen sheet was beneath her. He tugged at her shoes, lowered her stockings, and pulled them from her toes, rubbing the wrinkles from her feet, long confined within the leather half-boots she wore. His hands slid the length of her feet to clasp her ankles, admiring the fragile bones and slender conformation. His palms formed themselves to the curve of her legs and she drew them together, an instinctive movement. She was an enigma, her modesty proclaimed by each gesture, each response, and yet her desire for him went beyond the veil of innocence that was ingrained in her being.

He knew, as surely as he lived and breathed, he knew she would welcome him tonight, that her body would open to his possession.

Vainly, he yearned for the light from the parlor to be lit, the better to glimpse the hidden secrets of her body, but some inner sense told him to wait for another time, that his mouth and hands would be the instruments of sight he must use for this coming together. It was more than enough, he decided, lying beside her, leaning over her once more. She was soft, receptive, her skin smooth, her form rounded and pleasing to his touch. And she allowed his every caress, obeyed each whispered command, rose to the firm stroke of long, callused fingers, her body eagerly responding to the caressing rhythm he impelled her to follow.

Then her hands sought him, fingers tracing the muscles of his arms and back, returning his adoration of her flesh with soft, subtle movements of her own.

Her fingers explored him, slowly, but with purpose, as if she must seek and touch what she had only seen the night before. His arousal throbbed, surging against her thigh, and she searched it out, her fingers enclosing him with a firm caress he encouraged, moving within her clasp. She followed his bidding, and he gasped as sensations he had thought to hold in abeyance brought him to the brink of release.

It was sooner than he had planned, his readiness urging him to take his bride, and he submitted to his body's need, rolling her beneath himself, rising over her, capturing her hands. Smiling, her mouth damp from his kisses, her eyes languid with pleasure, she watched, and he nuzzled her throat, and buried his face in the golden waves of scented hair surrounding her.

It was a mating he'd only hoped for, an embrace of his manhood he'd yearned to receive, and in her eager, reaching arms, he found joy and satisfaction he'd thought never to know. She moved beneath him, unaware of the pleasure he yearned to grant her, and he held her fast, hands on her hips, guiding her as he filled her with the very essence of his being.

A cry of wonder escaped her lips, and her legs tightened their clasp on his hips, her arms circling his neck, her face buried in his throat, and he held her closely, wishing foolishly that she might crawl inside his skin and become a part of him. She shuddered in his grasp, her limbs slackening their hold, and he rolled to his side, taking her with him, unwilling to allow a hairbreadth to come between their damp bodies.

From deep in her throat, a sob hiccupped forth, and Wes was struck with a pang of regret. He'd rushed her, perhaps been rough with his taking of her tender flesh. "Lena? I'm sorry, honey. I know I was too quick. I should have taken more time, been easier with you." As apologies went, it wasn't the best he'd ever given, but then, this was in itself a first for him.

Always before, in his few encounters with women, he'd been on the other end of the stick, spending hurried moments in a bed that had held others before him and would be a place of pleasure to those who would follow in his path.

"Lena?" He nudged her with his index finger, needing his fears allayed, and she responded, her smile a pardon for his guilt. Having a wife was a wondrous thing, he decided, his lips curving with satisfaction. His palm swept her hair from her forehead, baring a spot for his lips, and he lingered there, silently wondering at the generosity of the woman he had married.

"Lena? It will be better next time. I won't be in such a hurry, I promise."

She shook her head, a sudden movement denying his worry. "You didn't hurt me, Wes. I wanted you to make me your wife. I needed to have you be a part of me."

"You weren't afraid? *He* wasn't there in your mind?" His greatest fear for this night was spoken aloud, the words hovering between them, and he waited, his breathing stilled as she peered up at him in the light of stars and moon that shed their glow through the windows.

"He's gone, Wes. I was so afraid his memory would haunt me, and I'd spoil it for you again." She caressed his cheek with her fingertips, her palm cupped his jaw, and her eyes were warmed with an expression of pleasure he could not fail to recognize. "All I feared has come to nothing."

She humbled him, this woman he had taken with haste, with his own pleasure foremost in mind. What little he had given her, she had accepted with joy, and his mind spun with visions of what he might offer her, of the days and nights to come.

Shuttered windows lent the farmhouse an abandoned air. It huddled beneath tall trees, its shaded porch at once inviting, yet abandoned, with no chairs sitting about, no swing dangling from the ceiling to offer a welcome. Wes drew the buggy to a halt some fifty yards from the empty building, and chanced a glance at the woman beside him. Perhaps she would cringe from the task of making a home here where no sound but the birds overhead broke the silence, where the nearest neighbor was a quarter mile down the road.

Her gaze met his, eyes glowing with anticipation. "Well? Aren't we going to go inside?"

He felt the grin stretch his mouth and he bent to snatch a kiss, his hesitation a thing of the past. "Sit still. You don't need to climb out here." A snap of his reins, and the mare moved forward. Angelena leaned toward him, her fingers squeezing his forearm.

"I can't believe it, Wes. To have a house of our own, where I can walk around in all the rooms and move things where I want them, and cook on my own stove." Her words were alive with awe and wonder, and he thought once more how easily this wife he had taken formed herself to his desires.

The buggy rolled past the side of the house, following the narrow lane to the back, where he drew it to a halt. Before he could tie the mare's lead rope to the hitching rail, Angelena slid from the buggy seat and was at his side, gripping his arm with both hands, urging him toward the entryway. A narrow porch led to the back door, and they crowded together before the weathered portal.

"Is it locked, do you think?" she asked, and he shook his head.

"I doubt it. Pace didn't give me a key. Nobody much locks their doors around here." His words proved true as he turned the knob and the door swung inward. A large kitchen lay before them, windows still adorned with flowered curtains, the sun splashing the worn floorboards with golden rays. A tall cabinet against the far wall and the black iron stove were the only furnishings remaining in the room. A long sinkboard with a red pitcher pump at one end was skirted with fabric to match the curtains.

"Looks like we'll have to get a table and chairs if we're plannin' on doin' much eatin' in here. I heard they sold a few things to the neighbors before they left," Wes said, crossing the floor to an open door across the room.

"I have some money," Angelena offered, fast on his heels.

He turned to her, hands grasping her shoulders. "Whatever money you've got stays in your pocket, Lena. I married you, and I'll take care of you. I've managed to put aside most everything I've earned over the past few years. Didn't have a hell of a lot to spend it on, to tell the truth."

Her eyes sparkled with what he suspected was a touch of defiance. "Well, as far as I'm concerned, we're partners in this, Mr. Tanner. If I want to buy things for my home, I guess there's not a whole lot you can do to stop me."

He grinned, more amused than insulted by her challenge. "I'll let you get all the fussy stuff you want, sweetheart. The furniture is my responsibility. I just thought you'd feel more secure if you had an nest egg of your own."

Angelena watched him, poised for an argument and nonplussed by his acceptance of her edict. *Fussy stuff?* She could buy the odds and ends and he'd handle the rest? At each turn, Wes Tanner offered new glimpses into the man she'd only begun to know. The arrogant, hard-edged sheriff was one and the same as this agreeable, nonchalant man who faced her in the hallway of the home he offered for her inspection. He wore two faces, a fact she'd suspected for some time. One for the public, who called him Sheriff Tanner, and another for the family who knew him as son and brother.

She had been privy to both, receiving scorn and harsh words, meshed with small glimpses into the inner man who found it difficult, sometimes impossible, to hold himself at a distance from her. A fact she found most gratifying.

It seemed now that she was granted entry into the exclusive group called family, for the chill of dark eyes darting and tangling with her own gaze was gone. Missing were the habitual glares of harsh judgment, cynical glances cast in her direction. Gone were the grim assessments of her face and form, as if he sought proof of wantonness upon her slender frame.

Somehow, in the mysteries of the marriage bed, in the revealing and accepting of her tattered memories and the blending of their bodies, he had left behind the misconceptions and doubts. At least for now, it seemed.

She looked up into his face, her heart warmed by his acceptance. For surely that was what his eyes offered, what his smile decreed. She was his wife, and though there might never be more than this affection between them, she could not fault him. He'd told her in no uncertain terms what it was he expected, what he would have of her, spelling out the terms of their marriage.

It was more than she had hoped for, those few short nights past, when her soul had shriveled in her breast at the lack of choices she faced. Wes Tanner was capable of kindness, generous in his passion, and for that she was grateful. A prayer of thanksgiving rose in her breast, her fingers pressing against her lips, and she vowed once more to be the wife this man needed.

The acquisition of their new home took less time than Angelena had thought. In two short weeks, a wagon, heavily laden with household goods, made the trek from town to the Murphy farm. Wes drove a new buggy, purchased from Bates Comstock, for Angelena's use, so that she would not be without transport of her own. They paused to admire the gateway to their farm, Wes's grin wide. Twin posts at the entrance from the main road boasted a new sign hung between them, freshly carved and varnished, stating that visitors were on Tanner land.

Angelena looked up at Homer Pagan's work, the stationmaster having spent his hours between trains making the wooden sign. *Wesley & Angelena Tanner.* The letters boldly proclaimed her as equal partner in this venture, a thing almost unheard of, that a wife should be so included.

"Like it?" Wes asked, his hands firm on the reins, holding the small mare to a walk as they followed the slower wagon down the lane.

"Oh, yes." Angelena whispered her pleasure, and her hand reached for his knee, squeezing with an intimacy she reveled in. "I can't believe you put my name on the deed with yours, Wes."

"I'm the sheriff, honey, with all the problems the job entails. If something should ever happen to me, there'll be no doubt that you've been a full partner in this place."

Her heart stuttered within her breast at his calm acceptance of his own mortality. "I don't want to hear you talk that way," she announced.

"I wouldn't be the first lawman to take a bullet, Lena. Hell, ranchers get gored by bulls, and bankers get shot by robbers. It's all a part of life."

"Yes, and women die in childbirth," she retorted, "but you probably don't want to think about that, do you?"

The reins were gathered up in one hand as he tucked her close to his side with a long arm. "I quit. You've had the last word, Mrs. Tanner." His hand tightened against her waist. "You're fillin' out, honey. I noticed last night—"

"Hush!" Her single word rang out sharply and he

laughed aloud. "You knew I'd be taking on weight, Wes Tanner." And the thought that he'd apparently accepted her condition continued to astound her.

"I like you, plump or not," he said, his hand sliding upward to cup the underside of her breast. "Especially here."

"Wesley!" She sat erect, pulling from his embrace, aware of the flush that rose to color her face.

"Lena!" he whispered, mocking her outrage. "You married a man who's mighty interested in your body, Mrs. Tanner. I told you that before you said 'I do' and I haven't changed much since."

"I remember," she said, his words vivid in her mind. *Am I gonna make love to my wife?…every chance I get!* He'd done just that. And what had begun as a threat of sorts, delivered with narrowed eyes and arrogant stance, had become a frequent blending of man and woman, one she could find no fault with.

"Complaining?" he asked, leaning back to meet her gaze, with just a hint of uncertainty shadowing his dark eyes.

A compelling need to reassure him, to give him whatever his masculine soul sought in her reply led her to defy her own rules of public behavior. Her palms held his face and she drew him closer, her lips claiming his with enthusiastic fervor. The reins fell from his hand and she was swept into his lap, skirts askew, his hands moving with precision, molding her against his muscular body.

The horse came to a halt, nosing at the grass beside the road, hampered by the bit in her mouth, but apparently willing to be idle. Such was not the case in the buggy. Angelena's answer to his single-word query was obviously what he'd needed, and Wes took full advantage of her willingness. His palm cupped her bottom, squeezing and forming her to himself, and for a wistful moment, she longed for the privacy and comfort of their bed.

His mouth savored hers, lovingly and tenderly exploring in a manner she'd come to appreciate, and his murmurs told her in broken phrases of all he yearned to do, the details bringing even more of a blush to her cheeks. The edges of his teeth teased the skin beneath her ear, and he muttered darkly about such things as buttons and laces and undergarments that deterred his purpose.

She giggled. There was no help for it. Her eyes crinkled with laughter, the sounds of mirth bubbled from her throat, and Wes growled words of warning against the front of her dress.

"Stop it!" she gasped. "You're getting my bodice all wet!" She grasped handfuls of his hair and tugged at him, laughter impeding her success.

His reply was a grunt of dissatisfaction as he lifted his head to glare darkly at the damage he'd done. "Serves you right, teasing me that way." He blew ineffectively at her breasts, and she laughed anew.

"It'll take more than that to dry me off. I'll have to cover up with something," she scolded, pouting prettily as he settled her back on the seat.

He lifted the reins and set the mare into motion, scooping his hat from his head and offering it with a bow. "Here, hold this over your front when you go in the house and hide somewhere till Bates and his boys get done totin' things in the house." His brows lowered, and his face was dark with a look she'd become familiar with.

"You just make sure when they leave you're waitin' for me on that new bed I put up yesterday," he told her. "And till they head back to town, I don't want to see hide nor hair of you, girl." His eyes flashed with a message she could not fail to read aright, dark and almost menacing.

His mouth tightened as his gaze followed the curves of her body and his nostrils flared.

"And if you don't find me waiting in your new bed? What then?" she asked, answering his look with a defiance that only added fuel to his desire. Her heart pounded, and deep in her belly a coiling, tingling warmth spread its heat, readying her for his taking. This game was a new one, and she entered into it with boldness, the excitement of being his prey filling her with a new depth of desire.

"Why then I'll have to come looking for you, won't I?" he said, the words an announcement of primitive intent. "Matter of fact, maybe you can find someplace even better than the bed," he said, challenging her, daring her to defy the edict he'd laid down.

The hat provided cover for the front of her dress and she scurried past the heavily laden wagon, through the back door and across the kitchen before Bates and his boys carried the first item into the house. As she scampered up the open stairway, she heard Wes issuing instructions and heard the answering replies, the four men joking and laughing as they struggled with the heavy furniture.

The bedroom they'd chosen for themselves was at the front of the house, and she closed the door behind herself, unwilling to be seen by any of the Comstock men, not with the damp residue of Wes's kisses staining her dress. She stood before the oval mirror centering her dresser, her hands pressed tightly to her breasts. They were full, aching not only with the tender swelling of her pregnancy, but with anticipation of the loving she knew would soon be hers to enjoy.

Her cheeks were rosy, her eyes alight, and she recognized the glow of desire that cast a patina of happiness over her features. Wes might never come to love her, might never whisper those words in her hearing. But he wanted her, needed the pleasure her body gave him, and made no bones about it.

"I love you, Wes Tanner." She watched as her mouth formed the words, listened as they fell on her ear with a winsome, wistful sound. "I love you," she repeated, whispering each syllable, closing her eyes the better to hear every nuance of her voice.

Would she have the courage to speak those same words aloud in his presence? Could she place herself at his mercy, open her heart only to have it broken by his denial of her pledge?

Or would he accept her words as his just due and fail to return even a semblance of the emotion that ruled her heart and soul? She bent her head, her hands pressing against the top of the dresser. Her mood of playfulness was gone, captured and disposed of, sent into limbo. Remaining was an ache that would only be eased by the embrace of the man who even now was outside the door.

His knuckle rapped sharply, and his voice boomed past the wooden barrier. "Angelena! Where do you want this big chest? The thing with all the quilts and stuff in it. And where does the funny little table with hinges holdin' it together go?"

Her hands flew to her cheeks and she raced to the door. Her drop-leaf parlor table, designed to hold a lamp at the end of her new parlor sofa. Solid oak and made to order by a carpenter Wes knew of, it was her prized possession. And the chest, lined with cedar she'd ordered from the Sears catalogue must not be bumped or scratched. How could she have thought to allow those *men* to carry her things in and place them appropriately?

The door swung open as she reached it and Wes stuck his head inside, his eyes narrowed as he scanned her face and form. "You want to show us where the last things go?" he asked, his eyes touching on her breasts, as if he could not help the direction of his gaze.

"Yes." She made to pass him in the doorway, but he stopped her, one hand on her shoulder.

"Stay behind me, and tell me what you want," he said, his grin only too apparent.

He leaned closer and whispered words for her hearing alone. "You waitin' for me?"

"Wes Tanner!" She hissed his given name, shoving him out the door and to the head of the stairs. He stood on the top step and she pushed him down another, the better to see over his shoulder.

"Put the small table in the parlor, please, and bring the chest up here to the back bedroom."

Bates paused to tug a bandanna from his back pocket, wiping his forehead and neck with a flourish. "You sure got us workin' up a sweat, Mrs. Tanner. We ain't carried such fancy pieces of furniture on our wagon in a long time. Bet you about bought out the Sears and Roebuck catalog, didn't you?"

"Not quite," she called back, her hands on Wes's shoulders. "Most of what you brought came from Shreveport." She peered toward the front door. "Are you about finished?"

"Yes, ma'am," Bates answered. "Only that cabinet with all the glass on the front, and we have to unwrap it first. I covered it good with blankets, so it wouldn't get broken."

Her china cabinet! She must go down and supervise its placing. Her hands tightened on Wes's shoulders and he turned his head, speaking in an undertone. "I'll take care of it. You just trot yourself back in our room and think nice thoughts. You hear?"

His eyes softened as she hesitated, and he twisted his head to drop a kiss on the back of her hand. "Go on, now. I take it all back about finding someplace different, honey. I want you on our bed, and I want to see you there in about five minutes flat."

She turned her hand away and he captured it, bringing her palm to his mouth. His lips were cool and dry and he kissed the tender flesh of her wrist, then visited a string of biting caresses across the flesh above her thumb. His eyes lowered, only his lashes and the line of his cheek visible to her.

He was hers. This man of complex emotions and primitive inclinations belonged to Angelena....

Whatever her name had been, it was Tanner now, and that thought alone was enough to erase the ponderings she'd struggled with. She was Angelena Tanner, and her husband was about to make love to her in her new house.

Chapter Thirteen

Bates Comstock lifted his head, setting aside his hammer and wiping his hands on the front of his leather apron. "Got some news for you, Sheriff." The glowing coals behind the man made the temperature soar, and Bates wore a sheen of sweat. A bandanna tied around his forehead was patchy with moisture, and his bare, muscular arms glistened in the sunlight.

He stepped away from the forge and looked up at Wes, who sat astride his black gelding. One big, callused hand rose to stroke the horse's neck, an automatic gesture. Bates had an affinity for horses. "Your pa's been workin' out at the old Thompson place, south of town." He peered up at Wes. "There's a new family livin' there, and just like I suspected, they never heard of Nate Pender before. Hired him on for field work. He's been there pretty near a month now."

Wes snorted his disbelief. "Two bits says he won't last long. Can't imagine Nate pitchin' hay or shockin' corn in the fields any longer than it'll take him to find an easy out." He leaned on his saddle horn and bent closer to Bates. "Did you talk to the folks about him?"

Bates's mouth took on a grim look. "Cal Hodges is the

fella who bought the place. I set him straight, and he said he'd keep an eye out. Field hands are hard to pick up these days, Wes, what with crops comin' in.''

Wes struggled with the tangled web of emotions any mention of Nate Pender set loose in his mind. For years he'd been free of the threat of this man, and now, just when life was offering him happiness, he was faced with the prospect of dealing with a man he'd wished dead years ago.

Bates untangled the gelding's mane, his huge hands strangely gentle. "Can't let him get to you, Wes. There's nothin' you can do about him, long as he's not breakin' the law, anyway. Might's well leave him be for now.'' He stepped back, picking up his hammer.

"I'll bet Miss Angelena's got everything all just so in your new place by now.''

Bates was making a hearty attempt at lifting his mood, and Wes struggled to be appreciative. "Yeah, she's knee-deep in beeswax and stove polish this morning. Yesterday, she cleaned lamp chimneys and ironed everything she could get her hands on.''

"You look like married life's agreein' with you,'' Bates said, with a sidelong look at him. A look that Wes decided held a multitude of speculation. "You know you're the envy of half the men hereabouts. Most of them would give their eyeteeth for a smile from the lady, and you're the one goin' home to her every night.''

Wes stiffened. "I don't want her named bandied about, Bates. The point is, she's all done bein' *Angel*, and settlin' in nicely as Mrs. Tanner. I want to keep it that way.''

"You think she'll ever sing again?'' Bates asked, his words hopeful. "Seems a shame to have that beautiful voice cooped up in a kitchen for the rest of her life.''

Wes had considered that problem himself, more than

once in the past little while, and had not found an answer that agreed with him. "Hard to say." His shrug ended the subject, and he lifted his reins. "I'm headin' out to see Cal Hodges. I'll put a bug in his ear. If Nate's behaving himself, I'll leave things be for now."

Bates lifted a hand in farewell, then turned back to his forge. The sound of hammer and tongs resounded in Wes's ears as he rode toward the south.

Cal Hodges was a young man with more work than he knew what to do with. His boys not being old enough to help with the heavy chores, he kept two field hands busy, while his wife tended four children. She looked about as frazzled as a woman could get, Wes thought privately. Yet she smiled and welcomed him, wiping careworn hands on her apron as a toddler gripped her skirts firmly.

"Cal's coming up from the barn now," she offered. "Won't you step up on the porch, and I'll get you some lemonade, Sheriff?"

Wes shook his head, not willing to add another task to her load. "I'll just walk out and meet him," he said, tipping his hat in a courtly gesture. "Thanks anyway, ma'am."

The young farmer heading his way looked puzzled, and Wes put his mind at ease quickly. "Just stopping by to see how you're doin' out here," he said. His sharp gaze scanned the open barn door and the pasture beyond. "Your men out cuttin' hay?"

Cal nodded. "I'm heading back out myself, soon as I get a jug of water and some food for their dinner." He eyed Wes curiously. "What can I do for you, Sheriff?"

Wes came to the point. "I heard you hired on Nate Pender. He workin' out all right?"

Cal grunted and slid his hands into his pockets, kicking

at a stone. "About as well as I figured he would. Tends to look for the easy way out, and whines a lot, but good field hands aren't all that easy to come by. We're getting by." His gaze was direct, and he turned it on Wes.

"Heard tell he's your pa."

Wes uttered an oath, short and succinct. "I don't like to admit it," he growled, "but he raised me—if that's what you can call it—for the first twelve years of my life. And that's pretty much why I'm here, Hodges. The man's trouble, and I don't mind sayin' so. I'd advise you to keep a good eye out, and don't let anything lay around you can't afford to lose."

"That bad?" Cal glanced toward the house. "Is my wife safe?" Dark color stained his cheeks. "Has Pender ever— you know…"

Wes shook his head. "No, not that I know of. Spent all his energy getting drunk all his life, and then turned out to be a horse thief, to boot. That's why he went to jail."

"He told me he was framed, said somebody lied about him," Cal said.

"Well," Wes drawled. "I'll let you form your own opinion. Just thought you might like a warning. If you can keep him workin', more power to you."

The farmer stuck out a hand, and Wes accepted the gesture. "Thanks, Sheriff. I appreciate the warning. I'd only planned on keeping him on till the hay was in and the corn all cut and shocked to dry in the fields. Guess maybe I had him figured about right."

The two men walked toward the house, and three children burst from the back door as their father approached. His wife was close behind them. Wes watched as the small family exchanged a few words, and the youngsters were dealt pats and hugs. Maybe they didn't have such a hard time of it after all, he decided, feeling a sharp pang of envy. Maybe one day… He looked away.

If only the child Angelena was carrying were his own. The thought jarred him, the presence of the baby within Lena's body a situation he'd only begun to face as a reality. One day that child would look to him, to Wes Tanner, for a father's love. Would it be as simple to accept a living, breathing reminder of Angelena's brush with a stranger then, as it was to ignore the gentle swelling of her belly now?

The sound of childish laughter spun him in place and he visualized himself as the man before him. Could he bend low over a golden-haired boy and brush a stubborn lock of hair back into place? Would his masculine pride allow him to take on the raising of another man's child as readily as he would his own?

"Be good for your mother, you hear?" The admonition penetrated his somber doubting, and Wes watched as the boy nodded his solemn agreement, then grinned shyly at the stranger who watched. Uncaring of his audience, Cal dropped a quick kiss on his wife's lips and turned from her. His hands full with a covered basket and a two-gallon jug of water, he headed for the barn.

"Thanks for coming by," he said to Wes. "I appreciate the advice." Wes watched Cal walk away, then hoisted himself atop his mount. He lifted a hand to his hat brim in a farewell salute to the woman and children who watched him.

And hoped that the filth of Nate Pender would not leave a stain behind when he left this place.

"You'll be needing some dresses that fit around your middle a little better pretty soon, Angelena. My new supply of yard goods came in this week, and I put a couple of bolts aside for you to look at.'' Pip dropped an arm across Angelena's shoulder and drew her across the store. "We'll just put them on the bill. You know Wesley won't mind.''

Geraldine Frombert looked up from the glass drawer of corsets she was examining, and peered at the two women over the top of her spectacles.

"Are you sure these are the latest thing, Phillipa?'' Her fingers sorted through the boned garments and she frowned, as if unhappy with the choice offered. "Bernice Comstock said she bought one here made from black sateen.''

"I see one just like it from here, Mrs. Frombert,'' Pip answered, bustling to where the banker's wife stood at the counter, too late remembering that the corset she recalled seeing would more likely fit Angelena than the stocky woman before her.

"Yes, I know. I don't think that one runs true to size though,'' Geraldine said petulantly. "And I won't settle for that drab color,'' she grumbled, pointing at the assortment before her.

Angelena had to agree that the hideous garments were all a rather nondescript hue, and she wondered briefly when it would be her fate in life to wear such a thing. Her mother had said she was most fortunate to be built with such slender lines, and yet the ladies in St. Louis… She drew in a breath. The ladies in St. Louis wore such garments, whether or not they needed the boning and cinching or not. It was the fashion, and her mind filled with the memory of shopping in stores that lined the streets of that city, looking at just such an assortment of corsets, arrayed in glass bins.

A veritable waterfall of sights and sounds assaulted her mind, trolley cars clanging, crowds filling the sidewalks, the smell of factory smoke and the sound of church bells on Sunday mornings awakening her after a Saturday night performance. She looked around, her mind swimming with so much detail it seemed she could barely begin to sort it out. Her eyes alighted upon the big rocking chair, and with a sigh of relief, she lowered her body into its comfort.

Pip caught her eye from across the store, and her brow furrowed. Angelena forced her lips into a semblance of a smile, waving her hand dismissively. She turned to look from the window, where farmers and townsfolk mingled. With little fashion in sight, only the everyday clothing of simple, small-town people in view, it was a direct contrast to the memories chasing through her mind. How could she have forgotten the hustle and bustle of city streets and hurrying crowds of people, all of them strangers to her?

Here, in Edgewood, Texas, she could pick out more than a few folks by name, and now that she was married to Wes Tanner, she received the courtesy of a nod and smile on occasion. Quite often, the old men sitting in front of the emporium grunted a greeting as she passed by. She glanced back at Geraldine Frombert, still fussing over the narrow choice of garments she was offered. Even Geraldine had a decent word to speak on occasion.

Pip's voice rose. "I have just the thing, Mrs. Frombert. I just remembered what came in this morning, fresh from Shreveport." Pip hurried to the back room and returned in seconds, bearing a long box. She lifted the cover and set aside a layer of tissue, revealing garments of creamy sateen, not quite white, but a richer color, almost like that of pearls.

"Now, that's just the thing," Geraldine said, nodding her head with satisfaction. "You just let me take a look."

Pip lifted a brow as she walked back across the store to where Angelena waited. "You all right?" she asked in an undertone. "You look kind of peaked."

Angelena nodded, and glanced again at the window. "I've lived in St. Louis, Pip. I remember walking down the street, and shopping in a large department store."

"St. Louis?" Pip's voice was strained as she spoke the syllables, and she cleared her throat. "What do you remember? Where you lived, perhaps?"

Angelena looked up quickly and shook her head. "No...well, maybe." It was gone, that single glimpse of a narrow house, tall, with a small porch and steps climbing to the door. "I thought I saw it, just for a second, Pip." A sense of outrage whipped through her veins, and she stood abruptly.

"It isn't fair!" The words were harshly spoken, but said in an undertone. "I need to know, Pip. I need to remember my mother's name, and where I sang, and why I came here." She twisted her hands together, idly aware of their trembling, their chilled surface. Her fingers brushed at her cheeks, and the tears were hot. "I won't even be able to tell my baby who his grandparents are, or where they are, for that matter. He won't have a family." Her final words erupted on a sob, and Pip moved into action, leading her toward the back room.

"Phillipa! Don't go away now," Geraldine Frombert called sharply. "I've about decided on—" Her words escalated in volume. "Phillipa! I'd like your attention out here."

Pip eased Angelena into the chair before her desk and pressed her firmly in place. "Don't you move," she warned her. "I'll be back in a few minutes, and we'll talk."

Angelena nodded, her tears under control. "I'm fine," she whispered. "Go take care of Mrs. Frombert, before she strains a gusset."

Pip giggled beneath her breath and hurried through the curtain. "I'm coming, ma'am."

"I'll need a corset cover to go with this, Phillipa," Geraldine announced. "What do you have? Preferably something in the same color, I think."

Angelena's head began to throb, a pounding, blinding headache that came from nowhere and took possession within seconds. She leaned forward, aware of nausea and a wave of dizziness. The buggy tied to the hitching rail in front of the store suddenly seemed miles away, and she wished vainly for Wes to appear.

And, as if her guardian angel attended her, the bell on Pip's door rang, announcing a customer, and Geraldine Frombert trilled a greeting.

"Good afternoon, Sheriff Tanner. I was just about to spend some time with your wife. It's been simply ages since we've had a chat."

"Where is she?" Wes asked, his words brisk and to the point.

Angelena stood, lest Wes should turn and leave before she could make her presence known. "I'm back here," she called, weaving in place. "Hurry, Wes!" she whispered, closing her eyes.

"Damn, you look like death warmed over," he grunted, grasping her hands and lowering her back into the chair. He squatted before her, his grip steady, his fingers warming hers. "What's wrong, Lena? What happened?" Tersely spoken, the words were barely whispered aloud, and he leaned closer, holding both of her hands in one of his, the other rising to touch her face.

She opened her eyes. "I remembered something."

"Well, if it makes you this puny lookin', I'd as soon you never brought to mind another thing, Angelena Tanner. Not one soul cares about where you came from or who you used to be. What you are today is what counts, and I'll be damned if I want you frettin' about this business anymore.''

Harsh though his words might be, his mouth lent a tender message to their delivery as he leaned forward and kissed her cheek. ''Look at me, baby,'' he urged, and her eyes widened at the endearment.

''Baby? Baby?'' she murmured wonderingly.

He felt a red flush climb his cheeks and ignored it. He'd found himself saying and doing things with Angelena he'd never experienced before. Including the use of pet names. ''Forget I said that,'' he muttered.

''Oh, no,'' she whispered, and her mouth twitched into a mere shadow of a smile. ''I liked that.'' One hand rose to rub at her forehead and she leaned closer, resting her face against his shoulder. ''I don't feel well, Wes, and I have a terrible headache. I wonder if you would bring the buggy to the back door of the store, so I won't have to go through the front.''

''What's wrong? Did someone say something to you? Was it Geraldine?'' And if she had, he'd be tempted to…do what? He shook his head at his own foolishness. This was no doubt some womanly thing, maybe to do with the child. If it made her ill now, what could they look forward to in the next months? he wondered glumly.

''Geraldine didn't say anything,'' Angelena told him. ''Just please get the buggy, so I can go home.''

He rose, patting her hands ineffectively, feeling more like a useless male in the face of feminine distress than ever before in his life. Stepping to the back door, he lifted the bar securing it, and then left the store, ignoring Pip's frantic waving behind Geraldine's back. He paid no mind to the men who greeted him on the street, intent only on tying his mount to the back of the buggy. Gripping the bridle, he led the mare down the street, around to the alleyway, and within minutes, he opened the back door of the emporium.

Angelena sat where he'd left her, head on the desk, silent and still.

"You sleepin'?" he asked quietly, stepping to her side. His hand rested for a moment on her shoulder, and he caught the minuscule movement of her head. "Let me help you up." His hands were careful as he helped her to her feet, guiding her to the door and lifting her to the buggy seat.

"Here's her things," Pip said from behind him, her hands full with Angelena's reticule, and an assortment of packages. "There's one more inside. I'll get it."

Wes was in the seat, Angelena leaning heavily against his shoulder, when Pip reappeared, and he nodded his thanks as he stowed the box near his feet.

"Wes?"

He held the reins still, intent on the woman who watched from the doorway, her look subdued, yet with a sense of elation dwelling behind her somber expression. There was more going on here than a headache, he'd stake his silver star on it.

"Don't ask her any questions for now," Pip said. "She'll be all right."

"She remembered something else?"

Pip nodded. "Yes, she remembered."

"St. Louis, Dex. She remembered St. Louis and she almost remembered the house she lived in." She clutched his arms, pressing herself against him. If it tore him from her, if he found his lost love because of this, her heart would break. But for Dex Sawyer she would surrender her happiness, if she must.

"Pip." He spoke her name gently, kindly, and his hands were tender as they held her. "You know, don't you? It's time for me to go. I need to know for certain, Pip. If Angelena is mine, I'll find out. Somehow, I'll hunt down Olivia Marie and hear the truth from her."

Pip nodded, her mouth turning to kiss his palm. "I'll pack your things, Dex. You can take the morning train." It was settled, but before he left, before he found evidence of another love, she would impress upon him the proof of her own.

"Come with me," she invited, leading him to the bed they'd shared for the past fourteen years. She undressed him, and he allowed it, his hands holding her face, bending to press kisses upon her tearstained cheeks.

Her own clothing was shed in moments, and together they slipped beneath the sheet, their arms locking them in an embrace that spoke of years of loving. He held her, comforted her, not totally aware of why she wept, only recognizing that her heart ached, and his departure was the cause of it.

"I'll be back, Pip. In just a few days—sooner maybe. It might only take a day or so to do what I must. Sweetheart." He bent low, his mouth avid on her skin, his hands skilled at the art of cherishing his woman. He found and conquered her weaknesses, giving unstintingly and with generous purpose, knowing he must reassure her tender heart of his love.

She accepted his offering and found within herself a fresh reserve of passion, a renewed awareness of the flame that dwelt just beneath the surface of their relationship. It was not enough that she tell him of the fount of love that overflowed daily on his behalf. Tonight, she must spend herself upon him, offering her devotion as a gift he would hold close to his heart.

They were as one in the shadows of their room, their bodies joined, their hearts united. And in the hours that led to dawn, they slept and woke, only to love again, until the sun rose above the horizon and this day of new beginnings was at hand.

Chapter Fourteen

"I've taken on a deputy," Wes said, leaning back in his chair, the empty plate in front of him giving evidence of Angelena's prowess at cooking. She crossed the kitchen floor, reaching to remove the plate, and his hand gripped her wrist, holding her fast.

"Don't you want to know why?" he asked, pushing back from the table, and easing her onto his lap.

She cocked her head, her eyes filled with his masculine beauty. "I'm sure you're going to tell me." He was far from perfect, but more and more she thanked her lucky stars that he'd pursued her so diligently. The life he'd given her, this home of her own, to do with as she liked, made up for any flaws in their marriage, and those few imperfections she was probably bound to live with anyway. Changing Wes Tanner was not a job for a woman with as little experience as she possessed.

"What are you thinking?" he asked. An arrogant smile crinkled his eyes and curved his mouth. Just once she'd like to see his eyes fill with more than admiration of her face and form, watch his lips utter words of love.

Be thankful for what you have. The words resounded in her mind, and she forced a smile to her mouth. Again, her mother. Daily it seemed, reminders of the woman who'd borne her filtered through her mind, and now was no exception.

"Nothing much," she lied. "Just wondering why you'd do such a thing. I wasn't sure there was enough to keep one man busy at the jailhouse."

"That's true enough," he agreed. "Edgewood's about the most peaceable town in Texas. Maybe that's why I've pretty near decided to work the farm," he said, his eyes watchful. "Would that suit you?"

To have him about, and close at hand, every living day? The whoop of celebration that threatened to erupt caused her reply to stutter from her lips. "I...I can't imagine..."

His grin wavered. "You'd rather not have me underfoot?" He waved a hand at the kitchen. "I thought I could help out here, and with a couple of hands to work the crops next year, we might make a go of it without me wearing a silver star."

"You want to help me in the house?" She could hardly fathom the idea.

Wes shook his head impatiently. "Not just that, but maybe painting or putting up new wallpaper, you know, just general fixing up while the weather holds. And there'd be plenty of heavy work to do during the winter. I'll need to set the barn and the rest of the outbuildings to rights.

"It's too late to do anything in the fields this year, but I thought I'd look around for some stock. We'll need a milk cow right off, and some chickens in the coop and probably a couple more horses to start with."

She was stunned. "You want to be a farmer." The thought of Wes Tanner as anything but the dapper sheriff of Edgewood, Texas was a bit much to consider. "I had the idea that your leaving town all those years ago was because you *didn't* want to live on a ranch."

"Who told you that?" His mouth was taut, his eyes narrowed, and he leaned back to look directly into her face. "I've never spoken to anyone about my reasons for running off."

She was hesitant, fearing to put Pip's friendship with Wes in jeopardy. "Pip just said that you left home at an early age. Probably I just assumed it was because you didn't want to live on a ranch."

He shook his head, and his eyes were flat, the dark centers expanding and deepening until she could see no trace of emotion lingering there. "That wasn't it, Lena. I left because I had to find out what sort of a man I really was." His jaw was taut, and the muscles of his thighs beneath her tensed as if his whole body prepared for pain.

"I was Scat Pender, the son of a drunkard. You know what my name means, Lena? Scat is something worthless, cattle dung, or mouse droppings, only fit to be thrown away."

She gasped aloud at his words, that any child should be so reviled by the name he bore. And yet he continued, as if her reaction to his revelation went unheard.

"I was beaten and cowed, and whipped to within an inch of my life. I lived by the skin of my teeth, and did my best to keep my little sister unharmed. I had a father I hated, the fine folks of Edgewood ignored my existence and my life was a misery."

Her heart clenched in her chest as she heard his recital of the cold, calculated facts as he remembered them. She'd guessed much of it before, when he'd intimated his beginnings. Now, they were laid before her in graphic detail, and her heart ached for the boy he had been.

He looked beyond her as he spoke, and she wondered if he was even aware of her existence as he continued, as if a dam had opened and he must lay before her the bare bones of the life he'd led. "One night I met Rosemary Gibson in the alley behind the saloon, and walked her home. She was like a heavenly being to my young eyes," he said quietly.

"That's about it, I guess. One day not long afterward, Rosemary rescued me and I became the chosen child of Gabe Tanner, who even gave me a new name, to go along with the new life they offered. I worked my tail off to prove myself to them, and I did such a good job turning Scat Pender into Wesley Tanner that by the time I was eighteen years old, I didn't even know who I was."

He focused on her finally, his eyes searching out her own, perhaps to find some trace of understanding there. "I had to find out how much of the Pender blood flowed in my veins, and how much of me was a neat and tidy wrapping, stuck in place by Rosemary Tanner." He shrugged, a flexing of wide shoulders, as if he shed the past with the telling of it.

"And so I left. Walked out the door and rode away."

Angelena released her breath, aware that she'd been holding it within her lungs as Wes spit out his succinct litany. "You sound bitter, Wes. And I know it must have hurt Rosemary and Gabe to see you leave that way." She wanted desperately to comfort him, ease his pain, but intuition told her he would not have that happen. For now, he was in the throes of recalling a part of his life that had changed all that he was up to that time, and perhaps made him the man she had married. Yet there were things she needed to know, in order to understand the moods and memories that ruled him.

She softened her voice, whispering her queries. "What happened to you? Where did you go?"

His brow raised consideringly, and she recognized his refusal before the words were spoken. "I'm not sure you really need to hear about my coming of age, Lena. Some of it isn't fit for your ears." He lifted her to her feet and shoved back from the table. "I've told you enough of my sad tale to last for the rest of your life. I'm back in town, I married a beautiful woman, and I've become a respectable citizen. What more do you want?"

The man who'd brought her home was gone. That tender, caring husband who'd helped her in the house, placed her on the bed and left her to rest for the whole of the afternoon had somehow become this harsh, brittle, angry being, whose every word pierced her heart. She could not let it go at this. If she allowed him to win this time, he might never loose his feelings in such a manner again.

Her legs trembled as she stood before him, refusing to heed his warning. "My ears may not be as tender as you think, Wes Tanner. You're my husband. For the first time, you've told me something about yourself. Do you think I can just ignore all of that and go about my business?"

The deep breath he drew flexed muscles in his chest, and he crossed his arms across that wide expanse, the action seeming to push her even farther from him. She compensated by stepping closer, her toes almost butting against his boots. "I mean it, Wes. Don't push me away like this."

His smile came without warning, and his white, even teeth gleamed between taut lips. "Why, sweetheart, I wouldn't think of it," he murmured, his voice dropping to a pitch as soft as dark, sleek velvet. He bent to her, swooping over her, resembling, to her mind, a great marauding hawk. His kiss was a greedy possession, offering neither gentle persuasion nor tender coaxing. Her lips were smothered, suckled and stroked, the invasion complete.

A harsh groan rose from his chest, and she shivered at the primitive sound, torn between the urge to shrink from his touch and the need to cling to the bulwark of his strength.

But he gave her no choice, his arms enfolding her, enclosing her slender body with muscular bonds she stood no chance of escaping. Breathless, she gasped against his open mouth, and he allowed the intake of air, only to resume anew the fervent molding and meshing of their lips.

Angelena was lifted against him, turned in his grip. He clasped her tightly to his chest, turning from the kitchen to seek out the hallway, and from there the wide, open stairway at the front of the house. With long steps that made short work of the risers, he climbed upward, his breathing barely changing as he shifted her to rest high against his chest. Tiny black dots swam before her eyes, and she struggled to catch a breath, turning her head to the side. He released her mouth and a shuddering gasp marked the return of a normal breath as she clung to his neck. Sweet air filled her lungs, tinged by the scent of male arousal emanating from his body.

Merciful heavens. The man was out of control, she decided. And perhaps that was not all bad. Her instincts were good, and for the first time in their marriage, she suspected she was being given a glimpse into the soul of the man.

She'd told him not to push her away, and he'd done just as she'd demanded, and far from casting her aside, he had possessed her with the strength of a man in the throes of anger, loosening a part of himself he'd kept inviolate and hidden from her sight, unleashing a primitive reaction to those few pleading words she'd uttered.

Or perhaps it had been a demand, she decided, wavering now between outright panic and the knowledge that Wes would not harm her. He turned to enter their bedroom and eased her through the doorway, protecting her head with his own. It was a short journey to the bed, and she was dumped there with a total lack of ceremony or delicacy.

Angelena sank into the feather tick, her skirts rucked up above her knees, her hair tumbling around her face, and with the perfect view of a man set on satisfaction leaning over her. His face was ruddy with the emotion driving him, his jaw tense, his eyes flashing dark fire. She'd mussed his hair, what with her hanging on so tightly as he strode up the stairway, and it hung over his forehead, giving him a youthful look that tempered the passionate mask he wore.

"I didn't mean for you to get this upset, Wes," she began, her words running together, all too aware of her position. She made a quick attempt to sit upright, but with a leveled index finger, he indicated she should not budge. Shifting her legs, she made a vain attempt to tuck her skirts down, and he shook his head, again halting her movement.

"Wes, I know you're angry with me, but—"

"You have no idea how I feel right now, Angelena." He leaned closer, one long finger tangling with a curl, tugging it upward, winding it around into a ringlet as she watched his action from wary eyes. "However," he murmured, "I think you're about to find out."

She sucked in a deep breath, aware of the tensing of all her muscles, her breasts taut beneath the cotton dress she wore, a creeping warmth settling deep in her belly. "Are you trying to frighten me?" she asked, frowning as her voice broke on the final word.

"Am I succeeding?" His big body weighted down the bed as he settled beside her, and she wrinkled her nose as his callused fingers tangled in her curls.

"I think what you're doing is pulling my hair," she told him, the law of gravity causing her to roll against him.

"And I think you're too smart and sassy for your own good."

She tried to find herself in his eyes, but to no avail. Heavy lids and lashes that kept his dark orbs half-hidden refused her scrutiny. His whiskers were rough beneath her fingers as she lifted a hand to touch his face, and his skin burned hot and dry against her fingers. A ruddy hue colored his cheeks and throat, and she sought in vain for a spark of humor in his final remark.

He bent to her, his mouth renewing the assault he'd begun only minutes ago. If he intended to dominate her, he was certainly going about it the right way, she thought, her own temper becoming honed to a fine edge. The man was holding her fast, and one hand was busily undoing her clothing, a task he'd become quite adept at over the past weeks.

"Wes! You're not being very nice," she complained dourly.

"No?" He held her down, breathing harshly, and she looked up at him warily. His mouth was wet, his teeth clenched, and he used both hands in a joint effort, stripping from her the layers of fabric she wore.

The last to go was her chemise, and she muttered a protest at his high-handedness. "I don't want you to—"

"Nobody asked you what you wanted, Mrs. Tanner," he growled, just before he undid the front of his denim trousers. "But I hope you'll notice I'm not pushing you away."

Indeed, just the opposite, she thought, fascinated by the thin line of control he exhibited. Her breasts were crushed against his shirtfront, and she winced as the coarse material rubbed her tender skin, and then felt the rippling response as a hot wire of desire spun from her swollen bosom to the depths of her feminine folds. Her head tilted back and her indrawn breath was a sharp, keening cry.

"That's it, baby," he growled, the words a guttural

sound. He lifted a bit, his body rising to relieve her from his greater weight, and she was struck by the need to urge him back, her breasts bereft without him there.

"Undo my shirt," he said bluntly, his words harsh and rasping, and she could think of no argument, her mind intent on revealing the hard, masculine lines of his chest, her fingers eager and trembling as they loosed his buttons.

"Yes...yes." She hissed the words beneath her breath, tugging at the fabric, impatient with the tight buttonholes, her whimper of aggravation calling forth harsh laughter from the man who held her.

His hand moved to join hers, and his shirt was opened with almost indecent haste, the undergarment given the same treatment and pulled from place. And then she was fully beneath him, his body covering her, effectively burying her in the feather tick. He held his weight on thick, masculine arms, rising higher above her, and she met his gaze, mesmerized by the taut lines of his face, lips drawn back, teeth clenched.

"Push down my pants," he snarled, his position allowing her room to maneuver, and she complied readily, her flesh warmed by his, yet beset by shivers that caused her fingers to quake at their task and set her mouth trembling. He closed his eyes as her hand brushed the firm flesh of his manhood, and his shuddering response was a revelation.

He was riding a sharp edge, his passion almost at its peak, and the lingering bit of apprehension he'd engendered fell prey to the overwhelming wave of love his vulnerability brought to life within her. She widened her legs beneath him, and he jolted, his manhood surging anew. He pressed against her, his hips driving forward as his instinct to mate found no barrier.

Angelena braced her feet, lifting the weight of her lower

body from the bed, her womanhood embracing the offering he could no longer withhold. She caught her breath, wincing for a moment at his entry, her tender flesh protesting the invasion.

"Lena." He stilled, deep shuddering gasps of air inflating his lungs, his head hanging, his arms taut with muscled strength. "Am I hurting you?" The words were rasping, harsh whispers, and she hastened to deny his worry.

"No, oh, no," she cried, aware of a hunger she'd only glimpsed before today. A need so urgent, so utterly chaotic, she could only clasp his shoulders, her fingernails gripping the steely muscles beneath satin flesh. "Wes!" Feverish with the whirlwind of sensation he imposed upon her body, she cried aloud again, her hips lifting in frantic movements to meet his turbulent thrusts.

"Wes!" As if his name were a talisman upon which she must throw herself with abandon, she chanted it beneath her breath, each whispering incantation bringing her closer to a peak so enormous, it might prove to be her doom.

Surely she could not survive the power of his possession. Certainly, she would not live through the maelstrom of sensation holding her prisoner in its grasp. Her breath became a hoarse cry, her cry a plea for mercy. And there was none to be had. All enveloping, the throbbing intensity he bestowed upon her seemed endless.

And in her struggling, groping, stretching and grasping for the pleasure he held within the power of his masculine possession, she rose to a majestic pinnacle of joy that shattered her yearning into a million shreds of rapture. Held suspended on the thin wire of delight he spun in her depths, she could only call his name, whispering words that expressed the overpowering emotion she could no longer contain.

"I love you." She murmured it against his throat, spoke

the syllables in fervent gasps as she took his lips captive. She repeated the litany as she suckled and bit at the flesh of his mouth, even as her body sought restlessly for the last shuddering spasm of release.

And then he bowed high over her, his head thrown back, his teeth gritted and clenched as he sought the culmination of their coming together. His frame quaked and trembled, the width of his shoulders seeming immense above her. She was swallowed up by his male strength, possessed by the force of his striving, her slender body receiving his seed.

With great shuddering gasps, he drove into her and she clung, exultantly aware that Wes Tanner's control was spent, his hunger unleashed, and she was the vessel for the strength and power of his passion.

She stood at the stove, lost in thought. Her hands moved automatically, pulling a pan of biscuits from the oven to place in the warmer above, then returning to lay thick slices of bacon in the skillet. Behind her the door opened, and her every sense was alert.

No need to turn and look. The presence of Wes Tanner was there. A faint whisper of fresh air accompanied him, along with his own indescribable scent, a masculine, teasing aroma she had inhaled throughout the night just past.

And now she yearned to face him, to find in his eyes some trace of approval, a small spark of affection that would pleasure her hungry heart. Her head turned and her gaze swept the length of the kitchen, falling at last upon the man watching her, encompassing his long, lean length. His hair was damp, looking as if long fingers had smoothed it into place. Below his hairline, his face was all hard, harsh lines, with nary a twitch of those full lips to assure her of his good humor. Far from it.

His eyes were dark and unfathomable, his expression grim, and all of Angelena's joy vanished in one slow breath.

She'd awakened alone, reaching a tentative hand toward Wes's pillow, only to find it empty, the white pillowcase still dented, but cool to her touch. Now he stood at the back door, watching her in a manner that certainly didn't induce any degree of happiness in her soul.

"What's wrong?" she asked, turning back to the stove, unable to look any longer at his face, for fear that his features might indicate anger or impatience with her. After yesterday afternoon and then last night, late, when the moon had risen and their room was flooded with its unearthly glow, she'd hoped...vainly perhaps, but still...

"Are you all right?" He'd moved rapidly, and his hand touched her shoulder. She glanced back at him again, surprised at his touch.

"Yes, of course." Her lips quivered as she attempted a smile, and his gaze swept from her suddenly tear-filled eyes to the trembling of her mouth.

"Aw, Lena. I knew it. I hurt you. I was too rough." His face paled before her eyes, and she shook her head forcefully, intent on denying his fear.

"No, Wes. Oh, no. You didn't hurt me."

His hands turned her to face him and he slid them to her back, holding her with care. "I was there, honey, remember? I didn't give you a chance, and I didn't even think about the baby until this morning. I might have hurt you, and don't shake your head at me again. I remember how you pulled back and cried out."

"It was just for a second, Wes. And it didn't really hurt. I was just..." How could she explain the exultation she'd felt at that moment when he'd lost control and possessed her with a passion she'd never before been privy to. "I'm fine, and the baby's fine." She lifted a hand to his face, and he turned his lips to her palm.

"I won't ever come after you that way again," he vowed. "I behaved badly, Lena."

She cupped his chin and her fingers dug into his jaw. "Don't you make me such a promise, Wes Tanner. I'll never forgive you if our whole married life goes by without another—" She lifted her chin bravely and spoke the words she'd thought herself too cowardly to voice aloud. "It was a night to remember, Wes. I hope it won't be the last."

He brushed her hand aside, his head lowering, his mouth taking possession of her lips, and she was lost in a haze of desire. Her flesh softened against his firm masculine body, and he molded her to himself. She clung to him, her arms entwined around his neck, her head nestling against the curve of his shoulder. The events of the night past made her brave and she whispered words of invitation, then held her breath as he drew back, his heavy-lidded appraisal giving her pause.

"You mean that?" he asked, and again she heard the dark, guttural tones that spoke of arousal and passion.

She was breathless with the knowledge of her love for him, and she murmured the only reply she was capable of giving. "I love you, Wes Tanner. I want to show you how much you mean to me."

He bent lower, his ear bare inches from her lips. "Say that again, Angelena. The first part anyway." He was immobile, barely breathing as he waited, and she closed her eyes. He'd not given her a pat reply last night, nor was he about to do so today, it appeared, but his reticence could not bring her to deny the power of her love for him, and she allowed it to pour forth.

"I've never loved a man before, Wes. I know that as

surely as I know the sun will rise and set tomorrow. When you walked into the saloon and watched me sing, I felt my heart come up in my throat. You frightened me out of my wits.''

"You? You looked cool as a cucumber, all dressed in white. Your mouth opened, and the music poured out, and those men looked like they'd been poleaxed. Every last one of them, slaverin' over you like a pack of wolves on the prowl."

She felt a bubble of laughter well up within her and allowed it freedom. "Oh, Wesley Tanner, you are a mess. Not a one of those men ever touched me. I wasn't afraid of them.''

"Only me, I suppose. You acted like you were scared to death of *me*.''

She shook her head, remembering the first time he'd come to her room. "I was fearful of myself. Not a one of the men who came to hear me sing made me feel the way you did.'' Her hands delved into his hair, caressing the back of his head. "When you kissed me, I wanted to kiss you back, but I didn't know how. You were way beyond me, Wes.''

She smiled at the memory she'd cherished for so long. "And then I teased you about your mother, remember? And you told me it was my future you were interested in.''

"You've got quite a memory, girl," he murmured, intrigued by the words she spoke. It seemed to him he'd intimidated her and frightened her, and to hear her talk, she recalled it fondly. "I just knew I wanted you in my bed, and I'd do most anything to get you there. Up to and including a touch of blackmail.''

"Well, you succeeded. And without resorting to blackmail.''

"I didn't give you a choice, Lena. I railroaded you into

a wedding, and turned you into Mrs. Tanner without you having a whole lot to say about things.''

"What you did was give me a home and a family, Wes. And a husband to love and look after.''

He eyed her cautiously, wary of pushing his luck. "You meant what you said a few minutes ago? About going upstairs and—''

She flushed, biting at her lip. "Perhaps I'm too forward. I shouldn't have...''

"You can't get too forward to please me, honey. I told you a long time ago that I'd make love to my wife every chance I got. And if you're willin', then I'm ready.''

He scooped her up and her hand fluttered toward the stove. "I'm making breakfast, Wes. The bacon's cooking.''

He held her firmly and bent closer to the iron range, one long arm reaching to rescue the bacon from ruin. A quick shove sent the pan flying to the back of the surface and he grinned his satisfaction. "It'll just keep warm that way. We'll eat later.''

She was secure in his embrace, and he held her closely, marching from the kitchen to the stairway. "Seems like we just did this,'' he told her, elation driving him upward as he scaled the stairs with ease.

Gone was the despair he'd felt upon entering the kitchen only minutes past. Absent was the fear engendered by the fragile stance of the woman he'd stripped and fallen upon last evening. She was stronger than he'd given her credit for, able to withstand his passion and the force of his need for her, more than willing to join with him in the acts of marriage he'd instigated throughout the long hours of the night.

He'd thought she might have second thoughts, might have been insulted by his blatant need for her body. He'd feared her reaction this morning, had hesitated to face her in the light of day, and then upon watching her in the kitchen, had recognized fully his need of Angelena Tanner. Not just her body, but the woman who dwelt within its confines.

A woman who might very well be his salvation.

Chapter Fifteen

"**Y**ou got any idea what Nate's up to?" Gabe Tanner stood before the shabby desk in the jailhouse, and Wes leaned back in his chair.

"Good morning to you, too," he said, unable to halt the curve of his lips, even though the look on his father's face spoke of trouble.

Gabe turned aside and shook his head. "Forgot my manners, didn't I? I reckon I've always had a habit of gettin' right to the point." He tossed Wes a salute, accompanied by a sheepish grin. "Haven't seen you in a couple of weeks, Wes."

His gaze raked the lean form behind the desk, and then focused on his son's face. "You're lookin' good." His grin widened. "In fact, looks to me like my boy's head over heels these days."

Wes allowed a slow chuckle to erupt. "I wouldn't let anybody else make that sort of a crack, you know. And from a man who knows all about women the way you do, I'd say you probably walked the same path yourself."

Tanner nodded. "Still am, for that matter. Rosemary keeps me in my place, you might say."

"Yeah, I've noticed that." Wes began to enjoy the conversation, noting the softening of Gabe's features, the easing of his stance. And then he watched him stiffen once more as he referred to the reason for this visit.

"What have you seen of old Nate? Any talk goin' around?"

Wes shook his head. "No, I don't know what he's up to. He's been in town a couple of times, but he's pretty much keepin' his nose clean, far as I can tell. Folks have mostly left him be, and so long as he behaves himself, I guess there's not much I can do about it."

Gabe strode to the window, his hands deep in his back pockets. "He's up to something. I'll guarantee it, Wes. The man's never been up-front and honest a day in his life, and he's not about to start now. Just keep an eye on things." He turned from the window and settled in the extra chair, bending one long leg to rest his boot on the other knee.

"Your mother wants you and Angelena to come out to the ranch for a meal. Said I shouldn't take no for an answer."

"I think Lena's drivin' the buggy in today," Wes said. "I got her some chickens and built a pen for them, and she's all excited about havin' eggs to sell. Pip told her she'd take all she could get. I expect she'll come rollin' down the road about noontime."

Gabe pulled his watch from his pocket and opened the lid. "I'll still be around. I've got some things to take care of at the bank, and Rosemary gave me a list for Pip. I'll try to catch her at the emporium, and ask her myself."

"Did you hear about the new deputy I hired?" Wes watched as his father settled deeper in the chair. "I'm about done with the silver star, Gabe. I think it's time to settle down and do some farming."

"Yeah," Gabe agreed, steepling his hands and watching Wes over the tips of his fingers. "I figured it would come to it one of these days, once you got rid of the restless streak.''

Wes nodded. ''I did a lot of wanderin' around, gettin' things sorted out for myself. Angelena said she figured I'd hurt you and Rosemary when I left home.''

''You told her about it? About everything?''

''No.'' The single word was sharp, succinct, and Wes shook his head for emphasis. ''I decided there were a few things she didn't need to know, but when it came to you and Rosemary, she knows all there is to say. We talked about Nate, and a little bit about Anna.''

''You tell her why you left home?''

He'd never noticed before how much Gabe's dark eyes resembled his own, their heavy lids narrowing until his gaze penetrated like the blade of a knife. It was uncanny that a man who held no blood tie with him should be truly a father to him, and that he should so closely resemble the man.

''Yeah, as a matter of fact, I did.'' And that was a conversation he'd as soon leave private. But another subject had arisen in his mind more than once over the past weeks, and now it swam to the forefront again, and he plunged in, his need for resolution in the matter making him brave.

''I've wondered about something, Gabe.'' He paused and flicked a glance at his father. He was impassive, waiting, his big body relaxed in the chair. ''You know Angelena's going to have a baby, don't you?''

''Yup. And I know it isn't yours.'' Gabe tilted back in the chair. ''Is that your problem, son?''

''Somewhat,'' Wes admitted. ''She's...fillin' out. You know, with the baby. Even when we're...you know—'' He inhaled, changing direction. ''Well, I can tell...uh, I can't help but notice...and I've been thinking.'' He paused and wished fervently he'd never taken this tack. ''Hell, you know what I'm talkin' about, Gabe. She's gonna have a child that isn't mine, and I'm worried sick I won't be able to—''

''You won't be able to be a father to another man's child?'' The chair legs hit the floor and Gabe stood, in one smooth motion becoming a man Wes remembered from a time long past. When man and boy had forged a link in a chain that bound them to this day.

''Do you doubt my feelings for you, son? Have you forgotten what you mean to your mother and me?'' He stepped closer, leaning over the desk, and Wes was assured and strengthened by the look of determination on Gabe Tanner's face.

''I took you when you were twelve years old and named you my child,'' Gabe reminded him. ''I had every fear you have, and probably a hell of a lot more. I knew where you came from. I knew the blood that flowed in your veins, and I vowed to forget everything that had ever happened in your past and concentrate on your future.''

He lifted his hand and pointed one long finger at Wes. ''Now, if you can't do that for the baby your wife is carrying, if you can't forget from this moment on that that child is not yours by blood, then, by God, you're not the man I thought you were.''

Wes stumbled to his feet and circled the desk, his throat tight with emotion. ''I don't think I've told you how much I appreciate what you and Rosemary did for me, Gabe. You've been more of a father to me than I deserved.''

''Hell, it was Rosemary who hauled you out of that cesspool you were livin' in,'' Gabe said forcefully. ''She made it a condition of our marriage that I take you and Anna in and treat you like my own. You think I wanted it that way?''

His frown turned to a smile of remembrance. ''If I

hadn't wanted your mother so badly, I'd have turned tail and walked away, Wes.''

"She blackmailed you?" Wes grinned widely. "I'll be damned!"

"Yeah, well, it all worked out," Gabe muttered. "And don't you dare tell your mother I let you in on that little secret, either. Matter of fact, by the time I agreed, I'd pretty much decided it was a good move all around."

Wes scanned his memory. "I think it was the day Nate got shot, and you talked to me about him that I really knew it was gonna be all right."

"Well," Gabe said slowly. "One of these days, you'll find your own turnaround point and realize that the baby Angelena's carrying is going to be your child, no matter who put the seed there."

"She doesn't know his name," Wes said quietly. "It was rape."

Gabe's eyes darkened. "I know. Rosemary told me, but we haven't said anything to anyone else. It's nobody's business but yours and Angelena's, son. And I have a notion it's gonna work out just fine."

He wrapped a long arm around Wes's shoulder. "Keep an eye on Nate, whatever you do. I don't feel good about him hangin' around. There's something fishy going on. Rosemary has a feeling about him, and she's usually right about these things."

His ride outside of town was far from productive, and by late afternoon, Wes was disgruntled and saddle weary. He'd poked and prodded through three campsites, where the remains of a fire and the trash left by careless inhabitants had provoked his ire. There was, as Rosemary thought, something fishy going on, and his frustration was at a high level as he headed back to town.

The new deputy, old Oscar Rhinehold's boy, was eager to take over the office, and by all rights Wes should have allowed him the privilege a couple of weeks ago. Instead, he'd hung on and made excuses, till August Rhinehold was about to lose patience at being relegated to walking the streets and keeping Duane Goody in line.

Being the perennial town drunk was an occupation Duane was really good at, and luckily for him his employer, Joseph Richardson, was a patient man.

A fight at the Golden Slipper the other night had brought a bit of excitement into the young deputy's life, and he'd drawn his gun and settled two men down in a move that Jason Stillwell had proclaimed as downright smooth. It seemed that the way was clear for Wes to empty his desk and head for the farm in earnest. Yet he dithered, uneasy for some nameless reason.

The bank was closing for the day as Wes rode the middle of the street, and he watched as Pace Frombert locked the heavy door, then shook the handle to ensure its security. Pace looked up and flagged him down. "Sheriff, got a minute? I need to talk to you."

Wes slid from his saddle and led his horse to where Pace waited, aware of a general air of agitation surrounding the man. "What's the problem?"

Pace looked down the sidewalk, then scanned the road before stepping closer to Wes. "You remember that fella that came in the bank, back, oh, maybe a couple months ago? He was there asking about opening an account, but we never saw him again. Remember?" His hands fumbled with the ring of keys he carried, and as Wes watched, Pace dropped them to the wooden walkway.

Wes bent to scoop them up and handed them back to the banker. The man's fingers were icy as he took the keys from Wes's hands and slid them hurriedly into his pocket.

"He was in the bank today," Pace said, his mouth moving nervously. "I'm not one to borrow trouble, Sheriff, but that fella's up to no good. I just know he's not what he seems."

A chill slid up Wes's spine and he glanced behind him, wondering for a moment if he was being watched. It was just that sort of a day, he decided, recalling his fruitless efforts all afternoon, riding in a lazy circle around the town. And yet, if there was something in what Pace said, and if Rosemary was right...

Naw, he was grabbing at straws this time, looking for trouble where none existed. "I'll keep an eye out for him, Pace," he said soothingly. "Probably just a gentleman lookin' to settle in these parts, and tryin' to locate a place to stash his money." And he sure as hell hoped that was all there was to it, Wes thought. Just when he was hoping to skin out of being sheriff and turn himself into a full-time farmer, Pace Frombert had to go getting himself in a dither.

"The problem is, Sheriff Tanner," Pace confided, bending closer, "when that man left the bank he walked across the road, and stood there talkin' to your—" He looked decidedly uncomfortable for a moment, and then his chin lifted. "Old Nate Pender was in town again, holding up a post in front of Pip Sawyer's place, and that fancy man stood about as near as you are to me, looking like he didn't know Nate. But I could see his mouth moving. And you tell me what they might have to talk about, Sheriff. You just figure that one out if you can."

Pace looked indignant, and if he'd had feathers, they'd have been all puffed up, Wes decided. He looked across the road to where Pace had designated the meeting spot, and an oath slid from between his lips. His head dropped, and he shook it once, his good mood shot to hell and back. "What do you mean, Nate was in town *again?*"

Pace held up a hand. "Now, don't get all in an uproar. I know the man has a right to come and go as he pleases, but he's been hanging around the past couple of days, and I don't like the feeling of it."

Wes felt the chill again, and his heart thumped at a faster clip. "I reckon you're right, Pace. Somethin's brewin', and I don't even want to guess what it might be. But I suspect I'd better take a run out to Cal Hodges's place in the morning and see if I can find Nate."

"We got a shipment coming in tomorrow morning, Sheriff," Pace confided, "and it's a tidy haul from the train to the bank. I surely don't want to worry about somebody showing up with robbery in mind."

Wes sighed, consigning Nate Pender and his like to perdition, and then turned back to Pace, reassuring him as well as he could. "I'll do what I can, Pace, and I'll leave my deputy in town to keep an eye out. I shouldn't be more than a couple of hours in the morning, gettin' hold of Nate."

Pip watched the banker bustle past her general store just as she locked the double doors from the inside. "Old man Frombert sure is in a hurry tonight. He looks fit to be tied," she said, her voice carrying to the back room, where Dex waited for her.

He held the baby in his arms, and was dressed in his best suit, a diaper thrown over his shoulder, lest the child should drool on the fine wool worsted. "Probably didn't balance at the end of the day," Dex murmured, his gaze intent on Pip's approach. "You know how much I missed you, woman?" he asked, one hand reaching for her waist, drawing her against himself.

The baby squawked loudly at his father's actions, and then subsided, apparently used to being held as a buffer between husband and wife as they took their ease for a moment. Pip leaned her head against Dex's shoulder, and he murmured words of intent against her fiery hair, his mouth brushing the unruly curls.

"I guess you did, Dex," she said, laughing at his shenanigans. "I thought you were only going to be gone for a few days, and you ended up stayin' over a week. No wonder you missed me." Her grin was sly as she ducked past him to hang her apron on a handy hook. "Let's get on home. I left the Worths' oldest girl there to get supper on. It ought to be ready by now."

They left by the back door, walking down the alleyway to where their large, two-story house stood at the end of the back street. Lights glowed from the window, where figures moved back and forth in the kitchen. Pip looked up at Dex, struck anew by her love for this handsome man, his golden hair neatly combed, his collar high, sporting a new four-in-hand draped on his shirtfront.

"I missed you, too," she admitted softly and was struck by the ambivalent look he sent her way. "What is it, Dex? You haven't said a word since you got off the train this afternoon. At least not about the reason for your trip. Did you find out anything? About Angelena, I mean?"

He nodded, and then held the gate for her as they reached their home. "I'll tell you about it after supper," he said. "When the boys are all in bed for the night."

Pip endured the meal, waited for endless minutes as the baby had his final nursing of the day, and found herself impatient as she listened to prayers and tucked the older boys into bed. Dex waited for her in their bedroom, stripped to his trousers, his suspenders hanging.

"You think I need to shave?" he asked, bending to peer at his image in the mirror over her dresser.

Pip closed the door, then leaned back against it. "I think

you need to talk to me, Dex Sawyer. I've been on pins and needles all evening and half the afternoon. I thought we'd never have a quiet minute.''

His gaze met hers in the mirror, and she stepped closer. ''You don't have to shave on my account,'' she said, her eyes cherishing the male beauty of the man watching her. ''I'll take you any way I can get you, Dex.''

''You think I don't know that, Pip? I've ached for you, and dreamed every night about holding you. Lady, I've missed you like the very dickens,'' he declared. ''But I had to stay in St. Louis for as long as it took to pin down every last detail I could come up with.'' He turned and faced her, and his eyes shone with unshed tears.

''Angelena is my daughter, Pip. Her mother was Olivia Marie Jordan, just as I suspected.'' His voice broke. ''She's my daughter, and I never knew she existed. Why would Olivia do such a thing, keeping her a secret from me?''

''We'll never know that, Dex.'' Her heart ached for him, and she yearned to give comfort, even as she recognized there was little she could offer that would soothe the ache in his heart.

His hands moved in a helpless gesture. ''I ran down every lead I could come up with, and found people who knew about Angelena. I talked to every last one of them.''

''They didn't know her? Only about her?'' Pip asked, puzzled.

''That's where the rub came in. Olivia Marie sent her away to school and then to a conservatory in New York for training. She'd only been back in St. Louis for a matter of weeks before her mother died.''

He took Pip's hand and led her to the bedside, sitting down and patting the mattress beside him. ''Come here, sweetheart.''

She obliged him, and waited as he opened his leather wallet, bringing out a neatly folded playbill with the name of a music hall on the front. "I'll warrant you this is the place Angelena remembered when she recalled singing on stage. She appeared there just a week before her mother died. And then no one knew where she went from there."

"She came here," Pip said quietly. "But how she knew to come here is what I'd like to know."

"My God!" Dex groaned, bending his head, resting it in his hands. "I might never have known, Pip. What if she'd stayed on that train?"

"But she didn't." And thank the Almighty for that, Pip thought. "When will you tell her?"

He lifted his head and met her gaze. "That's up to you. I think we should do it together, don't you?"

Pip nodded, and a sudden thought brought joy to her heart. "Dex! Do you realize that this means Angelena is my stepdaughter? I told her she could use your name on her wedding license, and she did." Her heart beat rapidly as the memory of that day came to mind. "It's almost as if I knew, Dex, even then."

He turned to her, his arms circling her, and drew her back on the sheets. "Maybe you did, honey. Maybe you did." He bent over her and his mouth found hers, and she was lost, aware only of the loving care bestowed on her by the man she loved.

The sun was high in the sky the next day when Wes made his way back to the farm where Angelena waited for him. He snatched a bite to eat while he told her of his morning, of striking out at the Hodges's farm. "Cal Hodges is up to his neck in work, and Nate just took off on him the other day. Said he had a better job offer." He bent to drop a quick kiss on her lips. "I'll meet you at the ranch before suppertime, honey. This may be a futile search, but I need to try. I think finding Nate will give me some answers.''

"I believe I'll leave early and give Rosemary a hand," Angelena told him, watching anxiously as he strapped on his gun belt. "I hate for you to wear that thing, Wes. Do you really think there's going to be trouble in town?"

He shook his head. "Naw, probably not. I just want to be prepared, Lena. Pace Frombert is hatchin' up a worrisome situation, and probably nothing will come of it, but it'll make him feel better if I'm walkin' around with my gun tied to my leg.''

She nodded, but her inner instinct told her he was weaving a tale to keep her happy. His mouth was taut, and his eyes were dark with some nameless emotion as he took his leave. Angelena waved until he was only a cloud of dust at the end of the lane, then turned back to the house, walking across the yard to the kitchen door.

The day dragged by slowly, and she found herself looking up at the least noise, her heart pounding as the chickens squawked loudly at a hawk flying overhead. They dove for cover, scampering inside the coop, and she smiled as she mocked her fear. "I'm leaving now," she muttered aloud. "Rosemary's place is loaded with people, and I'm in need of company."

She was ready in short order, her basket loaded in the buggy, and the mare between the traces. Wes was a good teacher, she decided, her fingers adept at the harnessing, the mare being a most cooperative animal. And then she set out, for the first time uncomfortable with the silence of the home she loved.

The trip took less than an hour, and Rosemary waited with open arms, her gaze narrowing as she scanned Angelena's figure. "You're filling out nicely," she announced, hugging her daughter-in-law with feeling. "I've been lonesome for the pair of you, and I told Gabe to deliver the message to Wes that I needed to see you."

Angelena laughed aloud. "I got the message, and I figured I'd set out a little early so I could give you a hand with supper. I brought some rice pudding with me."

Rosemary led the way to the house. "My boys all love it. I used to make it for Wes when he was first with us, trying to fatten him up." She opened the door and waited for Angelena to enter the big kitchen. "Come on in, honey. You can peel potatoes while I brown the meat. I baked bread this morning and the boys are out picking the last of the corn. We'll husk it on the porch."

It was a comfort, Angelena decided, listening to Rosemary ramble on, her voice bright, her smile contagious. No wonder Wes loved this place so much. It was a wonder to her he had had the courage to walk out the door and leave it behind, those many years ago.

She peeled a whole dishpan full of potatoes, listening as Rosemary brought her up to date on the family. It seemed Anna was considering going to Dallas to seek employment, although why she wanted to leave this beautiful home for a stint in the city was more than Angelena could understand.

And she said so. "I've remembered some things about St. Louis," she ventured, breaking a silence, as Rosemary put on a big kettle of water to heat for the corn. "I can't imagine trading life here for the city. I don't want to ever go back there."

Rosemary turned to glance at her, one eyebrow raised. "You don't think you'll want to go back someday? Maybe go on the stage there? You sure don't have much chance to sing in Edgewood."

"This is home now," Angelena said simply. "Maybe

sometime..." She shook her head. "But not for now. I'm going to have a baby, Rosemary, and that's the most important thing in the world."

"Well, Anna is set on trying her wings, and I'm fearful of it, but Gabe says we have to let her go, the same way we had to turn loose of Wesley." She blinked rapidly, and Angelena caught a glimpse of tears glittering from blue eyes.

"Do you suppose she'll come back? Wes did."

"Yes, and I'm thankful for that. And now that he's married you, I feel sure he'll stay put. Unless you decide to move on." And at that Rosemary gave Angelena a direct look that left no doubt as to her druthers on that subject.

"Rosemary, I've had little enough family in my life. I'm so happy to be a part of this one." Angelena looked out the screened door to where three young boys could be seen, arms filled with fresh sweet corn, laughing and stumbling their way to the kitchen porch. "Just look at those boys. They've got enough corn for a small army."

Rosemary went to the door and waved her sons up to the porch. "And that's about what I feel like I'm cooking for," she remarked, watching as the corn was deposited on the wooden stoop. She looked back at Angelena. "Come on, honey. We'll husk corn and have it ready by the time the water boils."

Supper was late, Wes arriving just as the family sat down, having waited for him for half an hour. He apologized nicely, washed up quickly and slid into a chair next to Angelena. He leaned over and kissed her loudly and she gasped, frowning at him. "It's all right, honey, we're married," he reminded her with a grin, and then proceeded to eat four ears of sweet corn before he loaded his plate with potatoes and meat.

"I see you haven't lost your appetite," Rosemary said,

her humor well in place, although Angelena suspected that his mother enjoyed watching Wes eat his meal.

He'd been gone for most of the day, and food had been the last thing on his mind, he'd told them. He'd followed tracks, and found another abandoned campsite, and was more than frustrated by the tracks of a number of horses that seemed to disappear at the edge of the wooded area east of town.

"I'm just as glad you didn't try to follow them into that woods, anyway," Gabe told him. "There've been rustlers hiding out there a couple of times over the years, and it's a good spot for keepin' out of sight."

"Well, I doubt that Nate and the gentleman stranger have gone too far away," Wes said, leaning back in his chair. He waved his hand as Rosemary offered another piece of beef. "Can't do it, Mother. I'm stuffed to the gills."

"I won't even have to cook breakfast, will I?" Angelena asked sweetly, batting her eyelashes at him.

His grin was quick. "Don't count on that, sweetheart. I'll probably work up an appetite before then."

Gabe cleared his throat loudly, and Angelena dropped her gaze to the table, pushing her chair back hastily as Wes reached for her. She glared a reproof in his direction and began clearing the table.

"I'll help you," Jenny announced from her seat on the other side of the table. "You scrape and I'll clear," the girl said, following suit as Angelena nodded her agreement. The dishes were carried to the drainboard, and Angelena cleaned them for washing, half listening to the conversation behind her. It was all a part of family, this give and take, talking and listening, the laughter, the occasional reprimand as the boys became boisterous and were sent outdoors to do their chores. She reveled in it, basked in the unconditional respect she was given. And if Wes could be believed, Rosemary had stated her love for the woman he'd married. The thought warmed her and she turned to the table, dishrag in hand.

"Move your elbows, Wes, so I can wipe up." She watched as he leaned back, then swiped the crumbs from before him, gathering them in her hand. His hand slid around her waist, and he held her fast.

"We'll need to head out, honey. I've got a long day tomorrow." His words were low, but Gabe heard him and nodded his agreement.

"I'm heading into town myself, son. Things are brewing, and I'd feel better stayin' close."

"I'm going to town tomorrow, too," Angelena announced. "I've got eggs to take in, and Pip is saving some new material for me to look at."

Gabe caught Wes's eye and an unspoken message traveled between the two men. "I don't know if that's a good idea, Lena," Wes said quietly.

"Do you want her to stay here?" Rosemary asked. "In fact you could both bed down in Anna's room. She's gone for a couple of days."

Angelena shook her head. "No, I have chores to do in the morning, and the cow can't be left unmilked."

Once more, Wes tied his horse to the back of the buggy, then climbed in next to his wife and took the reins in hand. Rosemary waved from the porch and Angelena called out to her. "Thanks for everything."

"Oh! You forgot your basket. And the rice bowl. Wait!" Rosemary scooted inside the house and reappeared a moment later, bustling out to where the buggy sat. She handed the basket up to Wes, and Angelena saw a look of warning pass between mother and son before final goodbyes were called out.

They'd reached the town road before Wes spoke. "You know, Lena. I've been thinking. Maybe you should stay at home tomorrow. Rosemary had me tie a bushel of tomatoes and some peppers on the back of the buggy. The tomatoes are dead ripe. You'll need to do something with them so they don't spoil."

She considered his words, and decided to be agreeable. "All right. I've got Rosemary's recipe for chili sauce. I'll see what I can do." If Wes and Rosemary were in agreement, she'd be foolish to make a fuss. Slipping tomato skins and setting the beautiful red fruit to cooking was an enjoyable task, one she remembered from somewhere in her past. And those memories were coming by the score. One day, she'd be able to match them together, like the pieces of a puzzle, and the woman who was Angelena would be complete.

Chapter Sixteen

Leaving his wife at home alone did not sit well with Wes. Neither did the idea of taking her to town with him, where she would be at odds and ends all day. His rooms above the jailhouse were almost empty, only a few pieces of furniture remaining to give witness to his stay there. She could, of course, spend the day with Pip, and be welcome. But even that idea did not appeal, his sense of danger on alert, giving warning that all was not well.

Nate Pender. The name reverberated in his mind. A man he'd hoped never to lay eyes on again was once more a part of his life, even though their paths had not crossed. Except for that one long look from his bedroom window, the first night Nate rode into town, Wes had not laid eyes on the man. But in the depths of his soul, he knew that trouble rode Nate's shoulders; now, as never before, the sixth sense he'd developed long before he became sheriff was on alert.

Yet he could not arrest Nate Pender for hanging around Edgewood, any more than he could chase him from town as an unsavory character. Hell, he hadn't even spent much time in town, for that matter. And fifteen years had dulled the memories of Edgewood's residents. Indeed, there were some who seemed oblivious to the fact of Nate's existence, and others who appeared willing to accept him in the area. And probably a whole lot more who weren't even aware he was around and about.

The man was a thorn in Wes's flesh. Even the presence of Angelena by his side was little comfort during the long night hours. A feeling of dread hung over him. Not fear of upholding the law, but rather a prevalent cloud of unease, knowing that Nate Pender was capable of evil. Evil far beyond the concept of many of the people Wes was sworn to protect.

Morning brought no respite to his spirit, and he rose from his bed with apprehension riding him. Angelena was quiet, making his breakfast with little to say, sensing his mood. Leaving her was difficult, but an hour after dawn edged the eastern sky, he rode from the barnyard, her kiss still warm on his lips.

Edgewood rose early, its inhabitants out and around, the storekeepers sweeping the sidewalks and a scattering of horse-drawn vehicles already on the road. Wes pulled his mount to a halt in front of the livery stable, where the forge glowed brightly and Bates Comstock worked at forming a horseshoe.

"Morning, Bates." He slid from the horse's back and watched as huge hands used hammer and tongs, amazed as always that the man could tolerate such intense heat.

"Morning, Sheriff." Men of few words on occasion, they nodded, then stood together, the clang of Bates's heavy hammer ringing in the clear morning air. The shoe formed quickly, and within minutes, hung on a rack near the anvil. Bates turned to the man who watched him.

"You're out and about early." He wiped his hands on his leather apron and put aside his tools. "Miss Angelena kick you out already?" His smile attested to the teasing he offered, and Wes grinned, willing to allow Bates the privilege.

"Naw, she's pretty well taken with me. Matter of fact, I'm about to start spending a whole lot more time with her."

Bates nodded. "I heard tell you're about to hang up your guns and pick up a plow. My youngest boy's thinkin' of askin' you for a job out at your place. He's quite taken with the idea of workin' a farm."

"I'll be ready to hire, come spring. Maybe even some through the winter, setting the place to rights. Old man Murphy didn't till the fields much the last couple of years. They pretty much just lived in the farmhouse. The outbuildings need a hammer and nails and new boards here and there."

Wes tilted his hat back, glancing toward the rows of storefronts and buildings that made up the town. Edgewood sat like an oasis in a small valley, the houses sprawling in a series of streets, circling the business section. In the years since his childhood, Wes had come to love the people who lived there, and he found himself voicing his sentiments aloud.

"It's a good town, Bates. I'll miss being here every day," he said quietly, his mood ambivalent this morning.

"You've been a good sheriff, Wes. But I can see where gettin' married has changed things for you. It's time to raise a family and make a life for yourself. Oscar's boy is takin' hold real good. Folks are accepting him, and his pa's pleased as punch, seein' his boy with a star on his vest." He cleared his throat. "How about coming on over to the house and havin' Bernice fix us a cup of coffee?"

"No." Wes shook his head regretfully. "I'm going to go by the jail and talk to August, and then I need to see

Sam Westcott. Him being mayor, I guess I'd see him about swearing in August as sheriff.''

"You're really gonna do it, aren't you?"

"Well," Wes said on an indrawn breath, "maybe not today, but right soon."

"I saw a couple of strangers late last night, Wes. Riding out of town after dark." Bates shoved his hands in his pockets, his apron pushed aside. "Nate was with them."

"Yeah, well, I'd expected something of this sort, I guess. He quit out at the Hodges place. Said he'd found a better job."

Bates's snort was answer enough. "I've got a good memory. The man never worked any more than he had to, back before—"

"I doubt he's changed any," Wes said dourly. "I still haven't seen him. He's stayin' out of my way."

"You haven't missed much." Bates turned back to his forge. "You suppose he's leavin' town?"

"That's too much to hope for."

"Well, he looked right at home with the fellas he was with. He might be well on his way to Dallas by now." Bates shrugged, picking up his hammer. "Guess I'll have to quit callin' you sheriff, won't I?" His grin was wide as his hammer clanged against the anvil. "You take good care of Miss Angelena, you hear?"

Wes mounted his horse and rode on into town, tipping his hat at Duncan Blackstone as the editor opened the newspaper office for the day. A young man swept the sidewalk before the hotel, and Sam Westcott stood in the wide doorway. He lifted a hand in greeting as Wes rode up.

"Morning, Sheriff. You stoppin' for breakfast?"

Wes shook his head. "I ate early on. I need to talk to you later, though. I'm heading for the train station, but I'll be by before noon, Sam."

Pip opened the doors of the emporium with a flourish, her broom in hand, and called to Wes as he rode past. "Is Angelena coming in today?"

He shook his head, bringing his horse to a stop before the store. "She's doing chili sauce. Rosemary sent her a bushel of tomatoes, and a peck of green peppers."

"She got canning jars? I think Mrs. Murphy got rid of all hers when she sold out her household goods."

He hadn't even thought of that, Wes admitted to himself. The intricacies of cooking and preserving food were far beyond his capabilities. He wasn't even sure Angelena knew what she was going to do with the task he'd given her. "Maybe I'd better take her some when I go home."

Pip laughed. "Not on the back of that horse, you won't, Wes. Likely she'll hitch up the buggy and come to town. Hope so. Dex and I need to talk to her." She paused, and her smile was one of anticipation. "We've got news for her, Wes. You, too, for that matter."

"You gonna have another baby, Pip?" It was common knowledge that Phillipa Sawyer had been surprised with the last boy she'd borne. Her red hair was sprinkled with silver here and there, and although the years sat lightly upon her, she'd made it clear that her days of having babies were about over.

"No, not exactly," she said vaguely. Her smile was wide. "Matter of fact, I'm really hopin' Angelena drives up this morning. I'm about to bust."

Wes answered her grin. It was an automatic reflex where Pip was concerned. He tipped his hat and rode on, his mind only briefly dwelling on the news Pip hinted at. She was probably anxious to get some dresses in the works for Lena, something that would fit over her expanding waistline.

The stationmaster sat on the platform as Wes approached

and nodded glumly, his lap holding a wooden carving he worked at with care. For a man so wizened and cheerless, Homer Pagan was the handiest man around when it came to a whittling tool. "Morning, Sheriff. You expectin' something on the morning train?"

Wes dismounted and squatted by Homer's side. "Nothing unusual. But I know there's a shipment comin' in to the bank today. Pace Frombert told me about it."

"Yup, happens 'bout once a month or so. Reckon he'll be down later on to see to it." Homer glanced up, his rheumy eyes suddenly piercing. "You suspecting trouble, Wes?"

"Hell, I don't know. I feel like I'm being set up, Homer. Things are all every which way for some reason. Maybe it's gettin' married that's got me so edgy."

"Maybe it's your pa comin' back to town that's done it," Homer said wisely. "I thought sure he was out of your hair. I can't think that him showin' up has made you feel like celebrating much."

"No, you're right, it hasn't," Wes admitted. He rose and stepped back beneath the sheltering eaves of the station. "It's gonna be a hot one, Homer. There's not a cloud in the sky."

"Yup." Homer bent low over his carving, and Wes led his horse back down the street and toward the jailhouse. A desk awaited him, with paperwork needing to be sorted through. He hadn't even looked at the last batch of Wanted posters. His steps quickened at that thought.

The sun was high in the sky, and the passengers from the morning train had long since dispersed by the time Angelena drove up the road into town. The savory chili sauce was on the back of the stove, barely simmering, and she'd dawdled as long as she could before harnessing the mare and setting out. Wes had not wanted her in town, and for the life of her, she couldn't figure out why. But the reasons for the trip were legitimate, and without canning jars enough to finish the job, there was no sense in beginning it.

Six blue Mason jars were the sum total of those she'd found in the pantry, and not a rubber ring on any of them. She knew enough about canning to know that she not only needed jars and lids, but that the heavy, red rings that sealed the jars were the most important part of the equipment. Besides that, the lure of new dress fabric was strong, and seeing Pip was inducement enough to make the trip.

She halted the buggy in front of the emporium and climbed down from the seat. The store was scattered with customers, and Pip stood behind the counter. Angelena approached, egg basket in hand. "I've got three dozen for you, Pip. Those hens Wes bought me are good layers."

Pip laughed. "Anybody else would have bought chicks and let you raise your own. Wes Tanner had to go out and buy you pullets ready to lay. I don't know what he thought you were going to do with all the eggs."

Angelena smiled broadly. "I suspect he knew it would give me an excuse to visit you. Not that I need one." She looked toward the back room. "Where's the baby?"

"Home with Dex. He'll bring him over when he brings dinner for us."

Angelena's mouth softened and her heart swelled within her breast. "He's a good husband for you, isn't he, Pip? Minding the baby and cooking, and all?"

"You bet, a good husband and a wonderful father. And a big help, keeping the books and doing all the heavy work in the store. He used to get teased about toting my dinner here every day, but he's so blissfully content that it didn't make a dent."

Angelena grimaced. "Blissfully content? I can't imagine ever hanging that label on Wes. He reminds me of a kettle set to boil most of the time." She walked to the counter where paper-wrapped bolts of fabric sat. "Is this the new material you got?"

Pip unloaded Angelena's basket, then placed the blue-speckled bowl of eggs on the counter. "I'll bet we can fill the basket for your trip home, once I take the wrappings off the top two pieces," she teased.

Geraldine Frombert approached from the far end of the store, where men's shirts and trousers were placed on shelves. "I'd think you'd go to the dress shop next door and buy your clothes, Mrs. Tanner. The modiste there does wonderful work."

"Pip is going to help me make a couple of dresses," Angelena said quietly, not willing to argue the point. She turned back to Pip. "I thought maybe I could come in and watch the store a couple of afternoons and you could cut them out for me and get me started. I remember sewing a little, but I think there was usually a woman who took care of my clothing, growing up, and even when I got older and had costumes to tend to."

"Costumes?" Geraldine asked, as if the word held a nasty connotation.

Angelena faced her fully, and her smile was forcibly sweet. "Yes, I sang on stage in St. Louis before I came here."

"In public?" Geraldine's eyebrows rose in drastic increments, almost touching the frizzled bangs on her forehead.

"Yes." Angelena turned away, watching as Pip carefully removed the brown paper covering, revealing a pale green fabric, with white flowers and darker green leaves tracing a design on its surface. "Oh, I love it, Pip," she breathed. "I'll wear it for church."

"You'll be attending church?" Geraldine asked dubiously.

"Wes and I have gone to vespers ever since we got married, Mrs. Frombert."

"Really. The mister and I don't attend evening services. His Monday-morning duties are rather heavy at the bank."

Pip rolled her eyes and worked at the second bolt, unwrapping the paper carefully, so as to keep it to use again. She glanced at the coins on the counter near Angelena's basket, and aimed the conversation in a new direction. "What are you going to do with all your egg money?"

"I'll have you know, it's going in the bank, along with my savings. I brought every penny along with me today. I'm going to open my own account."

"I'm not sure Mr. Frombert will allow a woman to have an account in her own name," Geraldine said stiffly. "He prefers to have the gentlemen take care of such things."

Angelena frowned. "Well, then, maybe I'd better go over and talk to him about it. I don't care if Wes has access, but I want my name on the account that holds my money. It's something I've been wanting to do for a long time, and today I'm going to make it to the bank."

Pip held up a length of the fabric and tossed the end over Angelena's shoulder. "You'll look good in this shade of blue," she judged, cocking her head to one side. "What do you think?"

"Fine." The single word was bluntly spoken, and Pip's eyes widened. "I'm going to walk over to the bank right now, Pip. I won't be long." Angelena scooped the coins from the counter and dropped them in her reticule, then walked quickly to the door. And if Pace Frombert knew what was good for him, she thought, he'd better get out a file card and put her name on the top line.

Jason pushed the swinging doors open and exited the Golden Slipper, stepping onto the boardwalk, directly into Angelena's path. She halted quickly, barely able to keep from barreling into him. "Jason! You startled me."

"Angel, it's good to see you. How are things on the farm?" His words were teasing, his smile genuine, and Angelena felt a rush of warmth at his words.

"It's wonderful. I'm going to put up chili sauce today, after I buy some glass jars from Pip, and all the assorted rings and lids to go with them. Rosemary gave me the recipe and I found a cookbook in Mrs. Murphy's cabinet, and it tells how to do the job. And Wes bought me some young chickens and…" She flushed brightly, her laughter ringing out.

"I don't usually run on like this. You'll have to forgive me."

Jason took her arm and stepped beside her. "On the contrary, Angel, I'm pleased that you're so enthusiastic about your new life. I'm assuming the chickens are providing you with eggs. Has he also bought you a cow and assorted piglets?"

She frowned at him, her mouth pursing a bit, her laughter gurgling in her throat. "Now you're teasing me. Yes, he just bought a cow last week, but he hasn't taught me to milk it yet, and he says the pigs will wait till winter's about over. Next thing I'm going to learn to do is churn butter."

"Is Wes treating you well, then?" He tugged her from the middle of the sidewalk to stand against the front window of the hotel, out of the way of other pedestrians, and his hand dropped from her arm. "I don't suppose it's proper for you to be speaking to me in public, Angel."

"You're my friend, Jason. I'll speak to you whenever and wherever I like. And as to Wes, yes, he's very good to me. He's been more than generous." She held up her reticule. "I'm to keep the egg money for my own. In fact, I'm on my way to the bank to open an account right now."

"With egg money? Surely you haven't saved so much already?"

"No," she said quietly. "But I saved all that you paid me, and it's enough to start with."

"Well, I'm heading that way myself," he told her. "I'll walk with you, and let the gossips have a field day."

Wes watched idly from his window, thinking of the multitude of chores he could be taking in hand at the farm. His mind focused on Angelena, and he closed his eyes, imagining her working in the big kitchen. Perhaps the work was too heavy for her, maybe he should have held off on the canning project until he could be there to lift kettles of water, or whatever women used when they did such things. The vision of her golden hair, glittering in the shards of sunlight from the windows, and the memory of blue eyes fixed upon him with desire shimmering in their depths was almost more than he could cope with, and he shook his head, jarring loose the images.

He needed to be at his best, his thoughts sharp and clear today. Forcibly, he removed Angelena from the forefront of his mind and opened his eyes.

Merciful God in heaven. The woman was standing right across the road, her eyes sparkling, her smile turned on Jason Stillwell. Hell's bells! They were heading toward the bank, and Lena was talking a mile a minute, and bustling right along, Jason's hand under her elbow.

"I told her to stay at home. Give the woman one stinkin' order to follow, and she turns around and does just as she damn well pleases." His gun belt in place, he tied the thong around his thigh and slammed his hat atop his head. The door stood open, letting the breeze through the building, and he stalked toward the opening.

Before him, several horsemen rode past, three of them pulling their mounts to a halt in front of the bank. The others rode on down the road, then turned and formed a group in front of the hotel. Wes watched, his eyes riveted on the form of his wife. Jason held the door open and she passed before him into the bank, the saloon owner at her heels.

The three horsemen dismounted and exchanged glances, one turning to scan the street and storefronts before he headed toward the bank's door. *Damn!* Nate Pender faced the street, and drew a folded kerchief up from his throat, then turned as all three men rushed through the doorway into the interior of Pace Frombert's bank.

Wes stood as though frozen in place. A vision of drawn guns permeated his mind. Another of Angelena facing such danger brought cold sweat to his body, and he all but burst from his office door. Only the knowledge that several men stood guard in the road kept him from darting across to the bank.

From the back door of the jailhouse a voice spoke his name. August Rhinehold appeared from the hallway leading to the cells. "Wes, we got trouble out in the road." He stepped into the office. "Ah, hell! I thought I might make it in here and pick up a long gun before they got inside the bank. I caught sight of them from between the buildings, and if I'm not mistaken, I saw your wife step in the bank, too."

"Yeah, Lena's in there, along with Jason and Lord knows who else."

Wes stood beside the window and peered at the four men who centered the road, their hats tilted forward, and knew that their guns were only half a second from being drawn and fired. In the window of the emporium, Dex appeared, then moved aside quickly. One of the double doors opened and Wes would have been willing to bet that Dex was right behind it, gun in hand. The appearance of a gun barrel through the narrow opening proved his theory and he breathed a sigh of relief.

Behind the watching men, Bates paced the sidewalk, Lenny beside him, both carrying shotguns. Bates waved a beefy fist to alert those on the wooden walkway to take cover. Things were looking up a bit, Wes decided, pointing out the approaching gunmen to August.

And then, from the narrow opening between the saloon and the barbershop, Gabe moved into sight, his gun drawn. He moved lithely, keeping within the shade of the saloon's overhanging porch roof, almost directly across the road from Bates and Lenny. The odds were definitely in his favor, Wes decided.

"When all hell breaks loose, I'll take the one on the right," he told August quietly. "You aim for the left side, and we'll leave the other two to Bates, Dex and my father. I sure hope Dex can aim that thing he's pointin'."

Wes stepped to the doorway, allowing himself to be seen. The rider he had chosen as his own scanned the road, then jerked in his saddle, drawing his gun in a swift, smooth motion. His bullet splintered the doorjamb, inches from Wes's head. The other three gunmen, weapons firing, circled and milled in the center of the road, and Gabe dove for cover. Bates and Lenny dropped to one knee, each behind an upright post, and in a split second Wes was struck by the grim humor of their bulk being protected by a four-inch piece of wood.

Whether his or another's bullet struck the man he aimed for, he could not tell. The front window of Pip's emporium shattered as one gunman shot wildly at Dex. A horse whinnied shrilly, then bucked and plunged, tossing his rider to the dirt. Gabe sprawled on the boardwalk in front of the barbershop. He took aim, then fired a last shot. The last of the four gunmen sprawled facedown, his body jerking twice. And Gabe was up and running.

"Let's go," Wes shouted, sprinting across the road, August at his heels.

The sound of multiple gunfire outside brought chaos within the walls of the bank. Pace Frombert pushed his desk chair back, facing three masked men, and was ordered to the floor. Angelena turned from the teller's window where she'd been about to place her hoard of cash on the counter, shrieking in sheer surprise. Jason gripped her by the wrist and tugged her against the wall, only to have her snatched from his grasp by one of the bandits.

"Let's get the hell out of here," the tallest of the trio growled, peering from the window in the door. "They got Dougie and Pete, and the other two don't look so good." He jerked the door open and crouched low, running for his horse, his partner fast on his heels, their guns firing wildly. August jerked, one arm hanging limp at his side, but the two would-be robbers were hit by bullets from four guns, and their bodies hit the ground before they reached their mounts.

Inside the bank, Angelena found herself held tightly against the front of the third member of the group, his arm almost lifting her from the floor. The cold muzzle of his gun brushed her face, then leveled toward the doorway.

"Come on, missy. You and me are goin' out there and get on my horse." His words were snarled against her ear, and she struggled to breathe, gagging as his rancid breath reached her. He leaned over her shoulder and shuffled his way to the open door.

In the street, directly before them, Wes and his deputy watched, guns drawn but helpless in the face of Angelena's situation. She wriggled with all her might, hoping to jar the pistol loose from the man who held her, but to no avail. His grip on her waist tightened, and she gasped for air.

His words were foul, guttural and abusive, and he lifted his gun again, the barrel aimed directly at Wes. "Move out of the way, sonny. I got me a pretty lady."

Wes dropped his pistol to his side and watched as the pair sidled through the doorway. There was a sudden silence, like the lull before a storm, and in the midst of the eerie stillness a single shot rang out. Angelena stumbled, lurching forward as her captor slumped and fell where he stood. Blood and gore splattered the boards of the sidewalk in front of her and she shuddered as she sprawled on the crimson stains.

"Angel!" Jason called from the bank, his small pistol still held in firing position.

Wes was silent, on his knees beside Angelena, turning her to her back and lifting her. A quick glance assured him that Nate Pender would no longer be a threat, and he turned his attentions to the woman he held in his arms. Bloodstains decorated the front of her dress, and his heart pounded in an irregular rhythm.

"Is she all right, son?" Gabe stood over him, his face set in harsh lines. "Damn, I don't even know who got the bastard."

"Angelena? Are you hurt? Did you get hit?" Wes's

words were terse, his voice trembling, and only the fluttering of her eyelids gave him the reassurance he needed.

"Wes?" She whispered his name. "Did you shoot him?"

"I did, Angel," Jason said from the doorway. "I had my derringer. I always carry it when I'm goin' to the bank. I took me a good shot when he leaned to one side. The only target I had was his head." He stepped out to stand by Wes. "It was your pa, Wesley. I killed him. I can't say I'm sorry, but I sure wouldn't have done it on purpose."

Wes shook his head at Jason. "You saved Lena's life. That's all that's important." Rising with Angelena in his arms, he turned away from the sight of Nate Pender's body. From the emporium, Pip and Dex ran toward them, Dex still carrying the shotgun in one hand.

"Is she hurt?" Pip cried. "I saw her fall."

Wes strode toward them. "I think she's all right. Let's take her inside the store."

Behind them, August Rhinchold was in charge, directing men to carry the bodies behind the jailhouse, instructing Bates's son to find the doctor for the lone wounded man, all the while allowing Lily to tie a length of white material around his wounded arm.

"Sounds to me like my deputy's got it all under control," Wes said to Gabe.

"Let's go see to my wife."

The kettle of sauce was cooling on the back of the stove, the fire having almost burned itself out. Angelena's buggy held two cartons filled with Mason jars and other assorted paraphernalia, along with her basket, forcing her to sit almost on Wes's lap. She'd sent him back to the bank to find her money, and to his surprise it was still in a pile in front of the teller's cage.

"I'll have to open my bank account another day, won't I?" she asked, trying to chase the gloom from Wes's expression.

"We need to talk," he told her, helping her from the buggy, and half carrying her to the back door.

"Wes." She halted just inside the kitchen. "I know that that man was your father. Your real father, I mean. Pip told me when she was helping me wash up."

"You're wrong there, Lena. Gabe Tanner is my *real* father. Nate Pender was the man who happened to be in the picture before I was born."

She bit at her lip. "You know what I mean, Wes." She turned to him. "I don't know how to talk to you about it. You fired a gun today and men are dead because of it, and I know that has to upset you. Even as a lawman, it must bruise your soul to take a man's life."

He settled her on a kitchen chair and knelt before her, his hands removing her shoes and stripping her stockings from place. "I reckon it's something a man has to learn to live with, honey. Yeah, it bothers me." He looked up at her. "Maybe that's one reason I'm ready to be a farmer. It doesn't bother me as much as it did the first time I killed a man, down in Abilene."

His gaze searched her face as if he memorized each feature. "I'm all right, Lena. I'm aching inside, but I'm not near as bad off as I'd be if Nate had managed to get you on a horse." His hands clasped hers and he buried his face in her lap. His words were muffled, and she bent low to hear him.

"I would have crawled in the grave with you if one of those bullets had killed you, Lena. I was so scared." His shoulders shook and she lifted his head, her mouth pressing kisses against his brow and cheek.

"I'm fine, Wes. You did what you had to do, and so did Jason and Gabe, and the rest of them."

He nodded, his eyes shiny with unshed tears. "I love you, Angelena Tanner. I felt so bad that I'd never told you. It was all I could think of when Nate came out that door with you in front of him. I've never said the words to you, and I was afraid I'd never get the chance."

"You can tell me again, right now, if you like," she whispered, and waited expectantly, until his voice spoke the message she longed to hear.

"I love you, sweetheart. I love you."

It was enough, enough to last her a lifetime, she decided. And the sight of Wes Tanner on his knees was not one she wanted to remember. He'd been bent and almost broken today. She wanted him healed and whole, his hurting at an end.

"Do you love me enough to help me put that sauce in jars?" she asked meekly.

He looked up, surprise lighting his eyes. "Are you sure you're up to it?"

"If you'll bring in the jars, I'll put wood in the stove, and get the kettle boiling. Before you know it, we'll have the job done," she told him. "I'd hate to tell Rosemary I let those tomatoes go to waste."

If her movements were a little shaky, and if his need to be near her hampered her efforts, neither of them minded. The jars were washed and scalded, then filled with boiling sauce, rings put in place and lids screwed on tightly. The kettle was put to soak, and Wes took his wife up the stairs to bed.

She held him, offering the comfort of her body, yearning to heal the wounds of his soul, and he allowed it. His murmured memories were told anew, his past years of hatred and despair put to rest. He rested in her arms, and she whispered her love, caressing him with tender strength.

They watched the moon rise, a thin sliver against the midnight sky, counted the stars over the roof of the barn and then spoke of their future as the night birds sang in the trees outside the window.

And then he slept, and Angelena curled against him, holding his hand firmly between her breasts.

Chapter Seventeen

"I brought you a present." Wes's long strides carried him from the wagon to the porch quickly, and Angelena rose from the swing to face him, laying aside the dress she'd been hemming. He held his hat, brim up, in front of him, one hand covering the opening of its crown, and she watched, her curiosity aroused as he climbed the steps to where she waited.

"What is it, Wes?" She rose on tiptoes, peering down at the back of his hand. "What are you hiding?"

A soft mewling sound answered her query, and she felt a joyous bubble rise within her. "A kitten? Is it a kitten?" Her hands tugged at his, and he teased her, laughing at her eager efforts.

"Now, what would you do with a kitten? With all the work you've got around here, you sure don't have time to waste on feedin' a cat, and havin' to let it in and out the door all the time."

His hand relaxed and she peeled it from his hat, revealing an enchanting face with black and white markings. Small ears twitched and the velvet nose snuffled her fingers, a raspy tongue tasting the tip of her thumb. She lifted the tiny creature from Wes's hat, and cuddled it against her breast. The body was tricolored, orange and black markings resplendent against a pure white background.

"She's a calico. How wonderful, Wes. I had a calico cat once, back in New York." She blinked, then smiled, as a vision opened in her mind. "I lived in New York, Wes. I went to conservatory there, and learned to sing. I had a cat, and I hid her from the landlady, because we weren't supposed to have pets."

"New York? How about that!" And then his expression sobered, and he spoke with solemn appreciation of her talent. "You knew how to sing before that, Lena. I'll guarantee it. They might have given you a few pointers, but your voice is a gift. Some teacher in New York might have improved on it a little, but you were born with a voice."

The bursts of memory were more frequent now, barely a day passing that Angelena didn't recall some trifle, or a flash of places she'd been. The final gap, that of the time before she'd arrived in Edgewood was still blank, but it no longer mattered. She'd set it aside, her joy overcoming the fear of her past.

The kitten meowed plaintively and Angelena lifted it to her face. "She's hungry, I'll bet. Let's take her inside and find a bowl for milk," she said, turning to the kitchen door. "Where did you get her?" she asked, as Wes followed her into the house.

"Bates has a barn cat at the livery stable, and she's about as productive as they come. He's forever givin' away her litters. When I saw this one, I thought you might like her. Besides, we're gonna need a cat in the barn before long, to keep the critters under control."

"Well, she's too little to turn loose yet," Angelena said stoutly. "We'll keep her in the house till she gets bigger."

"You're not supposed to spoil farm animals, Lena,"

Wes told her. "They forget where they belong if you make pets out of them."

She turned to him, and he was beguiled by the radiance of her smile. "You've spoiled *me,* Wes Tanner. Has it hurt me any?"

The sun gleamed brightly through the kitchen window, casting radiance throughout the waving length of her hair, and he was enthralled by the sight. Angelena was a beauty. He'd decided that the night he first saw her. But it wasn't until some time later that he began to recognize the grace and elegance of the woman he'd come to need with every fiber of his being.

No matter now that she'd come to him with another man's seed growing in her belly. He would be the father to that babe, as Gabe Tanner had been to him. The memory of Gabe's harsh words made him wince, though the thought of this child Lena bore pained him no longer. Her son or daughter was as much the child of Wes Tanner as if he had been there at its conception.

He was stunned by the knowledge. Hovering in the back of his mind, it had finally, finally made itself known, and he welcomed the joy of acceptance. Not only his willingness to afford home and shelter and love to the mother, but also to the child who would come into their home. The kitten cried again, and a thought entered his mind, one he'd pondered on the ride home from town.

"We'll need to get us a dog, too." His arms circled Lena's waist and he held her loosely, the kitten peering over her hand, tail lashing and ears twitching, as if her curiosity would not be contained.

"A dog? For helping with the cows?" Lena slipped from his grasp and placed the tiny creature on the floor, laughing as it scampered toward the woodbox, and clawed its way atop the pieces of firewood. Then, with a long look of speculation, she slid into his arms again, and circled his neck with her arms.

"Now, tell me about this dog we're going to get."

He twined a curl around his forefinger and brought it to his nose, lifting the scent she wore, inhaling its faint perfume. "We'll need to train it to watch over the baby when he gets here. You know, so we don't have to worry about varmints or snakes or—"

"That's enough!" she wailed. "I don't want to think of my child being in danger, Wes. I may just wrap her up in tissue paper and keep her in a box on the kitchen floor, so I can keep her safe."

He laughed at her fanciful speech, and swung her in his arms. "We need a dog anyway, Lena. All boys need a dog, don't you know that?"

"Boys? What if we have a girl?"

"Then we'll have a boy the next time," he told her patiently. "I have this long-term plan, honey."

She eyed him askance and leaned back in his embrace. "I think maybe I need to know what you're plotting, Wes Tanner."

From the barn a horse nickered, and outside the house another answered its call. Wes turned to the door, looking out to where a two-seated surrey approached. "Looks like we have company, Lena. Pip and Dex, and all the young'uns, comin' to call. Now how do you suppose they got away from the store in the middle of the afternoon?"

Angelena peered past him, then pushed him impatiently. "Let me out, Wes. Maybe something's wrong."

"Naw," he answered. "Take a good look at Pip. She's grinnin' to beat the band."

The visitors piled from the surrey, young Dexter leading the group, Dex bringing up the rear with Toby in his arms. The other two boys wrestled for a moment, until Pip spoke sharply, and then they nodded obediently, even as one gave the other a final jab.

"We've come to talk," Pip announced, climbing the steps to the porch. She turned to the three oldest boys. "Y'all behave now, hear? Go play by the creek, but don't get your britches wet."

They ran as if released from school on the final day, heading for the line of willows that hid the creek bank from sight. "Don't get your britches wet?" Dex said mockingly. "That's a joke."

"Well, it'll keep them in the shallows anyway," Pip said, following Angelena into the big kitchen. "Got the tomatoes canned, I see. They look beautiful in the sunlight, don't they?"

The jars were lined up on the buffet, eighteen in all, and Angelena ran her fingers across the tops of them. "The cookbook said to let them sit for twenty-four hours before you put them away."

"I wouldn't know," Pip said, settled in a chair, and taking the baby from Dex. "I'm not one to do much in the kitchen. Dex can swear to that." She looked up at her husband, her eyes dancing. "Dex has something to say to you, Angelena."

Her brow furrowed, Angelena turned to the golden-haired man who had befriended her. "What is it? Has something happened?"

He stepped toward her and grasped her hands in his. "Yes, sweetheart. Something wonderful." His eyes glowed, their color that of the bluebirds that nested along the fencerow. She looked deeply into their depths for a moment, recognizing something there, some faint reminder of a face she'd seen, perhaps, or a friend she'd known.

"I've been on a trip, Angelena."

She nodded. "Pip said you had to go to the city."

"St. Louis. I went there to find some answers...both for myself, and for you."

"For me?" She was truly puzzled now, and her gaze flew to Wes, who watched with narrowed eyes, his jaw firm, his mouth unsmiling. His nod reassured her, and she met Dex's gaze once more. "What did you find out?"

"I located people who had known your mother, Angelena. I found out that she died just a few months ago." He paused, and Angelena squeezed his hands.

"Go on, Dex. I want to hear it all." Tears flowed down her cheeks as she spoke, but her words urged him on.

"Her name was Olivia Marie Jordan, honey, and I found her grave in St. John's Cemetery. I had a photographer take a picture of the stone for you. I thought you might like to keep it." He lifted her hands to his mouth and kissed the back of each, in a solemn manner.

"Oh, yes," she said eagerly. "I need to see her name on it. I ordered it before I left St. Louis." Her words halted, and she felt a sigh of relief ease through her lips. "I remember, Dex. I remember the funeral and ordering the stone, and I remember the letter she left for me."

"Then perhaps you already know what I'm about to tell you, honey. I knew your mother. She and I were very close, twenty years ago, when we were both very young."

Her breath caught in her throat and she nodded. "She told me in the letter, Dex."

"What did she say?" His eyes were hopeful, his mouth curved in a tender smile, and Angelena had never felt such love engulf her from another human being as she did that very moment.

Dexter Sawyer is your father. The words were alive in her memory, and she closed her eyes, reading with her mind's eye, from memory, the letter she'd found just days after her mother's death, months past. *He went away before he knew I was to have a child, and I found out that he settled in Edgewood, a small Texas town. He married a woman there and has a family, Angelena. But if he is the same man I knew years ago, he will welcome you. Now that I am gone, I want you to go to him.*

She opened her eyes. "I was coming here, Dex. I was so excited, and at the same time, so filled with grief."

"You'd only just buried Olivia. That was to be expected."

Angelena was swept with a wave of sadness and remorse. "I barely knew her, Dex. After I grew up, and she was more in demand, she sent me away to school. Oh, not because she didn't love me, but because she felt the life was too harsh for a child to endure." She bit at her lip and glanced at Wes.

"I know she loved me. She really did. It was just that she couldn't..." Her hands withdrew from Dex's hold and she wiped her fingers across her cheeks in an attempt to halt the flow of tears. "It's all right now. I understood, later, when I came back to St. Louis and sang last year." Memories of late nights and noisy crowds and the constant grind of rehearsals and costume fittings ran like a kaleidoscope through her mind.

She looked deeply into Dex's eyes. "She wanted me to come to you, Dex. She said you'd welcome me," repeating the words her mother had written.

"Do you doubt that?" he asked.

She shook her head. "Not for a minute." She stepped back from him and knelt before Pip. Toby reached to touch her hair and she took his pudgy hand and kissed it. "You're my little brother, Toby." The baby chortled and leaned toward her, and she snatched a quick kiss from his rosebud mouth.

"Remember the day when you told me I could take your

name, Pip? When I signed the marriage lines as Angelena Sawyer?'' Her smile wobbled as she spoke, and she saw Pip's mouth compress, as if she held back an emotion so enormous she could only savor it within herself. ''I really was your child, even then, Pip. And Dex's.''

She looked up at the men who stood side by side, watching the women they loved. ''I can't believe this could be. It's too good to be true.''

''It's true, honey,'' Dex said quietly. ''I think I felt something between us the first time we met, and I told Pip soon afterward that there was a bond there. She thought it was the music, but now I know that it was more than that.''

Angelena looked up at Pip. ''What shall we do? When can we tell Rosemary and Gabe? We'll want them to know right away. And what shall I call you, Dex?'' she asked, her eyes now able to see the familiar shape of her face in his, the color of her hair reflecting the golden hue his own bore. And his eyes, those same eyes that greeted her in the mirror each morning. Each part of the puzzle fell in place, and she recognized herself in its form.

''You can call me whatever you like, honey,'' Dex told her. ''Maybe one day, when it comes more easily to you, it will be Father, or maybe it'll always be Dex. And that's all right, too.''

She shook her head. ''No, I yearned for years to have a father. My mother said you were dead.'' Another part fell into its slot, and Angelena recognized the sadness she'd felt in those long-ago years. ''What do your boys call you?''

His grin was wide. ''Something I never thought to answer to. *Papa.* It's what Pip calls her father, and they picked it up.''

''Papa.'' She tried it on her tongue, and smiled. ''It may

take some getting used to, but if I'm going to be a part of your family, I might as well do it right."

Six plain, pine coffins were lowered into the ground at the far end of the cemetery, and only two men watched as the final box settled six feet below the surface. "Which one is Nate?" Gabe asked his son.

Wes shrugged. "I don't know. I guess it really doesn't matter, does it? Maybe I should have had him put beside my mother, but somehow I don't think she'll miss havin' him there. He was meaner than a skunk to her, and I've wondered over the past years if she didn't die just to get away from him."

"I'm kinda surprised you wanted to be here today," Gabe said as they turned away. "Does Angelena know you came?"

"No, I didn't tell her yet. But, she'll probably know before the night is over. I have a habit of givin' her a detailed account of most everything I've done all day when we're lyin' there in the dark, and—" He shot a quick glance at his father. "I suspect you know what I'm talkin' about, don't you?"

Gabe grinned. "Yeah, I guess I do. Rosemary could always worm every livin' thing out of me."

"I had to see him in the ground, Gabe. It didn't matter which box he was in. Those men were all alike as far as I'm concerned. He chose his path, I chose mine." He grinned wryly. "With a little help."

"How's August doin'?" Gabe asked, mounting his big stallion outside the cemetery gates.

Wes lifted into his saddle. "He's prouder'n punch to be wearin' his pa's badge. He didn't want the new one I had. Sam Westcott swore him in this morning, and that old bent and battered tin badge shines up like brand-new."

"You got enough help to get your corncrib fixed up, Wes? I'll bring my hands and the boys along one day next week and give you a hand with that and the chicken coop. Have Angelena fix us noon dinner, and I'll haul over a wagonload of hay for your stock, too."

There was no use trying to argue with Gabe Tanner. If he wanted to share his hay crop, Wes knew better than to protest. "I'd appreciate the hay. We're too late to cut any this year. And the way things look, I'm going to need help with building stalls in the barn."

He rode quietly beside Gabe for a moment, then cleared his throat. It had been all he could do to remain silent this morning, but it was Angelena's secret, and he'd not steal her thunder. "We've got something to celebrate, Gabe. Maybe you'd better make it tomorrow, if you can sort out your chores. Be sure Rosemary and Jenny come, too."

Gabe tossed him a sharp glance. "Celebrate? We know about the baby, son. You got somethin' else in the fire?"

Wes grinned widely. "We'll be lookin' for you before dinner. Think you can make it?"

Gabe laughed aloud. "What do you think Rosemary will say when I tell her? She'll be up half the night packin' baskets of food and what have you to take along."

The hay made a satisfying mound in the hayloft, and the men's hammers pounded in a symphony of labor all during the afternoon. With Rosemary's fried chicken under their belts, and Angelena's pies for dessert, the group of men and boys made short work of the chores Wes had barely had time to begin. Supper was leftover chicken, served with potato salad and bowls of applesauce.

Again, the men and boys ate with gusto, while Rosemary, Anna and Angelena served them. There were not enough chairs in her kitchen for everyone to be seated, but

they managed to scrape up a long plank and two saw-
horses, and the little boys shared the makeshift bench on
one side of the table, Jenny in their midst. Talk and laughter rang out and Angelena stood by the cupboard, eating
her second chicken leg. It was enough to make a body
weep, she thought, her heart filled with the joy of belonging.

"I think we've got company comin'," Wes announced.
"Got enough food for five more, Lena?"

She met his gaze and relished the twinkle in his eyes.
He was enjoying this immensely. "I think we can scrape
up something," she said agreeably.

Voices in the yard announced Pip and Dex's arrival, and
Rosemary flashed a quick look at Angelena. "This is the
surprise?"

"You could say that." So filled with sheer anticipation,
she could scarcely breathe, Angelena went to the screened
door, holding it wide for the visitors to come in. "Pip.
Dex. We've got plenty left. Sit down at the table."

"Dex told me he wasn't cooking and I had to close the
store an hour early, so you'd better have plenty." Pip
hugged Rosemary, then Angelena, adding an extra squeeze
for good measure, whispering in her ear. "Have you told
them?" And then answered her own question. "No, of
course you haven't."

"Told us what?" Rosemary asked, then darted a look
at Gabe. "Do you know what's going on?"

He shook his head. "I'm as much in the dark as you
are, honey."

Dex stood just inside the door and motioned Angelena
to his side. She obeyed and held her breath as he placed
his arm across her shoulder and smiled at her. "We're
celebrating today, folks." His eyes began to mist and he
grimaced, whispering to Angelena. "I promised myself I

wouldn't do that.'' With a great clearing of his throat, he began again.

"This is a special day for Pip and me, and our boys. I'd like to introduce all of you—Gabe, Rosemary and the whole family…this is my daughter, Angelena Sawyer Tanner.''

The winter was mild, which was a good thing as far as Wes Tanner was concerned. By late January, he was certain he'd married a veritable whirlwind in the guise of a woman. Angelena had scrubbed and scoured every square inch of the farmhouse, and he'd been coerced and persuaded into hanging wallpaper and painting cabinets until he was sure he was adept enough to make a living at it.

She'd bought a new sewing machine with her egg money. At least she'd paid for part of it, Wes supplying the greater share. She'd been willing to settle for the Success model, selling for $8.50, from the Sears and Roebuck catalogue, but Wes wouldn't hear of it. When the freight was unloaded from the morning train just after the first of the new year, the machine inside proved to be Sears and Roebuck's top-of-the-line $27.45 model, with a drop-desk cabinet and all attachments and accessories.

Angelena had declared it to be Christmas morning all over again. Both Pip and Rosemary came to the farm to help her get started, and then, to Wes's amusement, there was no stopping her.

"She's nesting,'' Rosemary explained to her perplexed son, one morning late in January. "It's the mother urge, son. You might as well learn to put up with it.''

For all his muttering, Wes was enchanted with the flow of curtains and pillow covers his wife produced. She sewed hems on diapers, seams on baby kimonos and put together patches for quilt tops. One was a blend of flannel pieces, and she spent long hours in her new rocking chair quilting it to a pale blue backing.

And then the snow began to melt, the ground putting forth pale-green sprigs of grass around the farmhouse, and the hay field coming to new life. Inside the house, Angelena found it slow going climbing the stairs at night. Wes watched her carefully, alert for any reason to bring the doctor from town.

But Angelena had different ideas, and when she decided that her time was short, she sent a note to Rosemary, and another to Pip, by way of Lenny Comstock.

Wes grumbled at the supper table. "Don't know where that boy went to. I was sharpenin' the plow blade and he up and disappeared. He'd better watch his step I don't get after him good, leavin' me in the lurch that way." His fork, filled with mashed potatoes, disappeared into his mouth, and he speared a bite of pork chop next. "I might need him to send for the doctor one of these days, and he'd better be available, that's all I've got to say."

Angelena nodded wisely, pushing her food around on her plate, already weary from the back pains that had plagued her all day long. They'd switched around to the front before supper, and now she found herself holding her breath as a particularly harsh pain hit her broadside. Her gasp alerted Wes, and he stopped chewing, his eyes sharp as he watched her.

"What's goin' on, Lena? Are you havin' pains? And you didn't tell me?" He pushed away from the table. "Do I need to go for the doctor?"

She shook her head, catching her breath. "I don't think so, Wes. I've got two women probably on their way here already. Between us, I think we can handle it."

"Who?" He stood over her, his face flushed, his nostrils

flaring. "Why don't you want the doctor? I don't want anything to happen to you, Lena. Do you hear me?"

She reached for his hand. "Of course, I do, Wesley." Her lips kissed his palm and she placed it against her cheek. "I want your mother and mine both here to see this baby into the world. They've agreed, and they should be here any time now. I sent Lenny with messages almost two hours ago."

"Damn! And you let me sit here and grouse, and all the time…" He knelt beside her chair. "You're going to be all right, aren't you, Lena? I'll be there to help you, if you want me to. Are you ready to go to bed? Do you need to lie down now?"

She laughed quietly and then was struck by another pain, more intense than the last. "I'm all right for now, but when the mothers get here, they'll know what to do. I fear I'm an amateur at this, Wes."

"Well, how the hell do you think I feel?" he muttered. "I remember when Rosemary had the boys, and Jenny, and Gabe was about worn out by the time they were born. The doctor kept tellin' him he should wait outside the door, but Gabe laid down the law. He told Doc that he was good enough to be there when Adam was born, and he wasn't leavin' his wife on her own for the rest of her birthings. I'll tell you one thing, lady. I'm not waitin' in the parlor, either."

He was true to his word. He rubbed her back, and washed her face. He knelt by the bed and then sat behind her, holding her against his chest. He alternately coaxed and implored her when she began to despair. And then groaned when she cried aloud.

Finally, before midnight, when all the beds in the house were full of sleeping boys, and one small girl who would not be coaxed into sleeping but waited in the parlor, he shed tears of joy.

Pip held up a wrinkled, squalling specimen that Rosemary pronounced perfect. Once washed and dried, Wes thought his child looked amazingly like his wife, with golden hair and enormous blue eyes, unfocused but beautiful nonetheless.

He carried his precious bundle down the long, open stairway and presented it with a flourish, opening the blanket wide to reveal the result of Angelena's hours of labor.

"You're a better man than I am," Dex announced. "I heard one squeak from Pip when she had Dexter, and I was ready to leave home. I just couldn't stand the thought of her in pain. She chased me out, and I walked the floor like all good fathers should."

"Gabe didn't," Wes said quietly. "And I didn't have a choice. Angelena made me promise I'd stick with her."

"You haven't told us the important part," Gabe said impatiently. "Do I have a grandson or not?"

Wes grinned. "Sorry, gentlemen, but Angelena has broken the mold. Jenny has her niece."

Jenny stood quietly, her eyes wide as she listened to the men speaking, and then lifted one small hand to tug at Wes's sleeve. "Can I see her?"

"Better than that," he whispered. "Sit down here, and you can hold her. I'll help you."

The child scrambled up on the sofa and smoothed her dress across her lap, then held up her arms. Wes gently placed his daughter in Jenny's arms and straightened.

"What's her name?" Jenny asked, peering up at him. "I have to know what to call her."

"Angelena named her. Partly after her mother, and partly because she said she was so filled with joy before the baby was born, she thought it should be a part of her name. So, we're going to call her Joy Marie. Do you like that, Jenny?''

"Joy Marie." Jenny whispered the name and pronounced it good. "Yes, it's beautiful," she said, drawing out the syllables.

Epilogue

The church in Edgewood was filled to capacity as the newest member of the congregation was brought forward to be baptized and named. On either side of the parents stood a line of family, both grandparents and uncles, with one very small aunt beside Angelena. Anna had gone to Dallas, and so missed the occasion, but Angelena's pocket held a letter from her addressed to her first niece.

The ceremony was brief, and the baby was held aloft, and duly admired by the townsfolk.

"I always knew that girl would make a mark. She has good bones," Geraldine Frombert said from the front pew, nodding her approval.

"And a wonderful father," Pip whispered in Dex's direction.

"Are you happy?" Wes asked Angelena, taking her arm and leading her to the family pew.

"Do you need to ask?" she murmured, shooting a grin in his direction. "I'm about as close to heaven as I'll ever get," she whispered. "At least for the next fifty years or so."

The chores done and the house closed up for the night, Wes climbed the stairs. From their bedroom, he heard Angelena singing to the baby, and he hesitated, listening as her voice held a note, then whispered soft words to the infant in her arms.

With silent footsteps, he walked down the hallway, and entered their room, as always smitten anew by the sight of Angelena's golden beauty. She rocked slowly in a rocking chair Dex had delivered to the house the day after Joy's birth, decreeing that she needed one upstairs as well as in the kitchen. The baby nursed in a languid fashion, her hunger abating, her tiny fingers pressing against the firm flesh of Angelena's breast.

The sight ignited a flame Wes had been careful to keep under control, and he halted several feet away, feasting on the sight of his woman's soft curves. She looked up and her smile flashed into being, as if his presence alone was enough to bring her happiness.

"She's almost asleep, Wes. I'll put her in her bed in a minute."

He settled on the end of the bed, watching. "No hurry, Lena. I enjoy watching her nurse."

"Do you now?" Her mouth curved in a teasing moue, and she leaned her head back as she rocked. "Do you know that it's been more than a month since Joy was born?" she asked idly, as if it were a fact to be noted and commented upon.

"She'll be five weeks old tomorrow," he said. "I've been keeping track. Gabe told me to leave you be for a few weeks. Said six weeks was about his limit when Rosemary was havin' babies. He couldn't hold out any longer than that."

"I think five weeks is plenty long enough," Angelena told him.

His masculine flesh throbbed as he reflected on her words. "You think maybe tomorrow?" he asked.

She shook her head. "No, I think maybe tonight." She

tilted her head and looked at him through her lashes, and he recognized the teasing expression she was wont to turn in his direction.

He rose quickly. "I'll put her to bed for you, honey. Let me have her, and I'll pat her back a little and wrap her up nice and neat, and she'll be set for the night. She knows her daddy's touch." His hands were gentle as he cuddled the infant against his shoulder, and he pressed warm kisses against her rosy cheek, patting her back and waiting for the soft bubble to rise from her stomach.

Angelena watched him closely, her eyes taking in his every movement. "You really love her, don't you?" Her whisper touched him, wrapped tendrils of gentle concern around his heart, and he pondered his reply. It could only be the truth.

"She's mine, Lena. Of course I love her."

She nodded, then walked to the wardrobe and slid from her dress, hanging it inside the wooden cupboard. Her petticoat was next, then her shoes and stockings. She took longer than usual to undress, Wes thought, folding her underthings carefully, bending to place her best shoes on the floor of the wardrobe.

He watched, enthralled by the slender lines of her arms and legs, the rounding of her hips and the fullness of her breasts. His eyes followed each movement as she bent to remove a sleeping gown from her dresser drawer, his gaze drawn to the pouting outline of her breasts through the sheer fabric of her chemise. And then she stripped from the last items she wore, folding her drawers neatly, and her chemise on top of them. Without glancing in his direction, she slipped the gown over her head, and he rued the presence of the concealing garment.

Wes crossed the room to the baby's bed and bent to place her on her side, his hands gentle as he covered her. Then his gaze turned once more to his wife. "You don't need to wear the nightgown, Lena.'' His voice sounded gruff, and she looked over her shoulder at him, hairbrush in hand. The baby snuggled down beneath her quilt, and he patted her absentmindedly for a moment.

"It's cold outside tonight, Wes. I think we may get frost by morning.'' Her smile enticed him, and he turned to face her. His hands began the task of stripping his clothing from his body, and the job was completed in seconds. Her hairbrush slowed, her eyes on his every move, and as his drawers were kicked aside, she dropped the hairbrush on her dresser.

"I'll keep you warm,'' he told her, only too aware of the thrusting power of his manhood. Her gaze touched him there and he throbbed anew.

"Promise?'' she asked, the flirting smile in place. Her hands drew the folds of her gown over her head, and she placed it at the foot of their bed. "In case the baby wakes up,'' she murmured.

They nestled together in the center of the big bed, content for a few moments to enjoy the luxury of flesh against flesh. But his time without her had been long, and she knew his urgency would not be contained. Their hands sought and found the places of pleasure they knew so well. Their mouths brushed lightly, then meshed, lips suckling, teeth nibbling, tongues tasting. He nuzzled her throat and she sighed her pleasure. She teased the taut flesh of his back and hips, and he groaned his need in her ear.

The candle burned low, and in its flickering glow their bodies met and melded, his rising above her, then sinking to form a single shadow, his arousal thrusting into the depths of her womanhood. She cried out, her joyous note of completion reaching his ear, and he sought his own pleasure, ever careful of the tender flesh he inhabited.

It was a coming together such as they had not known during their months of marriage. A blending of mind and body, a union of souls. He whispered his love, and she responded. He praised her beauty, and she told him of her yearning for him and him alone. For long hours they communed, with foolish words and languid caresses. Then, when their bodies were surfeited by the hours of loving, they fell asleep.

The candle had long since guttered and the wax grown cold. Across the room, their child slept peacefully, and Wes awoke in the stillness, his arms filled with the woman he loved. She turned to him, perhaps sensing his restlessness, and her mouth sought his.

"I love you," she whispered. "You know what? My name is Angelena Tanner, and I know who I am."

"Do you now?" he asked, wondering if she spoke in her sleep.

"Yes." She nodded, her hair brushing his cheek. "I know who I am, Wesley Tanner. I know the days of my past, and I'm not afraid of the future. In fact, I'd say I'm about the happiest woman in Texas."

"Well, that makes us a pair then," he told her, wondering if he could keep her awake long enough to make her just a little bit happier.

* * * * *

In October 2000, be sure to look for the third and final story in Carolyn's Edgewood, Texas *miniseries,*

"WISH UPON A STAR"

This short story is part of the Harlequin Historical Inline Christmas Anthology,

ONE CHRISTMAS WISH,

and features Wesley's sister, Anna Tanner, and the wealthy Dallas entrepreneur who follows her back to Edgewood when he realizes he can't live without her!

If you enjoyed what you just read,
then we've got an offer you can't resist!

Take 2 bestselling love stories FREE!

Plus get a FREE surprise gift!

Explore the American frontier
with these rugged Westerns from

On sale May 2000

THE CAPTIVE HEART
by **Cheryl Reavis**
(North Carolina frontier, 1750s)

TANNER STAKES HIS CLAIM
by **Carolyn Davidson**
(Texas, 1800s)

On sale June 2000

BANDERA'S BRIDE
by **Mary McBride**
(Texas, 1870s)

MOLLY'S HERO
by **Susan Amarillas**
(Wyoming, 1870s)

Harlequin Historicals
The way the past *should* have been.

Available at your favorite retail outlet.

Visit us at www.romance.net

HHWEST7